"Do you know how very special you've become to me?" Quenton asked.

Olivia was afraid to speak, for fear of spoiling the moment.

"I must kiss you, Olivia." He bent to her and brushed his lips over hers. It was the merest whisper of mouth to mouth. And yet it sent heat pouring through her veins. Her heart swelled with so much love she feared it would burst.

On a gasp she started to pull away. He changed the angle of the kiss and moved his hands along her back, soothing, arousing.

"Quenton."

"Shh. A minute more." He pressed soft, moist kisses to her temple, her cheek, the tip of her nose. His mouth followed the line of her jaw, teasing the corner of her lips until, unable to wait any longer, she turned her face and felt his lips cover hers once more.

The kiss was no longer gentle. With a guttural sound they came together in a fierce heat that threatened to consume them both....

Dear Reader,

This month we've covered all the bases. You'll laugh, you'll cry, *you'll find romance.* Our big news this month is the return of Ruth Langan with *Blackthorne,* her first medieval novel in nearly four years! Packed with intrigue and emotion, this is the tale of a haunted widower, the lord of Blackthorne, whose child's governess teaches him how to love again. It's great!

Be sure to look for *Apache Fire* by longtime author Elizabeth Lane. In this stirring Western, a Native American army scout on the run from vigilantes finds shelter in the arms of a beautiful young widow. In *Lost Acres Bride* by rising talent Lynna Banning, a rugged, by-the-book rancher must contend with the female spitfire who inherits a piece of his land—and gets a piece of his heart! Don't miss this fun and frolicking Western.

Rounding out the month is *Three Dog Knight* by the versatile Tori Phillips. This clever "prequel" to *Midsummer's Knight* is about a painfully shy earl whose marriage of convenience to an illegitimate noblewoman must survive the schemes of an evil sister-in-law.

Whatever your tastes in reading, you'll be sure to find a romantic journey back to the past between the covers of a Harlequin Historicals® novel.

Sincerely,

Tracy Farrell, Senior Editor

Please address questions and book requests to:
Harlequin Reader Service
U.S.: 3010 Walden Ave., P.O. Box 1325, Buffalo, NY 14269
Canadian: P.O. Box 609, Fort Erie, Ont. L2A 5X3

RUTH LANGAN
BLACKTHORNE

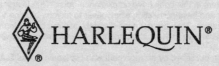

HARLEQUIN®

TORONTO • NEW YORK • LONDON
AMSTERDAM • PARIS • SYDNEY • HAMBURG
STOCKHOLM • ATHENS • TOKYO • MILAN • MADRID
PRAGUE • WARSAW • BUDAPEST • AUCKLAND

ISBN 0-373-29035-7

BLACKTHORNE

Copyright © 1998 by Ruth Ryan Langan

Books by Ruth Langan

RUTH LANGAN

traces her ancestry to Scotland and Ireland. It is no surprise, then, that she feels a kinship with the characters in her historical novels.

Married to her childhood sweetheart, she has raised five children and lives in Michigan, the state where she was born and raised.

To Riley Erin Langan
And her proud parents, Mike and Patty
And her big sister, Kelly

And, as always, to Tom
Who owns my heart.

Chapter One

Cornwall, 1662

Evening shadows cloaked the rolling hills and verdant meadows dotted with sheep. Tenant farmers, weary after a day in the fields, paused behind their flocks to watch as an elegant carriage rolled toward the manor house in the distance.

"So. The blackheart has returned." An old man leaned on his staff and turned to his son. "It isn't enough that he murdered his bride and tossed his brother from the cliffs, leaving him mute and crippled. Or that he fled England for a life of crime on the high seas, leaving the old lord to clean up his mess. Now he thinks his friendship with the king gives him the right to just come back and claim his inheritance as though nothing has happened."

"Who's to stop him?" the younger man muttered.

"Aye. Who indeed? The rich live by their own rules." The old man's eyes narrowed, watching the carriage roll to a stop in the distant courtyard. "It's bad enough that our sweat and blood contribute to his wealth. Pity those who must actually live under his roof at Blackthorne."

"God save us! His lordship has arrived." Mistress Thornton, housekeeper at Blackthorne, the estate of Quenton, Lord Stamford, clapped her hands for attention, then began summoning the servants in her squeaky, high-pitched voice. The more agitated she became, the higher her voice. "Edlyn, you vain, idleheaded minnow. Stop preening and move along with the others."

As the servants spilled out the front entrance and formed a long column in the courtyard, she and Pembroke, the head of the household staff, stepped forward. They made a comical picture. Where Mistress Thornton was as round as she was tall, with a soiled apron tied crookedly around her middle and a ruffled cap perched upon tousled white curls, Pembroke was tall and thin as a stick, with every dark hair in place and his clothing meticulously pressed. Her voice had the screech of rusty wheels. His was as cultured as royalty.

The driver brought the team to a halt, then leapt down and opened the door to the carriage. A cloaked figure stepped out, barely glancing at the assembled staff.

"Welcome home, my lord," Pembroke called, after clearing his throat loudly.

"I hope yer journey was a pleasant one," the housekeeper added.

"Allow me to present your servants, my lord." Pembroke turned to see that the maids bowed properly and the lads removed their caps.

Lord Stamford acknowledged each one with a

brusque nod, then turned back as a little boy stepped down from the carriage.

Pembroke remained ramrod straight, no sign of surprise visible on his features. But his gaze flicked over the sun-bronzed skin, jet-black hair and wide dark eyes of the lad.

For his part, the boy stared around in bewilderment at the imposing fortress with its acres of manicured lawns and its turreted towers that caught the last rays of the fading sun.

The driver began unlashing trunks and dropping them to the ground. At a snap of Pembroke's fingers several of the staff hurried forward to deal with the lord's baggage.

"Ye'll be wanting a late supper, m'lord," Mistress Thornton said nervously.

"Nay. Nothing."

As the cloaked figure moved past her she called to his back, "Your rooms are ready for you, m'lord. We've prepared your grandfather's rooms for your arrival."

He paused. Without turning he said, "I would prefer my old rooms, Mistress Thornton."

"Your old...? But, m'lord, beggin' your pardon, they're a bit small for the likes of...I mean, now that you're the new lord of the manor and all..."

He turned.

Seeing the scowl on his face she couldn't help taking a step backward. "At once, m'lord. I'll see to it myself."

He gave a curt nod. "I will wish to visit my grandfather's grave, Pembroke."

"Aye, my lord. On the morrow?"

"Now."

Pembroke swallowed. "At once. I'll take you there myself. But first, you may wish to greet your brother. When he heard that you were returning he became quite…animated."

Quenton glanced up. A man's face peered down from the upper window. In the reflected glow of firelight, it appeared ghostly-white.

He gave an audible sigh, the only hint of any emotion. "Aye. I'll go up to him."

As the two men turned away Mistress Thornton gathered her courage and asked, "What of the boy, m'lord? Where shall we put him?"

He gave a negligent shrug. "The east wing, I suppose."

"Aye, m'lord." The plump housekeeper glanced at the boy, who continued to stand hesitantly beside the carriage. "Come, lad. I'll show you to yer rooms."

He moved along at her side as they entered the imposing foyer. Mistress Thornton noted that he seemed properly awed by the gleaming chandeliers, ablaze with the light of hundreds of candles, and, as they began to climb the wide staircase, wildly interested in the colorful tapestries that lined the walls.

"Are ye hungry, lad?" She knew not what to call him, since the lord had not bothered to introduce him, and the lad had spoken nary a word.

He nodded.

"Well then, after I take ye to yer rooms, I'll see that ye have a fine meal brought up." When they reached the east wing, she flung open double doors and led him inside a set of rooms that included a sitting chamber and bedchamber.

"This is Edlyn."

A scowling serving wench, who had been coaxing

a fire on the grate, got to her feet, dusting off her skirts.

"This lumpish, knotty-pated strumpet will help you unpack and see that you're made comfortable."

The boy giggled at the housekeeper's colorful choice of words, unsure of their meaning.

"And what is yer name, young master?" Edlyn asked.

"Liat." His voice had a musical quality as he spoke the word in two syllables. He made his way to the balcony, where he climbed onto a trunk in order to stare at the green, rolling land below.

"Liat? What sort of mammering, hedge-born, heathen name is that?" the housekeeper muttered under her breath. She crossed herself, then turned away with a sigh. "I'll have his supper sent up on a tray."

As she hurried away, her mind was filled with troubling thoughts. Too much had happened too soon. The old earl had been so loved until his unexpected death. It was well-known that his grandson had been reluctant to return from sea to take over the estate. Already the rumors were flying about the return of Lord Stamford to his ancestral home, Blackthorne. Now, to add fuel to the rumors, he had brought with him a lad of questionable parentage. She had no idea what to expect anymore. But this much she knew. Life here at Blackthorne would never be the same again.

Oxford, 1662

THE CEMETERY WAS little more than a bleak, windswept stretch of hill beside the country chapel. Through a curtain of mist could be glimpsed the rooftops of the university buildings and picturesque houses nestled in a green valley below.

The vicar, a stooped gnome of a man, intoned the words meant to comfort the bereaved. But the words he'd spoken a hundred times or more had little meaning to Olivia St. John, who stood with head bowed, tears flowing freely.

It was almost beyond comprehension. Mum and Papa, falling to their deaths during one of their daily climbs. Still young and vital and full of life and love. And now they were gone. And she was alone. Alone. The word reverberated, like a litany, through her mind. No parents, nor grandparents, nor brothers or sisters. Alone, except for this aunt and uncle, who were complete strangers to her.

She glanced toward her mother's sister, Agatha, Lady Lindsey, who stood beside her dour-faced husband, Robert. As the two simple wooden boxes were lowered into the gaping holes in the earth, husband and wife turned their backs, hastening toward their waiting carriage to escape the elements. As if on cue, the heavens darkened and the rain began.

Olivia stood alone, unmindful of the cold rain that soaked her clothes and turned the open grave into a sea of mud at her feet. It seemed fitting somehow that it should rain. "The angels in heaven are weeping," Mum had often said of the frequent English rains.

She couldn't tear her gaze from the two caskets as the village gravedigger slowly covered them with earth. Even when the task was completed, she continued to stand alone, grieving as though her heart would break.

"Come, girl. Your aunt will catch a chill." It was the rough grasp of her uncle's hand upon her wrist that had her turning away. As soon as she was seated, a whip cracked and the carriage lurched ahead.

Her aunt's words, spoken through gritted teeth, penetrated Olivia's layers of pain. "I told Margaret that she was marrying beneath her station, but she would not listen. Her inheritance has been badly mismanaged."

"Inheritance?"

"Alas, there is little enough left. You are practically penniless."

"We were forced to live quite frugally, Aunt Agatha. Mum said that her money was in London, and under your control. Yours and Uncle Robert's."

Her uncle's lips thinned. "You can be grateful for that, young lady, or it would all be gone. Had it not been for our son Wyatt's careful scrutiny, that befuddled father of yours, with his nose stuck in dusty old books, would have squandered his wife's inheritance years ago."

"Papa had no interest in Mum's money."

"That was plain enough. As it is, there's barely enough left to pay your keep, though I suppose we can get something for the sale of your cottage."

Her husband gave a snort of disgust. "According to the vicar, even that will fetch no coin because your niece insists upon giving it away."

"Giving it…?"

As her aunt began to issue a protest, Olivia struggled to keep the rising anger from her voice. "I have already offered it to the widow Dillingham, who is a dear friend of ours. Since the death of her son, she has no one to see to her. I know that Mum and Papa would have wanted to share what little they had with her."

"No matter." Her uncle dismissed her with a wave of his hand. "It would fetch little, since it is no more than a hovel."

The cruel words brought a fresh stab of pain to Olivia's heart. "It is the only home I have ever known."

"And now you have none," Agatha said with a sigh of impatience. "Out of respect for my sister's memory, I suppose I shall have to take you back to London."

"That isn't necessary. I can take care of myself here in Oxford. I don't wish to be a burden, Aunt Agatha."

"Nor will I permit it." The woman's eyes glittered with shrewdness. She took note of the coarse, shapeless gown, the worn, shabby boots, the threadbare traveling cloak. The figure inside the clothes was equally unimpressive. Small and slight, with few womanly curves. Dark damp hair, tucked beneath a nondescript bonnet. If this girl had inherited her mother's striking beauty, she kept it well hidden. Perhaps, Agatha thought, the unfortunate girl had inherited her father's eccentric behavior instead.

How could this creature possibly fit in with the wealthy, titled women of London? Agatha thought of her own children, a daughter, Catherine, betrothed to the Earl of Gathwick, and a son, Wyatt, who shared his mother's fondness for amassing a fortune. Thanks to Wyatt's careful management of their estates, they had become one of the most prosperous families in England, and had even been invited to dine with the king. That had been one of Agatha's proudest moments.

"At least you can earn your keep. The vicar told us that you have a fine mind, and that your father saw to your education. I suppose I can find you a position with one of our better families in London."

London. Olivia thought about her impressions of the city on her single visit some years ago. Row upon row of town houses. Carriages clattering along narrow, dirty streets. Vendors, and parades of people, and parks filled with nannies and children. She had returned to her quiet country home and breathed a sigh of relief. "I cannot go to London. I prefer to remain here."

"It is out of the question. As your mother's only kin, I have no choice but to take you back."

The carriage rolled to a stop in front of a modest cottage. "Pack your things, girl," Agatha said sharply.

"Now?"

"Of course," Agatha snapped. "Did you think we would make another trip just to fetch you later?"

"Will you come inside?" Olivia struggled to remember her manners. "And perhaps have some tea while I pack?"

Agatha's reply was curt. "No, girl. Now move quickly." She folded her arms across her ample bosom. "We are eager to return to London. We've suffered quite enough discomfort."

Olivia was relieved that her aunt had refused her invitation. She was in desperate need to be alone. To gather her thoughts. To fill herself with the scents and sights and sounds of her home. To allow her heart a moment to grieve.

As she closed the door and leaned against it, her eyes filled with fresh tears. How she loved this place. For as long as she could remember, it had been her home. A home filled with love.

She touched a hand to the shelf that held her parents' precious manuscripts. She had instructed the vicar to see that their papers were given to the university.

Perhaps to others the St. Johns had seemed odd.

Always walking about the countryside, sketching the wild creatures, observing and recording in a journal. But scholars had held both husband and wife in high esteem. As for Olivia, she adored them both, and had enjoyed nothing so much as the time spent in their company.

Hearing the impatient stomp of the horses, she hurried to her room and began to pack. There was little enough to take with her to London. Two serviceable gowns, one gray, one blue. A shawl, a bonnet, a parasol. As for the rest, she knew the widow Dillingham would distribute them among the needy of the village.

On a sudden whim she walked to her parents' room and carefully folded the small, embroidered coverlet that lay across the foot of their bed. Her mother had made it before her wedding. Olivia pressed it to her face, inhaling the scent of her parents that lingered in the folds.

"Are you ready, girl?" came her uncle's irritable voice.

She raced back to her own room and picked up her valise. As she stared around the little cottage, she had to swallow the lump that was threatening to choke her. How could she leave all that she held dear? How could she just walk away from her memories, her childhood, her life?

She glanced at the two crude rocking chairs, fashioned by her father's hand, placed side by side in front of the fireplace. She could hear, inside her head, her mother's voice. "The mind is a wonderful gift, Livvy. In it we carry all of life's treasures. All the laughter, all the love. And so long as they are tucked safely away in our mind, they are always there when we need to take them out, to remember, to savor..."

"Come along now," her uncle called sharply.

Olivia lifted her chin higher and strode out to the waiting carriage. The driver helped her inside and stowed her valise. As soon as her uncle settled himself beside his wife, they began to move.

She turned her head, drinking in her last glimpse of her beloved home. As they rounded a bend she strained until, at last, the little cottage slipped from view. She glanced up. Seeing her aunt's penetrating stare, she bit her quivering lip until she tasted blood. She was determined that these two people would witness no further sign of weakness. But as she closed her eyes against the pain, she began to recall some of her treasured memories of her life with her gentle parents. They were not gone, she consoled herself; they would live on forever in her mind.

Chapter Two

"Beggin' yer pardon, m'lord." Mistress Thornton swallowed twice while Lord Stamford looked up from the ledgers on his desk.

"What is it?"

"It's about the lad."

"What about him?"

The housekeeper shrugged. She'd been rehearsing this for days. But now that she was facing that dark, penetrating stare, words failed her.

"Well?" He was clearly exasperated. "Is he ill?"

"Nay, m'lord. But he…he has no one to look out for him," she blurted.

"Then order a servant to see to it."

"I have." She saw him pick up his quill, and began talking faster. "I've told that saucy, dizzy-eyed baggage Edlyn to watch out for him. But she does no more than is necessary. And with her household duties as well, 'tis easy to forget about one small boy. Especially one as quiet as that. And if I may say, m'lord, it isn't good for a young lad to spend all his time in his room. He seems to have grown pale and…sickly."

"Nonsense. I looked in on him last night. I found

nothing wrong." He returned his attention to the ledgers.

"There's something else, m'lord."

He waited, without looking up.

"The lad appears bright enough. But he needs to be educated."

"You're right, of course. Perhaps a monastery...?"

"Nay, m'lord. Why, he can't be much more than four or five years." She waited, hoping to be given an exact age. When Lord Stamford didn't bother to respond, she added, "That's much too young to be sent away."

His tone was growing impatient. "Then what do you suggest, Mistress Thornton?"

"A nursemaid, m'lord. One who can be both nurse and teacher. It seems the most likely solution."

"A nursemaid." He seemed to weigh the thought for a moment, then nodded. "A governess. See to it."

"But how, m'lord?"

He turned the page in the ledger and adjusted a candle for light. "However that sort of thing is done. Tell the servants to ask around. Perhaps someone in a nearby village or shire..."

"Most of them know little more than Edlyn, m'lord." She thought a moment. "I have a cousin in London. Perhaps she could ask..."

"Excellent suggestion. See to it, Mistress Thornton."

The housekeeper watched as he returned his attention to the accounts in the ledger.

A short time later, as the plump housekeeper made her way below stairs, she fretted that her duties seemed to increase with each passing day. Ever since

Lord Stamford had returned, life had become extremely complicated.

London

Olivia descended the stairs of her aunt and uncle's sumptuous house and followed the directions that had been given her by Letty, an elderly upstairs maid.

'I knew at once who ye were, miss." Letty's smile was the first genuine smile she'd seen in days.

"And how would you know me?"

"Why, ye'r the image of yer mum when she was yer age."

"You knew my mother?"

"Oh, yes, miss. She was so fine and sweet. All the servants missed her when she went away to marry her professor."

"You mean my mother lived in this fine, big house?"

"Indeed. You didn't know?"

Olivia was stunned. "She told me very little about her childhood. I sensed there were things that caused her pain."

"She and her sister..." The servant thought better about what she'd been about to say and finished lamely, "...were very different." She glanced around uneasily. "You must go now, miss. You would not care to keep Lady Agatha waiting."

"Thank you, Letty. I hope we can talk again later."

"Aye, miss. I'd like that. Ye remind me of yer mum, ye do."

"Thank you, Letty," she called over her shoulder. "That's the nicest thing you could have said."

This was Olivia's first chance to actually view the house, since her aunt had insisted upon confining her to the guest room with orders to remain there and even to take all her meals there. Olivia was more than willing, since their arrival had been a most unpleasant affair. Agatha had railed against the cold, driving rain, the lateness of the hour and even the fact that her sister and brother-in-law had inconvenienced her by dying at such a time as this. It had taken all of Olivia's strength of will to hold her tongue through her aunt's angry tirade.

If their journey was unpleasant, their arrival in London had been even worse. An elegant young woman in a pink gown that must surely have been made for a princess, had greeted her parents, not with a hug, but with a complaint that she was missing much-needed sleep. And when Olivia had been introduced to her cousin Catherine, the young woman's manner had become even more abusive. Her features had become as twisted and bitter as those of her mother. Except for a curt nod, she had spoken not a word before going up to her room and leaving Olivia to fend for herself.

But it was a new day. Birds could be heard chirping outside the windows. Sunshine had chased away the clouds. Olivia decided to blame the short tempers on the unexpected turn of events. After all, if she was distraught over the loss of her parents, Agatha must be equally distraught over the death of her only sister. Surely after a few days of rest both Agatha and her daughter would have softened their attitude.

Olivia paused outside the dining room, breathing in the wonderful fragrance of freshly baked bread. From the sideboard steam could be seen rising from a silver tray heaped high with thinly sliced beef. A maid paused beside the table, ladling something from a silver urn.

With a wide smile upon her lips, Olivia brushed down the skirts of her simple gray gown. But as she took a step forward, she caught sight of a tall, sunbronzed man striding across the room to embrace Agatha.

"Wyatt!" Agatha jumped to her feet, all warm smiles and eager embraces. "Oh, when did you arrive? Let me look at you."

Olivia pulled back out of sight and leaned against the wall. It seemed wrong somehow to intrude upon this homecoming of her aunt and uncle's only son. Though her stomach grumbled over the lack of food, she decided to hold off her arrival until the family had a moment alone.

"My ship arrived in port nearly a fortnight ago," came the deep rumble of her cousin's voice.

"A fortnight? Then why have you waited until now to come calling?" This was Robert's voice, raised in challenge.

"I had business to attend to, Father."

"Of course you did." Agatha's tone left no doubt that she would always side with her son. "If a man is to remain successful, he must put business affairs ahead of all others."

"So you have always said, Mother. And I have become more successful than ever. Now tell me. What has happened while I was away?"

"Mother and Father had to journey to Oxford to bury Mother's sister." Olivia recognized Catherine's whining tones. "And you'll never guess who they brought home with them."

Before Wyatt could respond she continued, "Our spinster cousin from the country."

Olivia's face flamed. Greatly distressed, she pressed her palms to her burning cheeks as the voice continued, "I warn you, Mother, I won't have that plain, horrid creature wearing my clothes."

"It's only for a few days, Catherine, until I can have the dressmaker replace those pitiful rags she brought with her."

"She can go naked for all I care. I'm not sharing my things with her. And why have you put her in the guest suite?"

"Where would you suggest I put her? In the servants' quarters?"

"That would be too good for her. Have you forgotten, Mother? Ian and his family will be coming to pay a visit soon. I won't have the Earl of Gathwick being introduced to her. I would simply die if my intended and his mother knew we were related to...to...that bumpkin."

"Don't worry your pretty head about it, my princess. Nothing will ruin your chances with the earl and his family." Agatha's tone was soothing. "Your father and I don't want her here any more than you do. I'll find someone to take her off our hands, even if she has to muck stalls to earn her keep."

Stunned and horrified at what she'd overheard, Olivia began to back away, determined to hide herself in the guest suite until she could pack her bags and flee this hateful place.

Bringing a hand to her trembling lips she turned away. But even as she raced along the hallway, the cruel laughter followed, mocking her.

Minutes later, in her room, she heard a voice from the doorway. "So, here's our little mouse."

Olivia looked up from the valise into which she was hastily stuffing her belongings. A tall man with sandy hair and pale blue eyes leaned against the open door, his arms folded over his chest.

"I figured, after overhearing all that business below stairs, that you'd be packing."

"How did you know…?" Feeling her cheeks flame, she ducked her head and resumed her activity.

"I saw the hem of a skirt fluttering in the doorway. Who, I asked myself, but our little country cousin, would have tried to slip away without revealing herself?"

"You seem quite smug. Is that why you're here? To accuse me of eavesdropping?" She folded her blue gown, the one she'd intended to wear tonight to sup with her aunt and uncle and cousins.

"On the contrary. I am appalled at my sister's behavior. And I came here to make amends." He walked up to her and extended his hand. "Hello, cousin. I am Wyatt Lindsey. Could we begin afresh?"

For the space of several seconds Olivia stared at his hand, then into his face. Despite the elegant cut of his clothes, there was a certain boyishness to his smile. She sensed that he was very aware of his charms, and accustomed to using them. "I…suppose we could." She offered her hand. "I am Olivia St. John."

He continued holding her hand a moment longer than necessary, until, flustered, she forcibly removed it.

He chuckled at the color that flooded her cheeks, though he couldn't tell if she was flattered by his attentions or angry.

He was more than a little surprised by what he'd found. Pleasantly so. When Catherine had called their cousin a spinster, he had imagined a much older, plainer woman. Why this lovely creature was unmarried was a mystery. But as long as he intended to spend a few days here before returning to his country home, he planned to sample his pretty little cousin's wares.

He nodded toward the valise. "Where are you planning on going?"

"I have no thought, other than that I must leave this place, where I am so unwelcome."

"Perhaps I could...help you." He touched a hand to a tendril of dark hair that had fallen loose from the neat knot at her nape.

At once she pulled back from his touch. "In what way can you help?"

He smiled. She was not going to make this easy. No matter. He enjoyed a challenge. He reached into his waistcoat and removed a rolled parchment. Unrolling it, he walked to the writing table and handed her a quill.

"First, you will sign your name to this document."

Mystified, she moved closer. "What is it?"

"Nothing of any importance. It merely names me executor of your estate."

"My estate?" She gave a harsh laugh. "Your parents informed me I was penniless."

"And you are. It's merely a formality. But as a solicitor, I prefer everything to be tidy. Sign here."

She eyed the document, then shook her head. "The words have my head spinning. I would rather take my time and read it. Perhaps if you'd care to leave it..."

His smile, which only moments earlier had been

warm and friendly, suddenly looked dangerous. He took a step closer and watched as she backed away. He took another step, and she did the same, until her back was pressed against the wall.

"You don't want to anger me, cousin. I make it my business to know all of the wealthy and titled here in London." He pressed his palms to the wall on either side of her face and leaned close until his lips were mere inches from hers. "I might be…persuaded to help you secure a position. That is, if you are willing to be…very nice to me."

Outraged, Olivia tried to shove him away, but his strength surprised her. "I may be a country lass, unaccustomed to the ways of your London friends, but I understand what you're suggesting and I want no part of it."

At the last moment she managed to turn her face, so that his lips brushed her cheek.

"Stop this." Again she pushed against his chest, but she was no match for his strength. "Let me go, Wyatt, or I shall scream."

His eyes narrowed. "Go ahead and scream, little mouse. My parents are out in the garden. And the servants would never dare interfere."

As she started to protest, his mouth covered hers, stifling her words. His hot breath filled her lungs.

A sense of panic welled inside her. This couldn't be happening. Not here in the home where her mother grew up. Not in a place where servants bustled about in the hallways just beyond the door.

She struggled, harder now, as the panic grew. She kicked and bit and scratched, managing to draw blood along his cheek. But each time she fought him, he became more aroused.

This was what he'd wanted. The chase. The duel. The chance to subdue his opponent. And then the humiliation. That final act of domination was, to him, the ultimate reward.

He moved so quickly she had no time to react. Within minutes he had thrown her to the floor. With one hand he pinned her arms up over her head while the other hand fumbled beneath her skirts.

The boyish smile had been replaced by a look of evil. "Now, cousin, I will show you how I intend to bid you welcome. And when I'm through, you will sign anything, if you know what's good for you." His eyes narrowed to slits as he straddled her and shot her a look of triumph.

He was suddenly doused with a bucket of cold water. It poured over his head, causing him to gasp in shock. As the water spilled down his tunic and immaculately tailored waistcoat, he rolled to one side, releasing his grip on Olivia. She sat up, shoving damp hair from her eyes.

Old Letty stood over them, holding an empty bucket.

"Forgive me, m'lord," she said apologetically. "I was coming in to help the young miss with her bath, and I seem to have stumbled over the rug."

"Why, you old hag! No one takes a cold bath." His voice thundered with rage.

"The young miss specifically requested cold water, is that not so, miss?"

"Y-yes. Indeed it is," Olivia managed to say as she struggled to her feet.

Wyatt's eyes were dark with fury. "You old witch. I ought to…"

"I summoned your father and mother." Letty's

eyes bored into his. "His lordship should be upstairs any moment."

"What is it, Letty?" came Robert's voice from the hallway.

At once Wyatt scrambled to his feet and rearranged his soaked clothing just as his father stepped through the doorway.

"A bit clumsy I was," the old servant explained. "And the young lord was kind enough to help me clean up my mess."

"So I see." Robert arched a brow at the puddles of water on the floor. Then he flicked a glance over Olivia, pale and trembling, and his son, one cheek scratched and bleeding, working frantically to straighten his soaked clothes. "Come along, Wyatt. Leave that for the servants."

Wyatt's eyes were chips of blue ice, his voice a whisper for Olivia's ears alone. "One day soon we'll meet again. Without the old hag to protect you. And then you'll pay. Oh, little cousin, how you'll pay."

When the two had gone, Olivia turned to Letty. "How can I ever thank you? I thought..." Without warning she began to weep.

"There now, young miss." The old woman drew her into her arms and held her until the tears had run their course. "Everyone here knows about Master Wyatt. He has despoiled many of our young servants. All of them fear him."

"Why doesn't someone tell his parents?"

"No need. They've seen for themselves. But they choose to look away, and blame others for their son's flaws. 'Tis always the servant's fault, and the poor young woman is dismissed and branded a slut."

"Is that what they will say about me?"

The servant shrugged, unwilling to inflict more pain on this distraught young woman than she already bore.

But though the words were unspoken, Olivia knew. "Why don't you fear him, Letty?"

The old servant sighed. "What can he do to the likes of me?"

"He can have you dismissed."

"Aye. And then I'll be forced to go to live with my brother, who is already overburdened with a sick wife. But I think Lady Lindsey has a need of me, or I'd have been gone long ago."

Olivia shuddered. "I can't stay here, Letty. I have to go."

"Aye. Ye'r not safe as long as Master Wyatt is here." The old woman thought a moment. "There may be a place, though from what I've heard, ye may be going from a fire to an inferno."

"Please, Letty. Tell me. I'll go anywhere, do anything."

The servant paused a moment longer, then seemed to come to a decision. "I'll speak to Lord Lindsey. If the past is any indication, he'll be eager to be rid of you. This will relieve him of his obligation to you, and free you, as well."

With a swish of skirts she was gone, leaving Olivia to huddle behind closed doors, jumping each time she heard a footstep along the hallway.

She knew, without a doubt, that she had seen, in Wyatt's cold, unemotional features, the face of pure evil. A cruel heartless creature who would take what he wanted. With no apology. No remorse.

The trembling started in her limbs, until her entire body shuddered. Still she forced herself to remain standing as she waited and watched and listened.

A short time later there was a rap on the door.

"Who...who is there?" Olivia kept the width of the room between herself and the door as it was thrust inward to admit the servant.

The old woman's heart went out to the girl who stood pale and shivering across the room.

"Lord Lindsey agrees that it would be best if you were to go quickly. Even now the coach is being prepared." Letty gave the young woman a sympathetic look. "Ye'll need a cloak, young miss. 'Tis a long, cold ride to Cornwall."

Chapter Three

Cornwall

The English countryside, shrouded in darkness, rushed past the windows of the carriage in a blur. Occasionally Olivia could glimpse the lights of houses in a distant village. Such scenes brought a lump to her throat.

How she missed her little cottage in Oxford where life had been so simple, so peaceful.

"Oh, Mum. Oh, Papa."

There had been no time to grieve. No time to bid a proper goodbye to the villagers who had been her friends and neighbors for a lifetime.

She leaned back in the carriage and closed her eyes. She had slept through part of the journey, but her dreams had been troubled, robbing her of rest. And so she sat on the hard seat of the swaying carriage, tense, frightened, overcome with emotions. She wondered if she would ever be able to put aside the humiliation she'd experienced at Wyatt's hands. Just thinking about it had her trembling again, and she closed her eyes and drew her cloak about her to ward off the chill. At once the image of her cousin's evil smile and cruel hands had her jolting upright. She struggled to put him out of her mind, but thoughts of him lingered like a foul stench.

She drew a deep breath and wondered again what lay before her. What sort of hellish place was Blackthorne? Letty had hinted at something dark and dangerous. Something even worse than the place she had just escaped. Was it possible? Could anything be worse than her aunt and uncle's house of horrors?

Olivia peered into the darkness and watched as the faint glow of lanterns grew brighter. It would appear that the carriage was nearing its destination at long last.

The light was closer now, and she could make out the darkened shape of what appeared to be a fortress. Turrets loomed against the night sky. There were few welcoming lights in the windows. Instead, a solitary figure stood in the courtyard, straight and tall as a soldier, holding aloft a single lantern.

As the carriage made its way along the curving drive, the wind seemed to pick up, causing trees to sway and dip like angry demons. As if on cue lightning cut a jagged path across the sky, followed by the rumble of thunder. And as the carriage rolled to a stop and the driver helped her to alight, the skies opened up with a torrent of rain.

In that instant she looked up and saw a man's face peering down at her from one of the windows. In the glow of candlelight his face appeared waxen, ghostlike.

She froze, unable to move.

"Welcome to Blackthorne, miss." Pembroke accepted her satchel from the driver and hurriedly led the way inside out of the rain.

"Thank you." She was shivering so violently, even her words trembled.

"My name is Pembroke."

"Pembroke. I...saw a man. In an upstairs room."

"That would be Master Bennett, the younger brother of Lord Quenton Stamford. He has trouble sleeping."

"His face looked...ghostly-white."

"Aye, miss. Master Bennett is...sickly." He turned away. "Your rooms are ready. If you'll follow me."

They seemed to walk forever. Through a darkened foyer, along an even darker hallway, where candles sputtered in pools of wax. Up a curving stairway, where Olivia glimpsed shadowed tapestries, then along another hallway, where a door was abruptly opened, spilling light into the darkness.

A man stepped through the doorway, directly into Olivia's path. She slammed against a solid wall of chest. Her breath came out in a whoosh of air. Strong hands closed over her upper arms, steadying her. As he drew her a little away she had a quick impression of a darkly handsome face, and eyes so piercing they held hers even when she tried to look away. He was scowling. His temper, simmering just below the surface, was a palpable thing.

A hound stood just behind him, looking as angry as its master, with lips pulled back in a snarl, teeth bared. A warning growl issued from its throat.

Fear, sharp as a razor, sliced through her.

"Lord Stamford." Pembroke's cultured voice broke the stunned silence. "This is Miss St. John. The lad's governess. She has just now arrived from London."

"Miss St. John." The voice was low and deep. The look he gave her was intense. Probing. With just a flash of surprise. He had been expecting to meet a pinch-faced, elderly nursemaid, much like the one who had ruled ironfisted over his own childhood, and that of his younger brother. It had never occurred to him that a nursemaid could be young and fresh, with eyes more green than blue, and dark hair curling damply around dimpled cheeks.

"Lord Stamford."

He felt her trembling reaction to his touch and deliberately kept his hold on her a moment longer than he'd intended before lowering his hands to his sides. There was a fragrance about her that was reminiscent of something half-forgotten from his childhood. He absorbed a quick jolt to his already-charged system as he watched her take a hasty step back.

"It's a rather dreary night to be sending a young woman on such a tiring journey. Why didn't your driver put up at an inn for the night?"

"This was the way my uncle wished it."

"I see." He could see a great deal more. She was afraid. Had actually trembled at his touch. But whether she was afraid of him, or men in general, he couldn't be certain. No matter. She wasn't here to mingle with men, but to assume the care of one small boy. It would be wise to keep that in mind. Especially since the touch of her had caused an unwanted reaction in him, as well. A reaction he hadn't felt toward a woman in a very long time.

"My housekeeper, Mistress Thornton, has told the boy about his new nursemaid. He is looking forward to meeting you."

"The boy?" Her tone was sharper than she'd intended. Perhaps it was the lateness of the hour. Or a need to mask her fears. Or the fact that fatigue had her in its grip. Whatever the reason, she found herself bristling at his casual dismissal of his young charge. "Does the boy have a name?"

His tone was equally curt. "He does. His name is Liat."

"Just Liat? Has he no other?"

Her impertinence was growing more annoying by the minute. "Nay." His eyes narrowed fractionally, issuing a challenge of their own. "You will want your rest, Miss St. John, since I expect you to give the boy your full attention on the morrow. I bid you goodnight."

"Good night, my lord." As she stepped past him she glanced into the room and caught a glimpse of a man's figure huddled in front of the fire. When he looked up, she caught her breath. It was the man she had seen from the carriage. A man whose face had lost all its color. But his eyes, so like Lord Stamford's, were dark and piercing. And haunted.

Before she could see more Lord Stamford abruptly pulled the door shut.

Even as she followed Pembroke, she could feel him still standing where she had left him, staring after her. She stiffened her spine. She'd had quite enough of men who flaunted wealth and power. Such men, she vowed, would never again see any sign of weakness in her.

Still, the thought of that dark, chilling gaze boring into her back had the hair at her nape prickling until they paused outside a closed door.

"Here we are, miss." Pembroke opened the door

and carried the lantern across the room where a fire blazed on the hearth. "This is your sitting room."

It was a large room with several comfortable chaises positioned in front of the fireplace, and a side table holding a decanter and several glasses. In an alcove were a desk and chairs.

"The lad's chambers are through those doors. And in here—" he opened another door and pointed "—is your sleeping chamber."

She couldn't seem to take it all in. Nodding dully, she crossed to the fire and held out her hands to the heat. She'd never felt so cold. As though her bones had turned to ice.

"Mistress Thornton is sending up a tray, miss. I expect you're hungry after your journey."

"Yes. Thank you."

"I'll say good-night now, miss."

"Good night, Pembroke."

She waited until the door closed behind him, then sank down into a chair and stared at the flames.

What had she gotten herself into? Who was this child she would be caring for? What had happened to the man with the pale skin and frightened, haunted look? And what had made the lord of the manor so tense and angry?

She had hoped that her arrival at Blackthorne would put all her fears to rest. Instead, she felt more alone, and more desolate than ever.

The hated dream returned. Cold, icy terror held her in its grip. Once again Olivia felt the strength in Wyatt's hands as they pinned hers. Though she struggled, it was impossible to dislodge the weight of his body from hers. His mouth clamped over hers and his breath, hot, ragged, had hers hitching in her throat.

Like one drowning, she fought her way up through the tangled weeds threatening to choke her. As if from a great distance Olivia heard muted, shuffling sounds. She jerked upright, embarrassed that a servant had found the new nursemaid asleep, and in the throes of a nightmare.

"Oh. Sorry." She shoved a lock of hair from her eye and struggled to brush away the cobwebs.

The servant was watching her closely. Too closely. She was pouting, obviously annoyed at having one more duty thrust upon her at such an hour. "Mistress Thornton said I should bring you some food." She pointed to a tray resting atop a nearby table

"Thank you. That was kind of Mistress Thornton. And I am indeed hungry. What is your name?"

"Edlyn." The servant tossed a log on the hearth, then straightened, wiping her hands on her apron.

Olivia poured herself some tea. "What can you tell me about Liat, Edlyn?"

"Not much to tell. He arrived here with Lord Stamford."

"Arrived? From where?"

The woman shrugged. "Some heathen island in the Caribbean. Some say—" she lowered her voice and her eyes narrowed thoughtfully "—the boy is Lord Stamford's bastard son. "

Olivia sucked in a breath. "I do not hold with idle rumors. What of the boy's mother?"

"The boy claims his mum is dead. Perhaps she met the same fate as Lord Stamford's wife."

"His wife?"

"Lady Stamford." Edlyn's tone hardened. "You'll

hear soon enough. It's all anyone talks about in the village. She was a great beauty. Lord Quenton's younger brother, Bennett, adored her, as did his grandfather. She was found dead at the foot of the cliffs. Master Bennett was found nearby, barely clinging to life.''

"Oh, how dreadful."

"Aye. Though Master Bennett survived, he cannot walk or talk, so he can never reveal what happened. He spends all his time seated at his bedroom window, staring out to sea. The king's own surgeon came to examine him, and said he exists in a world of his own. Shortly after the surgeon's visit Lord Stamford left.''

"Left?"

The woman frowned. "Went off to sea, leaving his grandfather to deal with the tragedy alone. No one had seen or heard from Lord Stamford again until his grandfather died and he returned to claim his inheritance. Not that we cared. Blackthorne was better off without the likes of him.''

Olivia was surprised at the servant's venomous tone. "I would think, if you value your position here, you would be more careful of the things you say about Lord Stamford."

"My position." The servant gave a harsh laugh. "I came to Blackthorne with Lady Stamford, as her ladyship's maid. After her death I was treated like a common servant, and sent to the scullery, to exist on little more than bread crusts and gruel.''

In such sumptuous surroundings, Olivia thought that highly unlikely. "And now?" she asked. "It would seem your position has improved."

The servant gave a snort of disgust. "Now that Lord Stamford has returned, I know not what my duties are.

Nor does anyone in this household. We await his lordship's bidding. At all hours of the day and night 'twould seem.''

The anger in this woman made Olivia extremely uncomfortable. She had heard much more than she wanted.

She abruptly changed the subject. "What sort of child is Liat?"

Edlyn shrugged. "Scared of his shadow, he is. Keeps to himself. Never laughs or cries. Or shouts or runs. Just hides away in his room." She lowered her voice. "Probably touched in the head." Satisfied that she'd relayed enough gossip for one night, she yawned loudly. "Will you be wanting anything else?"

"Nothing, Edlyn. Good night."

When the servant was gone, Olivia lifted the lid of a tureen and inhaled the fragrance of beef broth. Beneath a domed cover she found thin strips of beef swimming in gravy. In a silver basket were several thick slices of bread.

She sipped the soup, tasted the tender beef, bit into the crusty bread. But the troubling things she'd been told about Blackthorne and its inhabitants had stolen her appetite.

Feeling restless, she crossed to her valise, hoping to unpack. Strange, she thought as her clothes spilled onto the bed, that they seemed to be in disarray. Could that rustling sound that awakened her have been the servant, rummaging through her things? At once she dismissed such thoughts. A servant would realize that a simple governess had nothing of value. These fears were the result of Edlyn's tales of dark deeds. Such talk had her imagination running wild.

Sinking into a chair, she pressed her hands to her

cheeks and thought about all that she had seen and heard. She squeezed her eyes tightly shut to blot out the fears that seemed to be closing in on her. She would rest for a moment, before pulling herself together for the task ahead.

It was her last coherent thought as she gave in once more to the need to sleep.

The sound that awakened Olivia was unlike anything she had ever heard. A long piercing scream that chilled her blood and had her leaping to her feet in alarm. Surely this sound was not made by a human. A wild animal perhaps. Caught in a trap and about to give up its life.

But it was coming from inside the house. Somewhere along these very halls. That realization had the hairs at her nape prickling.

Olivia raced across the room and tore open the door. The sound was louder now, a long thin wail that went on and on until she was forced to cover her ears.

Without giving thought to what she was doing, she scurried along the hall until she came to the door of the man she had seen huddled in a chair.

The door was open, and Olivia could see Lord Stamford and a woman, her nightclothes in disarray, standing on either side of a bed. At the foot of the bed was a young, red-haired servant.

Lord Stamford bent down and gathered the blanketed figure of his brother in his arms while the woman held a cup to his lips.

"Do as Mistress Thornton bids you, Bennett." The voice coming from Lord Stamford's mouth was unlike the one Olivia had heard earlier. Gone was the haughty tone of arrogance. Now the words were soft, soothing, as a mother might croon to her infant.

The wailing abruptly ceased. The cup was drained. And then there was only a childlike sobbing that went on for several more minutes before silence prevailed.

"He will sleep now, m'lord," the woman said.

"Thank you, Mistress Thornton." Quenton looked to the foot of the bed. "And thank you, Minerva. I'm grateful that you got to him so quickly."

"You're welcome, my lord." The young servant smoothed the covers. "Have no fear. I'll stay with him now and see that he sleeps."

As Quenton turned away, he caught sight of Olivia standing in the open doorway. Without a word he crossed the space between them and swept her roughly into the hallway, pulling the door shut after him.

"Forgive me, Lord Stamford. I didn't mean to pry."

"But that is exactly what you were doing."

"I...heard the scream and had to investigate. I didn't know what I was hearing. I thought..." She bit her lip, unwilling to finish what she'd been about to say.

"It does take some time to get used to, Miss St. John." With his hand beneath her elbow he steered her along the hall toward her room. He seemed in a great hurry to be done with her. "My brother is very ill. He is haunted by old memories. Memories that manifest themselves in the night and cause him great anguish."

"Can nothing be done for him?"

Quenton shook his head. "The physicians who have examined him have assured me that they know of nothing that can help him."

She paused outside her doorway and for the first

time looked up into his dark eyes. There was such pain there. Such misery. It touched her heart. "I'm sorry, Lord Stamford."

She could see the flicker of annoyance. It was obvious that he didn't want her pity.

He started to turn away, then thought better of it and turned back to her. "The next time you hear my brother's cries, Miss St. John, I advise you to remain in your room." He gave a curt nod of his head. "I bid you good-night."

She watched as he made his way down the hall. Then she entered her room and closed the door, leaning wearily against it.

"Well," she whispered. "Welcome to Blackthorne, my girl."

Chapter Four

Scant hours later Olivia was up and preparing for her first day as nursemaid. Dressed in her simple gray gown, she had just finished tying back her hair into a neat knot at her nape when there was a knock on her door.

"Come."

Edlyn entered carrying a tray. If anything, her frown was even more pronounced. "Mistress Thornton said I was to bring you tea and biscuits."

"Thank you, Edlyn. That was kind of Mistress Thornton. If you don't mind, I'll take the tray with me and have my breakfast with Liat."

The servant turned away with a scowl. "I'll fetch it there myself or Mistress Thornton will have my head."

"There's no need." Olivia wanted to be alone when she met the lad for the first time. She wanted no distractions that might cause him to put up his guard. "I won't say anything to the housekeeper. I'm sure you have more than enough chores to see to."

"Aye. Especially when Mistress Thornton is in one of her moods." The woman rolled her eyes. "You've never been insulted until you've had your ears blistered by the old biddy."

"I'll keep that in mind."

Olivia waited until the servant had left before carrying the tray through the door to the boy's chambers. The connecting sitting room was much like hers, with a cheery fire blazing on the hearth, and several comfortable chairs and a chaise. There was a small table as well, which Olivia decided would make an excellent writing table for her young charge.

She knocked on his bedroom door, then opened it.

"Hello, Liat. My name is Olivia St. John." She paused in the doorway and watched as the little boy turned. He was perched on a trunk which he'd dragged over to an alcove. His feet were bare, and he was wearing short pants and a shirt made of some sort of colorful fabric. She made a mental note that the boy needed warmer clothing for the brisk English weather. "What are you looking at?"

The boy shrugged and held his silence.

Olivia crossed the room and paused beside him. "Ah. I see. The gardens. You have a very good view from here. My, they look very small when viewed from so high." She smiled at him. "Would you like to walk in the gardens?"

He shrank back.

"You mean you wouldn't like to go outside? Why, I should think a boy like you would enjoy running between the hedges, and chasing butterflies."

At that he perked up. "Butterflies?"

Ah, so she had managed to snag his attention. "You didn't think there were any butterflies in England?"

He shook his head.

She gave him a friendly smile. "Well, there are.

And deer and rabbits and squirrels. Wouldn't you like to see them?''

He nodded.

''Good. Then we'll stroll the garden as soon as we've broken our fast.''

He shook his head again. ''I'm afraid.'' His voice was little more than a whisper.

''Afraid of what?''

''Of the monsters.''

''What monsters?''

''The ones—'' he glanced around fearfully ''—that sweep in without warning and blot out the sun.''

Puzzled, Olivia was about to ask more questions when he suddenly pointed. ''Here comes one now.''

She turned her gaze to the window and watched as a bank of stormclouds covered the sun, shrouding the land in darkness. ''It's just a little rainstorm, Liat. Surely you saw such storms before you came to England.''

He vehemently shook his head. ''On my island the sun was always shining. And it was always warm.'' He shivered. ''There are monsters here that snatch away the sun and warmth. Just the way they snatched away my mama.''

Olivia's heart went out to the frightened little boy. If there was one thing she understood, it was the confusion that came from having loved ones snatched without warning. ''Come with me, Liat. Don't be afraid,'' she urged when he hesitated.

Taking his hand she helped him down from the trunk and led him across the room to where a fire burned on the hearth. She motioned for him to sit on the rug, then settled herself beside him, drawing up her knees. Filling two cups with tea and milk, she handed him one and sipped the other.

"I recently lost my father and mother, too."

"Did a monster come and snatch them?"

"No. They died. Now they're with the angels."

"Where?"

"In heaven."

"Do they like it there?"

She nodded. "Very much. They're happy in their new home."

"Do you think my mama is there with them?"

"I know she is. And though you can't see her, she's still looking out for you. Just as my parents are looking out for me."

"If she's looking out for me, why did she allow me to be taken away from my island and brought to this place?"

Olivia watched the way his lower lip quivered. How she longed to take this poor child into her arms and kiss away his fears. But, she reminded herself, she was his governess, not his mother or doting aunt. Her job was to help him cope with the situation. And perhaps toughen him up in the bargain.

"We don't know why things happen, Liat. But we must trust that all things happen for a reason."

He seemed to digest that for a long moment before looking up at her. "Have you always lived here at Blackthorne?"

She shook her head. "Like you, my home is far from here."

"Then why are you here?"

"I'm here to be your teacher and your nurse, and, if you'll let me, your friend."

"Do you like it here?"

"I don't really know yet. I've only just arrived. But I'm going to do my best to like it here."

As soon as she had spoken, she felt a strange sort of comfort. Odd, she'd meant only to soothe his fears. But her own burden seemed suddenly lighter. It was true. She did intend to do her best to make her stay here, and that of the lad, as pleasurable as possible.

"Here." She broke apart a biscuit and spooned fruit conserve over it before handing half to him.

He nibbled, gave her a faint smile of approval, then finished the rest.

"You see?" She sipped her tea and returned the smile. "Papa used to say that talking out your fears was an important first step. Then you must face them if you are to conquer them." She brushed her fingers across his cheek and gave him an encouraging smile. "We will face our fears together, Liat, until there are no fears left."

Quenton Stamford stood perfectly still, cautioning the hound at his heel to do the same. He hadn't meant to eavesdrop. In fact, he'd only come to handle the introductions between the boy and his new governess. But now, watching and listening, he wondered about the fates that had sent this young woman to Blackthorne. Upon his first view of her, he'd thought that she might prove to be too young and inexperienced for the job. Too fragile. And too filled with her own arrogance and uneasiness to be of any help to a lost, frightened child. Now he was beginning to hope she might be just what the boy needed.

It weighed heavily on his mind that the lad was so out of his element in England. But there had been few choices left. With the death of his grandfather, Quen-

ton had been forced to return to Blackthorne in haste.
Still, he had made the boy's mother a promise on her
deathbed to protect Liat from harm. The only way to
keep his promise was to bring the boy here.

He watched and listened a moment longer as Olivia's voice washed over him.

"Liat, my mother used to quote from the Great
Book, 'To all things there is a season. A time for plant-
ing, a time for reaping. A time for laughing, a time
for weeping. A time for living, a time for dying.' This,
then, is your time to grow, to learn and to let go of
your fears. And I shall do the same."

Quenton nodded. Very well. He would let her remain. For now.

He turned and left as quietly as he had arrived. The
hound moved soundlessly at his side.

If only the solutions to all his problems could be as
simple as this had proved to be. Now he could turn
his attention to those damnable ledgers, and the mess
his grandfather had left behind.

"Come, Liat." Olivia opened the door of his chambers and beckoned him to follow. "It's time for us to
explore Blackthorne."

As they made their way along the hall he whispered,
"The servants told me I must never go in there." He
pointed to Bennett's room.

"Why?"

He shuddered. "Edlyn said there's a monster living
in there."

More monsters. Olivia was determined that such
nonsense must stop at once. "He isn't a monster. He
is a young man. Come. I'll show you." Without wait-

ing to think about what she was doing, she knocked, then opened the door.

Inside, the pale young man looked up, startled, from his chair by the window. The servant, Minerva, looked equally startled.

"What are you doing, miss?"

"My name is Olivia St. John. And this is Liat. I thought…" She wondered what she could possibly say to excuse her impulsive behavior. "I thought we might sup with you this evening."

"Master Bennett always sups alone, miss."

"And so do we," she said with a smile that included the silent young man. "If we were to take our meal together, it would give Liat a chance to get to know you. And you to know us."

"I don't think…" Before the young servant could refuse, she caught sight of Bennett's eyes, wide and pleading. "Well…" She considered, wondering how the housekeeper would react when she heard about this. Still, Master Bennett looked almost eager. She relented. "Aye. I'll have Edlyn bring your trays. We eat at dusk."

Olivia nodded, then turned to smile at Bennett. "Until dusk, then."

She caught Liat's hand and led him from the room. He didn't volunteer a word until they reached the kitchen. Then, in a hushed voice, he said, "That was my first monster, ma'am."

Olivia bit back her smile. "Aye. And mine as well."

"Who are you and what are you doing in my kitchen?"

At the booming voice they both turned to face a woman who was at least as tall as Pembroke, with hands big enough to handle with ease a side of beef or a whole roasted pig. These hands were now planted at either side of enormous hips encased in a shapeless gown.

"My name is Olivia St. John."

"The new governess."

"Aye. And this is Liat."

"My name's Molly. Molly Malloy. But I'm known as Cook."

"Hello, Cook." Olivia grasped her hand. "We've just come from a walk around Blackthorne and hoped we could warm ourselves with a cup of tea."

"Then you've come to the right place. Sit." Cook indicated a scarred wooden table.

Within minutes there were steaming cups of tea in front of them, along with tarts still warm from the oven.

"You do know the way to Liat's heart," Olivia said as she gratefully sipped the tea.

"Like my tarts, do you, lad?"

Because his mouth was full, he merely nodded.

"When Bennett and Quenton were lads, they couldn't get enough of my tarts."

"You've known them since they were young?"

"All their lives. And their father before them. Good lads they were. And still are."

While she spoke she continued rolling dough and shaping it into small tarts. Mistress Thornton ambled in and poured herself a cup of tea, and within minutes Pembroke joined them as well.

"I see ye're getting acquainted with the lad and 'is governess," the housekeeper muttered as she helped herself to a tart.

"Aye." Cook handed a tart to the butler. "Been

telling them about the lord and his brother. Got into mischief when they were younger. But never anything mean-spirited."

Pembroke nodded. "They always looked out for each other. But they were full of energy."

"Do you recall the time the old lord had us hunting all over Blackthorne for his two grandsons? Turned the house upside down, we did."

"Where did you finally find them?" Olivia asked.

"In the stables, beside their favorite mare, who had just foaled. All three young ones, the lads and the foal, being licked and nuzzled until they had fallen asleep." Mistress Thornton, in her high-pitched voice, had them all laughing as she recalled the scene.

It was a most pleasant hour. And it gave Olivia a chance to see Lord Stamford in a whole new light.

"Miss St. John seems attentive enough, m'lord. She and the lad seem to be getting on. A bit bold though. Has no qualms about poking all round the place, chatting up the servants."

Mistress Thornton saw Lord Stamford glance up from his ledgers and started talking faster to hold his attention. "From what I can learn, she's educated. Her parents were scholars. Made their home in Oxford. And..."

"Thank you, Mistress Thornton." Quenton rubbed at his temple to relieve the dull throb of a headache, made worse by the shrill voice. "Tell her to bring the lad to sup with me tonight. I'll see for myself how they're getting on."

"Aye, m'lord." She twisted the apron in her hands as she gathered up her courage. "That might prove to be a bit of a problem."

"A problem?"

"She asked if she and the lad could take their meal with Master Bennett tonight."

He shot her an incredulous look. "My brother?"

The housekeeper looked away. "I told her it was impossible. Master Bennett always takes his meals alone in his room with one of the servants to assist him."

"Why did she wish to eat with my brother?"

Mistress Thornton shrugged. "She seems to think that having company will ease some of the young lad's fears."

His scowl deepened. The housekeeper braced herself for his wrath. Instead he said through gritted teeth, "Very well. Invite Miss St. John and the lad to sup with me. And have one of the servants bring along my brother as well."

"To dine with you?" The housekeeper was so startled she couldn't help staring.

Instead of responding, he merely glowered at her.

"Aye, m'lord. I'll see to it myself." She hurried away and sent a servant to inform the new governess that she would be expected to dine with Lord Stamford and his brother.

An honor indeed, seeing as how the heir to Blackthorne had dined alone every night since his return.

Minutes later there was a knock on Liat's door. "Miss St. John?"

Olivia looked up at the dour Edlyn. "Yes?"

"Mistress Thornton says you and the boy are to dine with Lord Quenton tonight."

"But I had hoped to dine with his brother."

"Master Bennett will join you."

"Thank you." Olivia stood and held out her hand to Liat. "Come. I'll help you wash and get ready."

He held back. "Must I go?"

"Don't you want to?"

He shook his head and studied the floor.

"Why?"

"I'm afraid."

"Of Lord Stamford?"

He nodded. In a very small voice he said, "He doesn't ever speak to me. Or smile. He just looks at me. And his eyes aren't happy."

"I see." She knelt, so that their faces were level. "I only met Lord Stamford twice. Both times were on the night I arrived. He was a bit abrupt with me as well. So I suppose I should be as frightened of him as you are."

"Are you?"

She nodded. There was no point in denying the truth. "I suppose we're always afraid of what we don't know. But I've heard he's a very fine man. And very fair." She hoped her little lie would be forgiven. In fact, she'd heard whispers from the servants that Lord Quenton Stamford spoke to them only when necessary, and that he was most often brusque and impatient.

There were rumors and mutterings about him being repeated in every room and hall of the great manor house. Talk that he had been a murdering, thieving pirate in the employ of King Charles. That he had led a life of debauchery in the port city of Jamaica. And that the lad, Liat, was just one of his many illegitimate children. Olivia was determined to turn a deaf ear to all. Her only concern was the well-being of Liat. But it was difficult to ignore the rumors.

She got to her feet. "Let's get ready and go to dinner together, shall we?" She offered her hand again. This time Liat accepted, and followed her to the basin of water.

A short time later they made their way downstairs.

"Good evening, miss." Pembroke stood guard in front of massive double doors. "His lordship is expecting you."

He opened the doors, then stepped aside, allowing Olivia and Liat to precede him.

The little boy's hand found its way into Olivia's. And though she gave him a bright smile, her heart was thundering.

The room suited the man. It was a formal dining hall, hung with tapestries and furnished in a lavish manner. On either end of the hall was an enormous fireplace with logs ablaze. A long wooden table, capable of seating a score of people, dominated the center of the room. A dozen lavish pewter candleholders bathed the room in light.

"Lord Stamford." Pembroke's cultured voice broke the silence.

Quenton Stamford stood in front of the fireplace, staring into the flames. At the sound of Pembroke's voice, he turned. The hound at his feet stood and issued a warning growl.

This time Olivia could see the man much more clearly than on her earlier meetings in a dimly lit hall. A dark angel. The thought jolted. He was very tall, with wide shoulders and narrow waist. The elegantly tailored jacket couldn't hide the ripple of muscle along his arms and shoulders. Dark hair curled over the collar of his shirt, framing a clean-shaven face that might have been handsome had it not seemed so stern. His jaw was square, with a hint of a cleft in the chin. In his hand was a silver goblet. Both his hands and face, she noted, were bronzed by the sun. From his years aboard ship, no doubt.

As always, his eyes, so dark and piercing, held her when she would have looked away.

"Miss St. John and the lad are here."

He swung his gaze to the older man. "Thank you, Pembroke. You may tell Mistress Thornton to hold off serving until my brother joins us."

"Aye, my lord." Pembroke stepped discreetly from the room and closed the doors.

"Will you have some ale, Miss St. John? Or some wine?"

"No, thank you." She wasn't aware that she was squeezing Liat's hand until he glanced up at her. At once she relaxed her grip. Then, annoyed that their host hadn't even acknowledged the child, she said boldly, "Perhaps Liat would like something."

He arched a brow. "Would you, boy? What do you drink?"

"M-milk, sir."

"Ah yes. Of course. I shall tell Mistress Thornton."

The door opened and the housekeeper bustled in, looking more frazzled than usual. Her dustcap was askew, ready to plop in her eye any moment. Her stained apron hung at an awkward angle, attesting to the fact that she'd been forced to deal with more than her usual duties.

Behind her walked one of the groundsmen, a village youth with a strong back and bulging muscles. In his arms he carried the lord's frail brother.

"Ye'll set Master Bennett here by the fire," the housekeeper ordered.

When that was accomplished, she began directing two serving wenches in her usual shrill manner.

"Not there, you mewling miscreant. Lord Stamford sits at this end of the table."

Olivia winced, then glanced at her host. He showed absolutely no emotion as his housekeeper continued to browbeat the servants.

"The china here. The crystal there. Not that one. His lordship prefers ale with his meal. Give me that, you pribbling flax-wench." She sent the two servants back to the kitchen while she finished preparing the table herself. When it was finished she was sweating profusely and dabbing at her forehead with the hem of her apron.

"Ye'll let me know when ye wish to eat, m'lord?"

"Aye, Mistress Thornton. And would you tell Cook that the lad prefers milk?"

"Milk?" She glanced at the boy, then muttered under her breath, "The lad desires milk." In a louder tone she called, "I'll send a servant to the cowshed at once."

"Thank you, Mistress Thornton."

She bowed her way out.

With the housekeeper gone, an awkward silence settled over the room and its occupants.

"Miss St. John, Liat, I understand you have already met my brother, Bennett."

Olivia smiled. "Yes. We had hoped to share a meal together tonight in Bennett's room. But this is much nicer, don't you think, Bennett?"

He stared at her in stunned surprise, as though he couldn't quite believe that she was speaking directly to him.

"I hope we'll be friends." She offered her hand and

he had no choice but to accept her handshake. The fingers touching hers were limp and pale and trembling.

In his innocence, Liat blurted, "Why doesn't he answer you, ma'am?"

"My brother can't speak," Quenton said simply.

"But I heard..." she began before Quenton cut her off with a warning look.

"He may make a few unintelligible sounds when he is asleep, but awake, he is incapable of speech. Would you care to take a seat?"

He indicated several chairs around the fireplace. Olivia perched on the edge of one. Liat climbed up to another, then settled himself back against the cushions.

Quenton was determined to be civil, if it killed him. "I'm told you lived in Oxford, Miss St. John."

"Yes." She felt a wave of pain that caught her by surprise. How she missed her home and her parents, and the friends she had known for a lifetime.

Quenton was watching her closely. As was his silent brother.

"Did your father teach at the university?"

She nodded, not trusting her voice. She swallowed twice before managing, "He was a professor of botany and zoology. My mother and I acted as his assistants."

"You assisted him? In what way?"

She flushed. "In very minor ways, I assure you. He taught me the names of plants and animals. When he took me into the fields, I was expected to watch for certain species, and collect them for his students."

"I see. And did you go into the fields often?"

"Every weekend." Her smile bloomed. "I did so enjoy those times. I thought...if you wouldn't mind, that is, I'd like to take Liat for walks around Blackthorne and see if he might learn the names of some of the plants and animals.''

He glanced at the lad. "Would you like that, boy?"

"I…suppose so, sir."

"Good. Then you have my permission, Miss St. John." His eyes narrowed. "I must insist, however, that you stay away from the cliffs."

"The cliffs?"

Before he could respond there was a knock on the door, and the housekeeper entered, followed by her serving wenches.

"Come, Miss St. John. Liat." Quenton signaled to the village youth, who hurried forward to carry Bennett to a seat at the table.

Olivia was left to ponder the wide range of emotions she could read in the two brothers' eyes before they had turned away so abruptly. A brooding, simmering fury in Quenton's. And in Bennett's, stark terror at the mention of the cliffs.

She thought again about what Edlyn had told her. Quenton's wife had been found dead at the foot of those cliffs. And Bennett had been found nearby, barely clinging to life.

Sadly, whatever Bennett knew about the tragedy was locked away in his battered mind.

Perhaps forever.

Chapter Five

Pembroke stood at attention behind Quenton, who sat at the head of the table. Bennett sat at his left side, with Olivia at his right side and Liat beside her. The housekeeper bustled around the table, directing the servants in the proper way to serve the guests.

Wine was poured in three goblets, though only Quenton tasted his. This was followed by a silver tray of biscuits so light they seemed to melt on the tongue. A second servant followed offering a tray of clotted cream and fruit conserves. There was a platter of new potatoes swimming in gravy, and a second platter of vegetables arranged in a clear liquid of broth.

As each course was offered, Olivia would spoon some onto her own plate and help Liat do the same.

When a serving wench approached the head of the table with a large platter, Quenton glanced at the servant, then at the housekeeper.

"What is this, Mistress Thornton?"

"Mutton, m'lord."

"Did you inform Cook that my brother dislikes mutton? I specifically told you that he prefers beef. Or kidney pie."

"Aye, m'lord. But Cook says yer grandfather preferred mutton. So much so that he ordered her to prepare it every night of his life."

"Then tell her to feed it to my grandfather. And tell her also, if she serves mutton again tomorrow, she may well be joining my grandfather in his grave."

"Aye, m'lord. I'll tell that churlish, boil-brained harpy myself." The housekeeper turned the full weight of her anger and embarrassment on the innocent servant. "Take this maggot-pie back to the scullery and feed it to the animals. That's all it's good for."

Shocked, Olivia looked from Lord Quenton to the housekeeper. "You can't mean that. You wouldn't feed this to the animals."

Quenton glowered at her. "And why not?"

"Because the servants are probably making do with little more than bread crusts and gruel." The words were out of her mouth before she could snatch them back. Too late, she remembered where such a seed had been planted. By the servant Edlyn. "They would probably consider such a meal as this heaven-sent."

The housekeeper's jaw dropped. In her entire life, no one had ever dared to speak to the lord in such a manner. She looked toward Lord Quenton, whose dark gaze was fixed on the young nursemaid with such intensity, everyone in the room could feel the heat.

"Are you suggesting that my mutton should be given to the servants?"

"Your mutton, my lord? I thought you said it was Cook's mutton? Did you not suggest you would have Cook's head if she should dare to fix it again?"

Bennett, whose plate was heaped with food, and who had yet to taste a bite of it, swiveled his head to stare at his brother. His eyes seemed too big in his pale face.

Behind Lord Quenton, Pembroke stood stiff as a fence post, his face showing no emotion. But he was watching this battle of wills with great interest.

"It may prove to be Cook's head. Or...someone else's," Quenton said pointedly. "But I'll remind you it is my food, Miss St. John. And I'll say who will eat it and who will not." He pounded a fist on the table. "Mistress Thornton."

The housekeeper cowered as she moved closer, anticipating an explosion.

"Is it true that the servants are eating bread and gruel?"

"N-nay, m'lord. Well...that is, rarely. Only when Cook's in a snit over something said by one of the servants. But they have meat and soup at least thrice a week. Ofttimes even more than that."

His lips thinned. "Then they are better fed than if they found employment somewhere else?"

"Oh, aye, my lord. All in the village are eager to serve at Blackthorne. It has been thus since the time of your great-grandfather."

"Thank you, Mistress Thornton. Take this to the servants' quarters." Though he was speaking to the housekeeper, he kept his gaze fixed on the insolent nursemaid. "Tell them I hope they enjoy the mutton."

For a moment Mistress Thornton was speechless. Then, recovering, she gave the serving wench a shove. "Go on with ye, now. Ye heard Lord Stamford. Tell all those yeasty, clay-brained mammets to be grateful for his lordship's generosity."

As the servant stumbled from the room the housekeeper snatched the arm of another servant and pushed her forward. "Perhaps ye and yer brother would like some fowl, m'lord."

For the space of several more seconds he glowered at Olivia. Then, dragging his gaze away, he helped himself to a joint of fowl and motioned for the wench to serve the others.

Olivia glanced at Bennett, who had not eaten a thing. "Would you like some help, Bennett?"

Quenton spoke through gritted teeth. "Have you no care for his feelings, Miss St. John? I told you my brother cannot speak."

"So you have said. But there is nothing wrong with his hearing, is there?" She turned toward his brother. "Would you like some help, Bennett?"

The young man glanced up at her, then looked away, before giving a slight nod of his head.

"I'll fetch Minerva," the housekeeper muttered nervously. "She's a young lass from the village. She has a way with 'im."

A few minutes later she returned, followed by the pretty little redheaded servant who had been at his bedside. She took a seat beside Bennett.

"Lost your appetite again?" the girl whispered.

He nodded.

"Cook probably prepared mutton again. I know how you hate it. Here. I'll help." She placed a fork in his hand and pointed it toward the plate. "You must try at least a little taste of everything on your plate."

With the gentleness of a new mother she coaxed and praised until he had managed to eat almost everything.

"I suggest you do the same, young man," Olivia said in an aside to Liat.

"Yes, ma'am." The boy chewed woodenly while he kept his gaze fixed on the table.

All the while, at the head of the table, Lord Stamford ate in stony silence, speaking neither to his brother nor to the infuriating nursemaid and her young charge.

When the meal was done the housekeeper, eager to atone for the mutton, motioned for a young servant to approach the table with a tray of tarts.

"Ye've not had dessert, m'lord."

Quenton waved her away and lifted his goblet, draining it.

When the serving wench approached Bennett, his eyes lit like a child's.

"Would you like one or two?" Minerva asked. Without waiting, she removed two from the tray and placed them on his plate.

"Young master?" The servant paused beside Liat's chair and the boy took one tart in each hand.

"It is proper to take only one," Olivia whispered.

"Bennett took two."

"Bennett may have taken two, but you may have only one."

"What if I'm still hungry after I eat it?"

"Then we shall see about a second tart."

Olivia sipped her tea and watched as the boy returned one of the tarts to the tray before nibbling at his pastry.

"So, boy." Quenton sat back and waited until a servant had removed his dishes. "What has Miss St. John taught you so far?"

At Quenton's booming question, the lad hastily chewed and gulped, then set aside the rest of his pastry and stared at the table. "She taught me—" he thought a moment "—not to be afraid of monsters."

"Monsters?" There was a long moment of silence. "Now there's a fine lesson." Quenton's sarcasm was not lost on Olivia. "What else has she taught you?"

Liat thought long and hard. Then he smiled as he lifted his head and met Quenton's direct look. "She taught me to take only one tart at a time."

A hint of amusement flickered in Quenton's eyes, then just as quickly was extinguished, leaving only his familiar frown. "So much knowledge, Miss St. John." He gave a mocking bow of his head. "I can hardly wait to see what he will know in a fortnight."

The harshness stung. But Olivia held her head high and refused to be goaded into another outburst. She was still mortified that she had allowed her temper to rule her tongue. Her sweet, docile parents would have understood her need to champion the hungry, but would have been sorely embarrassed at her lack of manners, as was she.

"Is the boy in need of anything, Miss St. John?"

It was on the tip of her tongue to remind him once more of the boy's name. But she cautioned herself that one scene was more than enough for this, her first dinner in his presence.

"Liat's clothing seems a bit inadequate for our English weather. Especially if he is to accompany me on walks through the countryside."

He nodded. "I'll have Pembroke take you and the lad to the village tomorrow. I'll trust you to buy him whatever he needs."

"Thank you."

Just then Liat slipped from his seat and walked around the table.

Quenton sent him a look of dark disapproval. "You did not ask to be excused, lad."

"Nay, sir. I am not leaving."

"Then where do you think you're going?"

Even Olivia was puzzled by the boy's action.

He paused beside Bennett. "I...don't like to talk much either. But if you'd like, I'll talk for you."

Bennett looked thunderstruck. The servant, Minerva, clapped a hand to her mouth. And Quenton's look darkened to fury. "You will take your seat at once, lad. And when we're finished here your governess and I will have a little..."

Before he could finish, Bennett reached a hand to Liat's. For a moment he merely stared into the boy's eyes. Then, with a barely perceptible nod of his head, he smiled.

There were several moments of stunned silence before Quenton pushed away from the table and got to his feet. "Mistress Thornton, have the stable lad return my brother to his room." He nodded toward Olivia. "If you'll excuse me, I have some ledgers to see to."

When he took his leave, Pembroke placed a decanter of whiskey and a box of cigars on a tray and followed. It was common knowledge that the lord worked late into the night on his grandfather's accounts.

Olivia watched as Bennett was carried up the stairs to his bedroom, followed by Minerva. It saddened her that Lord Quenton had made no attempt to speak to his brother. But, she amended, the loss was his.

Catching the boy's hand, Olivia trailed behind the others. "I was very proud of you, Liat. That was a very kind thing to do."

"I just wanted him to know that he isn't a monster. He's just a man who can't talk."

She had to swallow several times as they climbed the stairs.

"Sometimes I don't like to talk either. Especially when I'm feeling sad and lonely."

"I understand. I guess it's the same with everyone. Well," she whispered, when they reached their chambers. "tonight wasn't so bad, was it? Lord Stamford did look at you. He even spoke to you."

The lad nodded his head. "Aye, miss. But that may be even worse than before."

"Why?"

"Now I'll have to worry about answering his questions."

As Olivia led him to his bed and helped him into his nightclothes, she felt a kinship with this lad. She was beginning to think she would much prefer being ignored by the lord of the manor to being singled out for his wrath.

In the future, she would try to keep her thoughts to herself. With that resolve firmly in mind, she decided to go below stairs for a soothing cup of tea.

The hallway, like all the others at Blackthorne, was dimly lit, with candles guttering in pools of wax. As her footsteps echoed hollowly, Olivia paused. Had she heard someone behind her?

She turned, but could see no one. Feeling slightly foolish, she stiffened her spine and continued on. But the hair at the back of her neck prickled and she knew, without turning again, that there was indeed someone behind her.

Her stomach clenched, and it took all her willpower to keep from running. Still, determined to remain composed, she lifted her skirts and quickened her pace. And knew, with absolute certainty, that the one following her had also picked up speed.

"Pembroke? Mistress Thornton?" The slight quiver in her voice shamed her. But when she stopped and turned, she was certain she saw a shadow dart away.

This was nonsense. She was allowing some childish notion to overrule her common sense. What reason would anyone have for following her? Yet she was convinced that someone was.

The tea was forgotten. Now, all she wanted was to return to her own chambers and close herself inside. Despite her attempt at caution she was running now, darting looks over her shoulder, her breath coming in short gasps. As she rounded a corner she went crashing into solid muscle. Strong arms gripped her. She couldn't scream. Couldn't even cry out. All she could do was hold on while her breath tore at her lungs and she found herself looking up into Lord Stamford's scowling face.

"What's wrong?" He could feel the fear vibrating through her. Instinctively his arms tightened, and he ran a hand down her back to soothe, to comfort.

"I can't..." She sucked in a breath and struggled for calm. Her chest heaved from the effort. Her arms circled his waist and held on, grateful for his quiet strength. "Give me a moment, my lord."

"Shhh." Without thinking his voice softened, as did his touch. "Take all the time you need." The feel of her arms around him caused a jolt that was not at all unpleasant. In fact, he found himself enjoying the feeling far too much. She was so small, so fragile. So very feminine.

"I thought...I heard footsteps behind me."

"Of course you did." He breathed in the woman scent of her. Her hair smelled of rainwater and that half-remembered fragrance from his childhood.

The troublesome ledgers were forgotten. As was everything except this woman in his arms. "Probably one of the servants."

Now that he was holding her, she felt her fears evaporating. How could she have been so foolish? What could she possibly have to fear here at Blackthorne?

But even as her fears subsided, and her breathing returned to normal, she became aware of something else. The hands at her back had not stilled, but were moving along her spine in a most provocative manner. She looked up to see Lord Stamford staring down at her with a strange, intense look that had her heart starting to race again. This time it was a new and different sort of fear that gripped her.

"My lord…"

"You're fine now, Miss St. John. Nothing's remiss." Before the words were even out of his mouth, his lips lowered to hers.

It was a jolt to the system that had him reeling. He wasn't even sure how this had happened. One moment he'd been holding her, offering her comfort. The next his mouth was fused to hers in a kiss that robbed him of his senses.

She tasted as sweet, as fresh as morning mist. An innocent, untouched by the things of this world. If she knew what he was thinking she would be shocked to the core.

The touch of Lord Stamford's lips was so very different from the way Olivia had felt when Wyatt had tried to force her. Despite the aura of danger that surrounded this man, there was a feeling of safety here. And pleasure. And simmering passion. As he took the kiss deeper, she sighed and found herself slipping under the spell.

The hands at her shoulders tightened, and she could feel his heartbeat as wild, as erratic as her own. Could it be that he was feeling the same quivering need? As he lingered over her mouth, she lost the ability to think at all.

Quenton knew exactly when she became so caught up in the kiss that her fear faded and the first stirrings of passion flared. She sighed and he found himself thinking about things that had long been forgotten. The thought of taking her, here, now, had him pulling back abruptly.

Something flared in his eyes briefly before he blinked. His tone was rougher than he'd intended. "You'd best go to your room now, Miss St. John."

"Yes. Of course." It was an effort to speak. Her throat was dry, the words strained.

As she turned away he laid a hand on her arm. At once they both felt the heat.

"It might be best if you bolt the door."

She avoided his eyes.

"Just so you'll rest easier."

She nodded, then strode quickly away.

He continued to watch until she entered her suite and closed the door. He waited until he heard the bolt.

His hands were trembling, he noted. He clenched them into fists at his sides and strode quickly away. And cursed himself because, if truth be told, it wasn't some dark shadow that had him ordering her to lock her door. It was the knowledge that he didn't trust himself around her. Not tonight, with all the memories swirling in his mind.

She was too sweet. Too innocent. She stirred something in him. Something that was better off remaining buried forever.

Quenton stood on the windswept hillside, oblivious to the bite in the air. His feet were planted, steady, wide apart, as they had always been on the deck of his ship. Beside him, the hound's fur ruffled in the wind.

The sea had been his refuge. At sea he had not been treated with deference because of his name. He'd had to earn the respect of his men with sword and fist, and at times, with swift justice. But at least he'd been free to curse the storms and rage at the inhumanity he was forced to witness all around him. There, among men hardened by life's blows, he was just another rough seaman.

For a brief time, while he engaged in battles and found an outlet for all the anger and rage, he'd fooled himself into believing that he had put the past behind him. But upon his return, he'd discovered that he'd merely hidden all the pain and fury. And now the feelings seethed and bubbled just below the surface, threatening to erupt for the slightest reason, catching him by surprise.

His gaze swept the nearby graves. His parents, resting side by side. His young bride, so beautiful, so vital. He knelt beside the freshly dug mound. And now this dear old man, who had taken in his two grandsons after the untimely death of their parents and had raised them with discipline and love.

How had it all gone so wrong?

Perhaps the Stamfords had been born under some sort of curse. Or a dark cloud, which would always blot out the sunshine. It seemed the only explanation.

In Jamaica the paper-skinned, blackbird-eyed old woman had looked into her crystal and had told him to beware.

"There is one who wants what is yours. Not just your fortune," she had warned, "but everything you hold dear."

He'd managed a bitter laugh. "That may have been true at one time. Now I value nothing in life, except a ship under my feet and a moonless night in which to ply my trade for His Majesty." His remark had been tossed carelessly, causing the old woman's tone to frost over.

"You think to bury your heart so deeply it cannot be broken again. But you are wrong, my young friend. You are fooling only yourself. One day you will step out of the darkness. But only you can find the pathway back to the light."

"No, old woman. It is you who are wrong. You see, I much prefer the darkness."

He had tossed her a coin as carelessly as he had tossed his casual remarks. But her words had remained with him. And haunted him still.

He studied the marker over his wife's grave. With her he had been, in those first heady months, deliriously happy. What made it even more perfect was the fact that his grandfather and his younger brother adored her as much as he. Their family had seemed, in that brief time, to have reached a pinnacle of happiness.

And then it had all come crashing down. At first he'd been unwilling to admit the truth, even to himself.

But then, as she had become more distant and more riddled with guilt, there had been no room left for denial. Antonia had been unfaithful. The rumors and whispers of a secret lover were rampant. Even young Bennett was suspect, though Quenton adamantly refused to dignify such a suspicion.

Even now it wasn't anger or jealousy he felt whenever he looked at Bennett; it was shame. Shame that his brother had been there in his stead. And pity, for what the once young, handsome Bennett had become. A hard, cold knot of pity that ate at Quenton's soul. The sight of all that suffering and torment was tearing him apart.

Their loving family had been shattered beyond repair by grief and scandal and despair. Despite what the old woman had said, he could see no way back to the light.

He shivered and glanced up. Two figures strolling across a moor caught his eye. Even from this distance he could see the shiny blue-black cap of hair on the boy, and the wind-tossed curls of the nursemaid.

If he were to leave now, he could avoid running into them. That was his first thought. He had steadfastly ignored Olivia St. John since the night he had kissed her. But something made him stay where he was. Perhaps it was curiosity over the wild gesturing of the boy, as he pointed to something in the long grass. Or perhaps it was the way the young woman knelt down and guided the boy's hand to whatever had taken cover. Quenton remained very still, watching and listening.

Their voices carried on the breeze. The boy's soft, musical; hers low, cultured, with a gentle laugh that touched a chord deep inside him.

"It is a baby bird. See, his mother hovers nearby, scolding us. She was probably giving him a flying lesson when he fell to the ground."

"May I keep him?"

"Oh no, Liat. That wouldn't be right. He needs his mother. She's the only one who can properly feed him and teach him the things he needs to learn to survive on his own."

"May I hold him?"

"No, dear. His poor mother is nearly mad with worry. Listen to her heartbreaking cries."

The boy glanced up at the bird that was circling their heads.

"Let's leave him now, so his mother can sit beside him and satisfy herself that he's unharmed. Come. I'll race you to that rock." Olivia caught up the hem of her skirt and started running.

Liat followed suit.

Olivia slowed her pace to give her young charge a chance to pass her. He touched a hand to the stone and turned to her in triumph. "I beat you."

"So you did." Her cheeks were flushed from the effort. Her eyes crinkled with laughter.

Just then her eyes widened as Quenton shifted and the hound beside him gave a deep growl of warning. "Oh, Lord Stamford. Forgive me. I didn't see you there."

"It's quite all right, Miss St. John." The breeze caught a strand of her hair and he found himself staring at it. Not brown, as he'd first suspected, but a rich chestnut, with glints of honey and russet. The need to touch it, to allow those silken strands to sift through his fingers, had him clenching his hands at his sides.

"I see you found the boy the proper clothing." He

turned his gaze to Liat, noting the sturdy boots, the warm breeches and snug sweater. "How are you enjoying your walk, boy?"

"Fine, sir." His eyes, which only moments ago were dancing with unconcealed pleasure, now lowered, avoiding contact.

"I overheard you discussing a baby bird. Would you care to show it to me?"

The boy shrugged. "I suppose so."

Quenton began to follow the boy, taking perverse pleasure in the fact that the nursemaid had no choice but to go along. She lengthened her steps to keep up with his.

"Miss St. John said I couldn't keep it."

"She was quite right. Babies need their mothers."

As they approached the spot, the mother bird once again took flight, squawking and scolding. The baby lay in the grass, its little wings fluttering. At a word from Quenton, the hound remained several paces behind them, standing as still as a statue.

"What happens to baby birds that lose their mothers?" Liat asked.

"Someone else is obliged to take them home and care for them." Quenton knelt in the grass beside the boy. "But no matter how much care they are given, it is never the same as they would have received from their mother."

"I would know how to care for them."

"You would?"

Liat's tone, his manner, were hushed and solemn. "I would take the baby with me everywhere. And I would talk to it, and love it. And when the bird cried for its mother, I would sing to it just the way the mother bird sang."

Quenton sat back on his heels a moment, studying the boy with great interest. He had the feeling the boy was no longer just talking about the bird.

He got to his feet and glanced at the mother bird, hovering nearby. "We'd best move away, or this baby's mother won't be singing, but attacking with that sharp beak."

As they made their way across the moor Quenton asked, "Have you learned the names of any plants or animals, boy?"

Liat nodded. "Miss St. John pointed out Agri...Agri..."

"Agrimonia eupatoria," she prompted.

"Ah, yes." Quenton nodded. "Agrimony. The Greeks called it *philanthropos,* because the seeds would cling to the clothes of passersby."

Olivia was surprised at Quenton's store of knowledge. "You know of agrimony?"

"A little. My grandfather thought it an excellent cure for his ailing back."

"Very wise of your grandfather." Olivia's smile widened as she directed her words to her young charge. "You see, Liat, herbs like agrimony can be helpful for many things. For healing wounds. Even for curing a naughty liver."

"A better cure might be to give up drinking spirits," Quenton said dryly.

She shook her head. "Papa used to say that a nip of spirits at the end of a day warmed a man's blood, cleared his brain and soothed his soul."

He smiled. "I believe I would have liked your father."

"You would have had no choice." Her eyes danced

with unconcealed joy. "To know Papa was to love him."

"Then you are fortunate indeed, Miss St. John." He loved the way she looked, her skin glowing, dark hair wind-tossed. Without thinking he tucked a strand of her hair behind her ear.

Her eyes widened at the intimacy of his touch. She felt the heat rush to her cheeks and knew he could see it. Once again she was reminded of the kiss they had shared in the darkened hallway. A kiss that had caused her a very sleepless night.

"Miss St. John told me her parents are in heaven with my mama." Liat looked very serious as he added, "Miss St. John said heaven is where the souls of the just go when they die."

"Did she?" Quenton's manner turned suddenly brusque. He made a slight bow of his head to Olivia and the boy. "I'll say good-day now. You'll remember to stay clear of the cliffs."

Without another word he strode away, leaving the nursemaid and her young charge to stare after him.

What had caused his abrupt change of mood?

Was he thinking of Liat's mother? Olivia thought of what the servant Edlyn had told her on her first night here.

Or was it guilt that put the frown between his brows?

She felt suddenly chilled. "Come, Liat. Let's go inside and ask Cook for some tea."

As they made their way back to Blackthorne, she berated herself for the confusing feelings she experienced whenever Lord Stamford was near. He was, by all accounts, a heartless man. Yet, when she looked in his eyes, it wasn't coldness she saw, but pain. And deep-seated sorrow. A sorrow that touched something in her. Though she didn't understand why, she was drawn to him. And that knowledge greatly disturbed her.

She shivered again and brushed aside all thought of him. Lord Quenton Stamford was unworthy of her pity or her concern. She would concentrate instead on Liat.

"Come on." She lifted her skirts and quickened her pace. "Last one home is a—" her eyes danced as she thought of Mistress Thornton's constant insults to the servants "—beslubbering, beef-witted bugbear."

She and her young charge were giggling hysterically as they raced across the moor.

Chapter Six

"Hello, Minerva." Olivia paused on her way to the stairs.

"Miss St. John." Minerva, red curls bouncing, bobbed and curtsied as she stepped into the hall. "I was just going off to fetch Master Bennett some tea. The days are long for him, confined to his room and all."

"I'm just headed out to the gardens with Liat. Perhaps Bennett would like to join us."

The young woman shook her head. "Master Bennett hasn't been out of the house in years, miss."

"Is his health so fragile that he can't breathe the air?"

"I don't believe so. It's just…" She paused, biting her lip and glancing around before continuing, "He becomes highly agitated if anything disturbs his routine. I think he feels safe in his room."

"Safe. I see." Olivia glanced at the closed door, then came to a decision. "Papa used to say if we risk nothing, we gain nothing. I believe I shall invite Bennett along and leave the decision up to him."

Before the young servant could bar her way, she

knocked, then entered Bennett's room. He was seated in front of the window, hunched in a chair, a shawl draped around his shoulders.

"Good day, Bennett. Isn't it a lovely day?"

For a long moment he merely stared at her, as though unaccustomed to having anyone speak to him. Then he nodded.

She gave him a wide innocent smile. "Liat and I are going for a walk in the gardens. I wondered if you and Minerva might want to join us."

The young servant dashed in behind her. "Master Bennett, I tried to explain...."

Olivia cut her off with a gentle smile. "I could have one of the stable lads carry you downstairs and settle you on a bench. The sun's out this afternoon. A fine day to sit and admire the gardens."

He showed no emotion as he continued studying her, and she was about to admit defeat when he shyly nodded his head.

"You'd like to join us?"

He nodded again.

"Splendid." She turned to Minerva. "If you'll fetch a stable lad, I'll go on ahead with Liat and find a suitable bench in the sunlight."

"Yes, miss." The servant glanced uneasily from Bennett to the nursemaid, then hurried away, fearful of what the housekeeper would have to say about this.

"I intend to ride over every section of Stamford land and speak to the tenant farmers myself, Pembroke." Quenton paced the floor of his grandfather's study, hands behind his back. "As soon as I've had time to examine all the accounts."

"Very good, my lord."

"From what I've studied so far, it simply doesn't make sense." He stopped, frowned. "The land appears to be yielding rich crops. The herds appear to be thriving. Yet the Stamford accounts are actually dwindling."

"Old Lord Stamford's health was failing in the last years, my lord. Perhaps his figures are incorrect."

"That was my first thought. But so far I've found no errors on my grandfather's part." He began pacing again. "No matter. I'll get to the bottom of this. If I have to, I'll ride to London myself and speak with the solicitors about…" He looked up at the knock on the door. The housekeeper stepped in, looking even more frazzled than usual.

"Yes, Mistress Thornton?"

"It's about your brother, m'lord."

Quenton visibly paled. "Is he ill?"

"Nay, m'lord. But he's…he's insisted on going outdoors."

"You mean he spoke?"

"Nay, m'lord."

"Then how could he insist upon anything?"

"That elf-skinned, tickle-brained servant Minerva told me. She said Miss St. John invited Master Bennett to join her and the lad in the garden, and Master Bennett has set his mind on doing just that. You see?" She looked beyond him and pointed.

Quenton walked to the window and stared down at the strange procession. A muscular lad was carrying Bennett in his arms. Behind them trailed the young servant, Minerva, carrying an array of quilts and pillows. Following them was another lad toting a heavy arm chair.

"I agree that it seems a great deal of work for the

servants. But I don't see the harm, Mistress Thornton.''

''Yer brother hasn't been out of his room since...''
She paused and glanced at Pembroke for support. ''He
must be looked after like a child, m'lord.''

Quenton turned to Pembroke. ''Do you agree?''

The older man walked to the window, then sadly
nodded. ''Your grandfather feared Master Bennett
might take a chill. In his condition, he would be hard-
pressed to fight it. If you'd like, Mistress Thornton can
order the servants inside at once, my lord.''

''Nay.'' Quenton touched his arm, then hurried
across the room. ''You and I will see to it ourselves,
Pembroke.''

The butler followed reluctantly as Quenton made
his way downstairs and out to the garden. Quenton's
frown deepened. He had spotted the nursemaid on the
far side of the garden making her way toward the others. So, this entire foolish scheme had been her idea.
It would seem she was intent upon insinuating herself
into affairs that were of no concern to her. It was time
someone reminded her that her only duty lay in the
care and education of the boy.

As he approached he could hear Minerva's voice.

''I thought Master Bennett would be more comfortable in a chair than on one of these benches.'' The
young servant hastily arranged pillows to cushion
Bennett's seat and back, then settled one quilt over his
lap and another around his shoulders as the stable boy
set him down.

The two stable hands doffed their hats to Lord
Stamford and hurriedly returned to their chores.

''I'm so glad you agreed to join us, Bennett.'' Olivia paused beside his chair. ''There's something

soothing about the sounds and scents of a garden. Don't you agree, Minerva?''

"Yes, miss." The servant seemed tense and edgy, not at all certain she had done the right thing. She hovered behind Bennett's chair like a mother hen.

Both women looked up when a dark shadow fell over them.

"Well, well, Miss St. John." Quenton was positively scowling by the time he made his way across the garden and confronted her. "You've given poor Mistress Thornton heart palpitations."

"Whatever for?"

"For bringing my brother out here without her permission."

"But I asked Bennett, and he said he wanted to join us."

"And just how did he do that?"

"The same way anyone would." She turned to the young man, who huddled inside his quilts as though it were the dead of winter. "Bennett, do you wish to be here?"

He looked from his brother to the young woman, then hesitantly nodded his head.

She turned to Quenton with a smile.

But instead of admitting his error, his scowl deepened. He glanced around. "Where is the lad who is supposed to be under your watchful care?"

"Liat will be here any minute now. I expect he's skipping along the path. I encourage him to skip, hop, jump and run whenever he is outdoors."

"You do? And why is that?"

"Because I found him much too pale and subdued when I first arrived. Children need to run and frolic in the fresh air. And they need to shout once in a while, to exercise their lungs. Don't you agree, Bennett?''

The young man seemed surprised to be included again. Gathering his wits, he gave a half smile and nodded.

''You see?'' Olivia's smile widened. ''It's a shame our English summers are so short. But we just have to make the most of them. I've been trying to keep Liat outdoors from late morning until early evening. I find he's sleeping better. And his appetite has certainly increased.'' She turned to Bennett. ''You might want to do the same. It's amazing what a little fresh air can do.''

Quenton felt his temper rising. ''It was my grandfather's belief that fresh air can also bring chills, Miss St. John.''

''My parents never subscribed to that theory, Lord Stamford. In fact, they saw to it that I was raised in fresh air. Mum said I often took my naps under the shade of a tree while she and Papa sketched and studied the nearby plants. They allowed me to accompany them on climbing expeditions as soon as I was old enough to toddle after them. I don't recall ever having a chill.''

''Then you are fortunate indeed, to have been blessed with robust health, Miss St. John.'' Quenton's frown remained. ''But my concern is with a brother whose health is...fragile.''

''My point exactly.'' She shot him that dazzling smile that always seemed to do strange things to his heart. ''What possible harm could there be in enjoying a pleasant afternoon in the garden?''

''The harm is...''

''Ma'am! Ma'am!'' Liat's excited cries had Olivia

racing headlong across the garden, with Quenton and Pembroke in hot pursuit.

"What is it? What's wrong?" Olivia cried when she spotted the lad on his knees on a grassy walkway.

"Look, ma'am. A butterfly." He pointed to a cluster of crimson roses. Amid the petals could be seen a gentle flutter of pale wings in exquisite shades of iridescent pink and lavender.

"Well, Liat. You are fortunate indeed." Olivia caught her breath and knelt beside him. "That's a *Lycaena helle,* considered one of the loveliest of all butterflies."

"Truly, ma'am?"

"Yes." When the butterfly moved on to another flower she got to her feet, smoothing down her skirts as she did. "Why, I'm told the king himself considers them good fortune."

"He does?"

She nodded.

Beside her, Quenton shot her a look of amazement. "The king, Miss St. John? I suppose you have that on good authority?"

"The best. My father told me that King Charles has an extensive butterfly collection. And he sent out a request for a *Lycaena helle* because he was missing one, and his collection wouldn't be complete without it."

"Should we send him this one, ma'am?" the boy asked.

Liat looked so serious, Olivia had to laugh. "In order to do that, we would have to kill the butterfly. Is that what you'd like to do, Liat?"

The lad's eyes widened. "Oh, no. I could never do that."

"I'm glad. Neither could I." She thought a moment, then said, "Perhaps you would like to do what my father and mother did, when they were studying the various species. They drew pictures of them, identifying their colors, and where they were sighted. Would you like to try drawing the *Lycaena helle?*"

The boy nodded eagerly. "I'd like that, ma'am."

"Then come along and we'll fetch some drawing materials."

As they started back along the path, Liat skipped ahead, the hound bounding after him, leaving Olivia and Quenton to follow, with Pembroke trailing discreetly behind. With each step Olivia became more aware of Quenton's ominous silence. It would seem that he was holding his anger on a short leash.

As soon as he approached Bennett's chair Liat began chattering away, describing the butterfly in detail.

"It was pink and lavender and Miss St. John said it is called a...*Lycae*...*Lycaena helle,* one of the king's favorites. But I didn't want to kill it and send it to the king, so we're going to fetch some drawing materials so I can sketch it." He turned to his nursemaid. "Do you think I could send the sketch to the royal palace? King Charles could put it in his collection instead of the real butterfly."

Olivia gave him a gentle smile. "That's certainly something to think about. Though I imagine by now the king has probably spotted a few *Lycaenae* of his own."

She offered her hand. "Come along, Liat. We'll get those supplies."

"There's no need, Miss St. John." Quenton had been amazed, not only by the words spilling out of this once silent little boy's mouth, but also by the reaction of his brother to Liat's animated conversation. Bennett's eyes had widened at the vivid description of the butterfly. He had followed every movement of the lad's hands, had even nodded his approval at the suggestion of a sketch. Perhaps there was something more going on here than a simple visit in the garden.

He turned to Pembroke. "Have a servant fetch Miss St. John's sketching supplies."

"Very good, my lord." Stone-faced, Pembroke turned away.

"Perhaps I should take Master Bennett in for his tea now." Minerva cast a worried glance toward the house.

"There's no need. Pembroke," Quenton called to his butler's retreating back, "tell Mistress Thornton to bring us some tea and biscuits as well."

The butler stopped, turned. "Tea and biscuits? In the garden, my lord?"

"Aye." Quenton ignored the little note of disapproval in the older man's voice and waved a hand in dismissal.

A short time later a parade of servants arrived carting a table, linens, a tea service and a variety of biscuits and pastries as well as meats, cheeses, jams and jellies.

Liat was sprawled on his stomach in the grass, sketching the butterfly, which flitted from flower to flower. Bennett's chair was positioned beside him, so that he could watch as the picture took shape and was slowly filled in with color. Minerva hovered behind Bennett's chair, lifting the blanket when it slipped from his shoulders, attentive to his every need.

"Will you be staying for tea, m'lord?" Mistress

Thornton directed the servants as they arranged the food, then sent them scurrying back to the house.

Quenton thought about the ledgers in his grandfather's study. So much to be done. Yet he was reluctant to leave this place. Not for himself, of course. It certainly wasn't the presence of the pretty nursemaid that held him here. Or the jabbering of the boy. Or the pleasing scents of the flowers. He would stay for Bennett's sake, he thought idly. To make sure that these fool women didn't tax his frail brother's energy.

"Yes, of course, Mistress Thornton." With an air befitting the lord of the manor, he settled himself on one of the benches. The hound lay down at his feet.

"Very good, m'lord." The housekeeper poured tea, and passed around the cups. "If there's nothing else, I'm needed in the house."

"Thank you." Quenton waved her away and sipped his tea, thinking how pleasant the sun felt.

"There are biscuits, Liat," Olivia called.

"Yes, ma'am. May I finish my picture first?"

"By all means. Biscuits, Bennett?"

"Master Bennett doesn't take a midday meal," Minerva said softly. "But he may be willing to sip some tea."

"Nonsense." While Minerva handed him a cup of tea Olivia proceeded to fill a plate with meat, cheese, biscuits and pastries. "All this fresh air is bound to give you an appetite," she said as she handed him the plate.

To Quenton's astonishment, his brother accepted the plate and began to eat, all the while watching the butterfly take shape on Liat's paper. Without seeming to be aware of it, Bennett cleaned his plate.

"Would you like a bit more?" Minerva asked.

He nodded absently.

The servant approached the table, where Quenton and Olivia sat enjoying their tea. "I can't believe how much Master Bennett has eaten," she whispered.

"It's as I told you," Olivia said matter-of-factly. "Since our daily walks on the moors and our visits to the garden, Liat's appetite has increased, and his sleep is uninterrupted."

Minerva glanced at Quenton, then said in a low voice, "'Twould be truly a miracle if Master Bennett should ever sleep through the night without those awful dreams."

Quenton set down his cup with a clatter. At the mention of Bennett's night terrors, his own appetite had fled.

Olivia glanced at the young serving girl. "Do you stay the night with Bennett?"

"Aye. I sleep on the floor beside his bed, so I can be there whenever Master Bennett needs me."

"Such devotion." Olivia could see that she wasn't the only one surprised by Minerva's admission. Quenton was staring at her with a look of astonishment.

"I've always admired Master Bennett. When he was just a lad visiting our village with his grandfather, he was very kind to me. So when old Lord Stamford asked Mistress Thornton to assign a servant to his care, I asked if I could be the one."

"But you must get weary, caring for him day and night without relief." Olivia touched her hand. "I'm sure if you asked, Mistress Thornton would find someone to take your place from time to time."

"Oh no, miss. I want to do it. Truly I do. And no one else would ever be able to take care of him the way I do." She filled the plate and hurried to his side.

Watching her, Quenton muttered, "My brother is indeed fortunate to have such a loyal servant."

Olivia nodded. But she was beginning to think there was more than loyalty involved.

"Tell me about your home in Oxford, Miss St. John." Quenton sipped his tea and watched her expression go all soft.

"It was a lovely little cottage, no bigger than the cowshed here at Blackthorne. But it was cozy. And my parents were so happy with each other." She flushed under his scrutiny. "They took great delight in each other's work. And they encouraged me to take pride in my work as well."

"With such fond memories, what could ever have persuaded you to leave?"

"When my parents died, I discovered that their estate is administered by my cousin. It was his mother who took me to live with her in London." Olivia lowered her gaze. "But I couldn't stay there."

"Why is that?"

She looked off across the garden, not wanting to meet those dark, knowing eyes. "It was an…unhappy experience."

More than unhappy, he guessed. What would it take to drive a young woman so far from home? How desperate had she become, that she would accept a job as nursemaid to a stranger's child?

"I'm sorry it was an unhappy experience, Miss St. John. But it was most fortunate for us."

When she looked up at him he cleared his throat. "I mean, most fortunate for Liat."

Her smile returned. It was the first time he'd called the lad by name. "Then you're pleased with my work?"

When she aimed that smile on him, he found his thoughts clouding, and his blood running hot through his veins. Unwilling to trust his voice he merely nodded.

"I feel I'm making progress with the lad. He's opened up a bit. You see how he is with Bennett."

Quenton glanced over as the boy got to his feet and eagerly showed his drawing to Bennett and Minerva, smiling broadly at their approval.

"He's not so fearful now as when I first arrived," she said. "Though I still sense a sadness in him. A yearning for his life before he came here."

"Does he speak of it?"

"Not often."

"I'd prefer that you not ask him about his past, Miss St. John."

She sensed the sudden tension in the man seated across from her. But when, a moment later, Liat hurried up to show them his paper, Quenton studied the crude drawing and gave the boy a nod of approval.

"Well done, Liat. Anyone seeing this would know it's a *Lycaena helle*."

Olivia blinked. How had he switched moods so abruptly? Surely she'd only imagined his earlier tension. She turned to the boy. "Now that you've finished your butterfly, Liat, perhaps you'd like a biscuit?"

"Yes, please." The boy climbed up on a chair and helped himself to biscuits and jam. As always, in the background could be heard the pounding of the surf. He glanced at Quenton. "Why is the ocean so angry here in Cornwall?"

"It isn't angry. But the rocks at the bottom of the cliffs cause it to churn. And the churning causes it to make that roar."

"I hear it at night sometimes, when I wake up." The boy put aside his biscuit. "And the keening of the wind. At least that's what Miss St. John said it is. The first time I heard it I cried. I don't like the sound of it."

Quenton glanced at her and saw the slight flush on her cheeks. It would seem that even a lie told in innocence to keep the lad from worrying caused her to suffer guilt.

"I hear it, too, at night," Quenton said gravely. "And sometimes I don't like it either."

With a grave look Liat took another bite of biscuit. "Miss St. John told me there were pretty butterflies here in England, but I didn't believe her. I thought all the butterflies in the world lived only on my island."

Again Olivia saw the slight frown between Quenton's brows. Was this his reaction whenever he thought about Jamaica? Or was it the thought of Liat's mother that brought the unhappiness?

To avoid staring at him she ducked her head and bent to the hound at his feet. "Does he have a name?"

"Thor. But I would not advise you to pet him, Miss St. John. He's apt to bite."

"Hello, Thor. I bet you like having your ears scratched, don't you, boy?" She rubbed the spot behind his ears and was rewarded by the lick of a tongue.

"He likes you, ma'am," Liat said with delight.

"So it would seem." She broke off a section of biscuit and offered it to the dog, who swallowed it in a single bite. "Are you afraid of dogs, Liat?"

The little boy considered. "I don't think so. I think I remember having a dog on my island. But I'm not certain anymore."

Quenton abruptly pushed away from the table and stood. At once the hound got to his feet also.

"Bennett," Quenton called. "How about a quick stroll around the gardens before we go inside?"

Minerva glanced at the young man in the chair, then voiced his unspoken question. "A...stroll, my lord? The stable lads have returned to their chores."

"We don't need them. I'll carry him." Quenton crossed to his brother and lifted him easily from the chair.

When the blanket fell away, Minerva quickly tucked it around Bennett's shoulders.

Without waiting for the others, Quenton began a leisurely pace along the carefully manicured paths, pausing occasionally to allow his brother to inhale the fragrance of roses, or to admire a fountain in the middle of the garden.

"I want to go with them," Liat called.

"Don't you want to stay here and eat your biscuit?"

The little boy shook his head. "I'd rather go with Lord Quenton and Master Bennett."

"Very well." At Olivia's approval he raced after the others.

As Olivia set off on a brisk walk to join him, she found herself deep in thought.

Just a short time ago this little boy, whose haunting, mysterious past had left him afraid of monsters he saw in the clouds, would have preferred to remain alone in his room. Now he was running as fast as his little legs could carry him in order to catch up with two men whose lives were bound by some dark mysterious thread of shared tragedy.

She wondered again at the strange twist of fate that

had brought her to this place. Had she found a safe haven? Or, like the surf she could hear at the base of the cliffs, was there a chance that she would be tossed into the maelstrom?

Chapter Seven

The nightmare was back. In it, Olivia was once again trapped. Pinned beneath the weight of Wyatt's body. His hands were rough and bruising as they moved over her. She couldn't free herself. Then his face, a face filled with evil, loomed in front of her. She looked into eyes as hard, as cold as ice and his lips twisted into a grotesque smile. She thrashed about, desperate to escape his clutches. She tried to scream but found it impossible to make a sound.

She sat bolt upright in her bed. The room was dark except for the coals in the fireplace gleaming red-hot.

Her night shift was damp with sweat. Her heart was beating wildly, and her breathing was ragged.

She took several deep shuddering breaths, then tossed aside the covers and climbed from her bed. Crossing the room she began to pace. She hated that Wyatt still had the ability to hurt her. Even though he was far away in London, thoughts of him crept into her dreams, rendering her as terrified, as helpless as she had been at their first encounter.

Was this what had happened to Bennett? she wondered. Had he been hurt so deeply that it haunted him still? Could the same thing happen to her? Would her fears begin to paralyze her to the point of helplessness?

Nay, she thought angrily. She might be still frightened of Wyatt, but she wasn't helpless. This had been merely a dream. If it had been real, she would have dug deep within herself and this time, have found the strength and courage to fight him. It still pained her that it had been an elderly servant who had rescued her. If not for Letty... She shuddered to think how many innocent girls had been despoiled by her hateful cousin.

Calmer now, she stopped her pacing. Despite the fact that morning was still hours away, she knew it would be pointless to try to sleep.

She draped a shawl around her shoulders and walked from the room. Perhaps a cup of tea would soothe her jangled nerves.

In the hallway, the flickering light of candles sent distorted shadows dancing across the walls and ceiling. At once her heart skipped a beat. Was she being watched? Was someone following her?

She had to pause and gather her courage. Hadn't her papa often called her a fanciful child? She could see fairy dust in moonbeams. Or, like Liat, monsters in the shape of darkened tree branches. But there was a practical side to her as well. She was the product of two very sensible parents. She squared her shoulders and held her fears at bay as she descended the stairs. Her bare feet made no sound as she made her way to the huge refectory.

In the morning this room would be warmed by the heat of flames over which would be roasting whole pigs, lambs and platters of fowl. The ovens would give off the wonderful aroma of baking breads and biscuits. Servants would be scurrying about, devouring a hasty meal before beginning their daily chores. But now, in the small hours of the night, this room, like the rest of the manor house, lay slumbering and silent.

Olivia was pleased to see a fire still burning on the hearth. Padding across the room she emptied a pitcher of water into a kettle and set it over the fire to boil. But just as she turned from the fire she caught a glimpse of a towering figure half-hidden in the shadows.

She brought a hand to her mouth to stifle the cry that sprang to her lips. "Oh, Lord Stamford." She let out a long slow breath. "It's only you."

When Quenton took a step closer, with the hound at his heels, she backed up.

"Sorry to frighten you." He saw the fear flit across her features. Saw a look of terror in her eyes before she was able to compose herself. "I didn't expect to see anyone else up at this hour."

"I…couldn't sleep."

He knew the feeling. Too well. "And you thought a cup of tea would help."

She nodded. "Would you care for some?"

He lifted his hand and she saw the tumbler filled with amber liquid. In his other hand was a decanter. "I've found my own cure for sleepless nights, Miss St. John."

Not only sleepless but restless, she realized. His thick black hair was tousled, as though he'd dragged a hand through it more than once. The collar of his shirt was open, revealing a mat of dark hair. A silk scarf that had once been carefully knotted at his throat now hung carelessly around his neck. And the familiar scowl on his face told her, more than words, that he preferred to be alone.

At a loss for words she said the first thing that came to mind. "My father often enjoyed a brandy before retiring."

"Did he?"

She nodded. "Sometimes he even managed to persuade my mother to join him."

"How bold of your mother. Did she like it?"

Olivia couldn't help smiling at the memory. "She said it didn't do much to help her sleep. In fact, it made her feel extremely alert." Oh, why had she blurted such a thing? She hoped the blush on her cheeks would be blamed on the fire.

"How fortunate for your father." Though his features remained stern, his voice was warmed by unspoken laughter. He lifted the decanter. "Perhaps you would care to join me, Miss St. John. We could see if your reaction would be the same as your mother's."

"I prefer tea." She turned away, grateful that the boiling water gave her something to do. She was unaware that the light of the fire clearly outlined her body through the sheer fabric of the night shift. But Quenton was quick to notice.

He went very still, enjoying the view. Her shawl had parted, revealing the curve of high, firm breasts beneath the prim, buttoned-to-the neck bodice. Her waist was so small he was certain his hands would easily span it. Below the flare of her hips, her legs were long and slender. The sight of her bare toes peeking out from under the hem made him smile.

Her hair, usually bound up in a prim knot, now spilled down her shoulders in a tumble of dark waves.

The firelight turned the ends to flame. Just looking at it made his throat dry.

Perhaps there was something to be said for company on a sleepless night. Especially when the company was young and fresh and easy to look at.

When the tea was steeped, Olivia lifted the cup, hoping to find a gracious way to escape to the privacy of her room.

Quenton watched her stiff, awkward movements and knew that his presence was the cause of her discomfort. Like him, she had come here to be alone with her thoughts. Still, it seemed to give him a sort of perverse pleasure to watch her squirm.

"Sit here, Miss St. John." He indicated the small chaise positioned in front of the fire. "You may as well be warm and comfortable as you drink your tea."

Though she longed to flee, there was no way she could graciously refuse. She sat, knees together, spine stiff, holding the cup to her chest like a shield.

"Are you enjoying your work here, Miss St. John?" Quenton set the decanter on the mantel, then leaned against it as he turned to face her.

"Very much. Liat is a sweet boy. Eager to please. He has a bright, inquiring mind."

Quenton nodded. "You've been good for the lad. His walks have put some color in his cheeks." He stared down into his glass. "And you were right about the benefits of fresh air. Minerva reported that my brother slept through the night after his visit to the gardens. She said it was the first time in years that he hadn't been awakened by his demons."

Her bright smile returned. "I'm so glad to hear that. I'd been afraid that I might have overstepped my bounds." She glanced away, avoiding his eyes. "I know that Mistress Thornton wasn't pleased when I invited Bennett to join us.''

"Mistress Thornton has a sharp tongue." He saw Olivia purse her lips and added quickly, "But she has a good heart. She loves my brother in her own way. She saw him nearly destroyed, and because of it, has become very protective."

Olivia gave a slow nod of agreement. "I understand. I would react the same way if anything should harm Liat."

"I promise you no harm will come to the boy." The words were spoken through gritted teeth.

Olivia felt a little quiver of response at the passion in his tone. Was this feeling in the pit of her stomach fear of him? Or something much deeper and much more primitive? It occurred to her in that instant that Quenton Stamford would be a dangerous foe, with that quick temper and hot blood. Or a fiercely protective ally. And, she thought suddenly, a riveting, exciting lover.

Now where had such a thought come from? Annoyed with herself, she sloshed tea over the rim of her cup and let out a hiss of pain.

"You've burned yourself." He dropped to his knees in front of her and took the cup from her hand, setting it on a side table with his tumbler of brandy.

"It's nothing." She was more embarrassed than hurt. Mortified that it was her own silly thoughts that had caused such a fuss.

"Hold still." He slid the scarf from around his neck and pressed it to her hand.

At his touch heat danced up her arm and she instinctively pulled back. But instead of moving away and giving her a moment to compose herself, he leaned

closer and caught her hand between both of his.
"You're very fortunate." He bent his head to examine
her flesh. "There doesn't appear to be any burn."

She had the strangest urge to touch his hair. She
actually lifted her other hand and felt the tingling in
her fingers as they brushed lightly over his head.

Suddenly he stood up and drew her with him, still
holding her by the hand.

"Does it hurt?" His face was so close, she could
feel the warmth of his breath whispering across her
cheek.

Afraid to trust her voice, she merely shook her head.
But when she looked up, those dark, compelling eyes
held her, daring her to look away.

He continued watching her as he lifted her hand to
his lips. "I couldn't bear to see you hurt." The press
of his mouth against her flesh sent a flare of heat
through her limbs that left her trembling.

"Please, I…"

"Shhh." He turned her hand and pressed a kiss to
her palm that started her pulse racing. With his fingers
at her wrist, she was certain he could feel it.

She was too stunned to pull away. Stunned, not only
by his unexpected tenderness, but by her body's reaction to it as well.

"I see I've shocked you, Miss St. John." Instead of
releasing her, he cupped her face with his hands and
studied her features as though memorizing them. His
lips curved into a hint of a smile. "Since I've already
crossed the bounds of propriety, I may as well do
something that will shock you even more."

He lowered his face to hers. When she tried to pull
away he held her firmly and covered her mouth with
his.

Heat poured between them. Even the air seemed to sizzle and snap as his mouth moved over hers in a kiss so hot, so hungry, it nearly devoured them both.

Her first reaction was to bring her hands between them in the hope of pushing him away. The thought uppermost in her mind was that she must fight him. And fight her own attraction to this dark, dangerous man. But as soon as their lips mated, all thought fled. It was impossible to think while he was weaving such magic with his kisses.

There was nothing gentle about his touch or his lips. The hands that held her were strong enough to break her. She could feel the control he exerted to keep from using all his strength. His lips were warm and firm and persuasive, moving over hers with practiced ease.

She whimpered slightly as her fingers curled into the front of his shirt. Instead of releasing her, his arms closed around her, dragging her closer. With a growl of pleasure he took the kiss deeper.

The taste of him was potently male, as dark and mysterious as the night. His hands moved along her back, his strong fingers kneading, massaging, as he changed the angle of the kiss and poured out all the feelings he'd kept buried for so long. Loneliness. Emptiness. A hunger so deep, so demanding, there was nothing that would satisfy it.

She could taste his hunger, his loneliness. It matched her own. She responded to it instinctively, answering it the only way she knew how. Though her response was hesitant and unsure, she stopped fighting him. In his arms she became soft, pliant. The lips she offered him were warm and sweet. She opened to him like a flower.

It occurred to him that the game he was playing

was a dangerous one. The woman in his arms was an innocent. He had no right to the thoughts he was entertaining. And yet, though he'd always considered himself a sensible man, he couldn't seem to get his bearings around her. He had told himself he would steal but one kiss. And then he would step back. But here he was, taking the temptation to the limit, and still unwilling to end it.

As he lingered over her lips, the thought struck. That half-remembered fragrance. Lavender. She smelled like a summer garden. He filled his lungs with the scent of her and thought he would happily drown in it.

Calling on all his willpower, he managed to lift his head. He could see her eyes, looking too big for her face. Her lips were swollen, and thoroughly kissed.

"I'm sure you'll want to return to your room now, Miss St. John." He was surprised at how difficult it was to speak. His throat was dry as dust. But he had to end this now, before he made a terrible mistake.

"Yes. I…Yes." She was afraid to trust her voice. Her breathing was still too ragged.

He turned away, to avoid the confusion in her eyes. "Would you care for the rest of your tea?"

"No."

"I'll say good-night then." He picked up the tumbler. "I'd accompany you upstairs, but I still have some brandy to finish. I do so hate to waste good brandy."

"Of course." She stiffened her spine. If he could act as though nothing had just happened between them, she would do the same. "Good night." She turned away, praying her trembling legs wouldn't fail her. At least until she was safely out of sight.

"Good night." He watched her walk away, then lifted the tumbler to his lips and drank. His hand, he noted, was shaking.

He walked to the mantel and filled the tumbler, draining it in one long swallow. Maybe, if he was lucky, he'd manage to drink the entire decanter. And wash away the taste of sweetness and innocence that still lingered like the finest of wines.

He stared into the flames, his thoughts as dark as the sky outside the window. Although he'd hoped to put it off a while longer, tomorrow would be a good time to begin inspecting the Stamford lands. Perhaps, if he were lucky, he could stretch the trip into several weeks. It would take a grueling journey of at least that long to ease the longing this simple little nursemaid had aroused in him.

Still, he had no one to blame but himself. He was the one who'd moved too close to the flame. And had gotten scorched in the process.

"Good morning, miss." Pembroke greeted Olivia at the foot of the stairs.

"Good morning, Pembroke." Olivia struggled to shake the fear that had nagged at her all night. A fear that she had once again been followed when she'd left Quenton in the refectory.

She glanced around, wondering how she would react when she saw him again. She had spent the hours pacing, seeing in her mind the passionate scene they had shared. Even now her blood heated at the very thought of how she had felt in his arms. Her body was behaving in a strange way, her breasts tingling, her heart racing as though she'd just run across the moors.

She had taken great pains with her toilette this

morning, though she refused to admit it even to herself. She was wearing her blue dress and had fastened her hair back with combs. And just before she'd started down the stairs, she had pinched her cheeks, hoping to put some color in them. Vanity, she scolded herself. Simple female vanity. And all over a dour, angry man who had probably had a good laugh at the clumsy nursemaid.

"Liat and I are going for our morning walk. I thought perhaps Master Bennett and his brother might care to join us."

"You might check with the servant Minerva and Mistress Thornton about Master Bennett. As for Lord Quenton, he isn't here, miss."

"Not here?"

"Nay, miss. Lord Quenton left early this morning to inspect his lands. I expect he'll be gone a few weeks."

"I see." She turned away to hide her disappointment. "I suppose I'll have to go in search of Minerva then."

"You'll find her upstairs caring for Master Bennett."

"Thank you, Pembroke."

Olivia made her way up the stairs. The spring was gone from her step. What a fool she had been, thinking that somehow a worldly man like Quenton Stamford would be affected by something as simple as a kiss. She had somehow convinced herself that he would be standing around waiting to see her. Like a fool in love. Taking pleasure in the simple act of looking at her. For in truth, she enjoyed looking at him. He was surely the most handsome man she had ever seen. Sleek, and dark and dangerous as a panther.

She felt suddenly too warm, and touched her hands to her cheeks, struggling to sort through her troubling thoughts.

How could she feel such things for the lord of the manor? A man whose wife had met a cruel fate at the foot of the cliffs. A man who was rumored to be the father of the little boy she'd been brought here to tutor. If that were true, he was a pure rotter, who gave not a thought to his dead lover or her son.

And yet, Olivia had seen a tender side to him. A side she wouldn't have believed had she not seen it with her own eyes. When he wasn't ignoring his brother, he was tender and caring in his presence. Though he rarely looked at Liat, he had been fiercely protective about the boy's safety. And though he often treated her with gruff indifference, he had been genuinely concerned about her hand when he thought she'd burned herself.

Or was it all part of a charming act? Was she simply not looking? Perhaps, she berated herself, she was looking, not with her eyes, but with her heart.

She would have to keep a very careful watch over her foolish, irresponsible heart.

She was much too ignorant to know how to deal with a man like Lord Quenton Stamford.

When Olivia ascended the stairs Pembroke returned to the library. The hound looked up eagerly, then, seeing that it wasn't his master, rested his head between his paws and stared morosely into the fire.

"You're looking as sad as the young nursemaid." Pembroke bent down and absently scratched the dog's ears. "What you need is a bit of cheering up. Come with me."

He started toward the door and the big dog followed. At the door to the kitchen man and dog halted. Inside Mistress Thornton was berating the cook.

"There's no reason to be cooking all this food with his lordship gone. Who's going to eat it?"

"The staff." Cook faced her, hands on her hips. Despite the fact that she was taller and wider than most men, with hands as big and soft as bread dough, her voice was softer than usual.

"And why should you make a special meal just for them?"

"They've been complaining."

The housekeeper gave a snort of disapproval. "It's that spleeny, hasty-witted Edlyn, isn't it? She's been flapping those lips and stirring up the servants again."

"And what if she has? The lass is entitled to her say."

"If she has her say and riles me just once more I'll have her sent back to the village and she can support herself by slopping Lord Thane's pigs. Now you can…" She looked up at the figure in the doorway. "Aye, Pembroke? Is there something you need?"

He hesitated, then took a step inside this foreign domain. These two were always at it. Except, of course, when the little governess dropped by. She had a way of smoothing over rough edges, and bringing out the best in people. He wished she were here now. "A cup of tea would be nice. And a scrap for poor old Thor here."

The housekeeper's thin lips curved into what could almost be called a smile. Her whole demeanor softened. "I think I could scare up a bit of tea. And maybe even a scrap or two for the hound. Sit down, man."

Pembroke pulled out a chair and stretched his long

legs in front of him. While Cook scowled, Mistress Thornton moved around the kitchen, pouring tea, cutting slices from a steaming roast.

In no time the butler was sipping tea and nibbling meat and cheese, while the hound lay contentedly on the floor licking up the last of the scraps.

"Now what's this about sending Edlyn away?" Pembroke asked.

"The ill-nurtured clotpole is like a boil. Her anger always festering. She plants seeds of trouble, she does, then waits for them to grow."

"If you'd like, I'll keep an eye on her. See that she doesn't…plant any more seeds."

Surprised at his willingness to help, Mistress Thornton could only stare at him. "Now what's brought this on?"

He shook his head, finished his tea. "I don't know what you mean. I just thought I'd help."

"Aye. Well, I'd be grateful."

He nodded. "Thank you for the tea."

"Ye'r welcome."

As he strolled away, the dog at his heels, he pondered what had happened. In all the years he'd worked in the Stamford household, he'd never before wanted to insinuate himself in matters that didn't concern him. Live and let live. That had been the way he'd spent his entire life. Forty-five years he had been at Blackthorne. As had his father before him. He'd started out in the stables, wielding a shovel that had been bigger than he. And then he'd moved into the manor house, hauling logs, stoking fires and doing anything he could to please his demanding masters.

By the time his father was too old to carry on, Pembroke had acquired the necessary polish to step into the exalted position of butler.

And in all these years, he had always managed to stay out of the petty skirmishes that were bound to crop up in a household of this size. So, he wondered, why had he allowed himself to be caught up in this one?

Perhaps he knew the answer. Miss St. John. Since her arrival, nothing was the way it had been. And just maybe, he acknowledged, that was a good thing.

Chapter Eight

The days gentled as summer covered the land with its green, green grass and soft blue sky. The gardens were a riot of color. The air was perfumed with primrose and lavender.

Only the sea remained unchanged, crashing over the rocks at the base of the cliffs with a fury that resounded throughout all the rooms of Blackthorne. By day it was a symphony, punctuated by the song of seabirds wheeling overhead. By night it was a strange, haunting fugue, keeping time to the rhythmic heartbeats of a sleeping household.

Olivia and Liat were returning from their walk across the moors. Though she had never before seen such rugged, desolate country, she found herself fascinated by it. Slabs of stone, each as big as a ship, flung by the sea and leaning one against the other to form strange shapes. Gulls and wild birds haunted the cliffs, wheeling and diving, their cries echoing across the skies.

"Look, ma'am." Liat pointed to the splendid horse and rider approaching Blackthorne at a gallop. "Is it Lord Stamford?"

"It is." Olivia's heart gave a series of somersaults. "Returning from his tour of his lands."

They watched as he dismounted and one of the stable lads stepped forward smartly to take the reins. For a moment Quenton turned and scanned the surrounding hillside until he caught sight of them. Even from so great a distance Olivia felt the power of his dark gaze. The doors were thrown wide and Pembroke could be seen standing to one side as Thor bounded around his master's feet, barking a welcome. Quenton and the hound turned away and disappeared inside.

By the time Olivia and Liat made it back to the house, Quenton was already sequestered in his grandfather's library, going over his books and ledgers.

Later that day, Edlyn knocked on Olivia's door, looking more dour than usual. "Lord Stamford has requested that you and the lad sup with him tonight."

"Thank you, Edlyn. What about Master Bennett?"

"Aye. He's to be included." The servant gave a snort of disgust. "To hear Minerva tell it, he's been twitching like a leaf in a storm all afternoon."

Olivia understood completely. She was feeling slightly agitated herself. "Come along, Liat. Let's give you a good scrubbing. We wouldn't want you to present yourself to Lord Stamford with the dirt from the moors clinging to you."

By the time they had washed and dressed and made their way to the dining hall, Olivia had her nerves thoroughly under control. She would be cool and composed, she decided. And not at all interested in anything except Liat's behavior.

As always, Pembroke stood guard before the massive double doors.

"Good evening, Pembroke." Olivia gave him a wide smile as they approached.

Liat's hand sneaked into hers.

The houseman nodded. "Good evening, miss. Lad." He opened the doors and stood aside to allow them to precede him.

"My lord, Miss St. John and the lad are here."

"Thank you, Pembroke."

Olivia steeled herself as Quenton turned from the fire. She had been prepared for the handsome, aristocratic face, the piercing gaze, the familiar frown line between his brows. What she hadn't expected was the weariness etched in his eyes.

"Good evening, Miss St. John."

She gripped Liat's hand. "Lord Stamford. Welcome home."

He nearly smiled. What a pretty picture they made. The prim and proper nursemaid and her dark-eyed, copper-skinned little charge. The lad had been freshly washed. Tiny droplets of water still clung to his hair. The dark britches and crisp white shirt framed an impish face. His hand was tucked firmly in hers, seeking, Quenton supposed, a measure of courage.

He was relieved to see that she lived up to the image that had flitted through so many of his dreams. If anything, she was even lovelier than he'd remembered. She was wearing the same blue gown she'd worn dozens of times before. It occurred to Quenton that he had seen her in only two gowns. This blue one, and a simple gray. He would have to find a way to rectify this without bruising her pride.

The hound hurried up to her, hoping to get his ears scratched. He lolled at her feet, looking dazedly happy.

"Tea, Miss St. John?" Quenton indicated a lavish tea service on a round table.

"Thank you."

As she started across the room he nodded toward a pitcher.

"And milk for you, boy."

Liat blinked. Then a slow smile touched his mouth. "Aye, sir."

"Have you been studying while I was away, boy?"

Liat nodded and accepted a glass from his tutor. "I've been keeping a journal of all the plants and creatures I encounter on my walks. Miss St. John helps me with the words. But the drawings are all mine. Would you like to see it?"

"Very much. Perhaps later I'll drop by your chambers and you can show me."

The doors were opened and Pembroke intoned, "My lord, Master Bennett."

They looked up as a stable lad carried Bennett to a chair situated in front of the fire. Minerva trailed behind, carrying his blanket. When she had seen to Bennett's comfort, she turned to leave.

"Wait, Minerva," Quenton called. "You'll stay and sup with us."

"You mean I'll help Master Bennett with his meal."

Quenton shook his head. "You'll do that, of course. But you will eat as well. I noticed last time you ate not a thing."

"My lord." The little servant's face grew as red as her hair. "'Twouldn't be right."

"Are you saying you've already eaten?"

"Nay, my lord."

"Then you'll eat. I'll hear no more about it."

The girl fell silent.

Olivia glanced at Quenton with new respect. He was aware that the servant had to go without dinner in order to care for his brother. Though he had barked the invitation like an order, it was plain that he was looking out for Minerva's welfare. And doing it without making it look like an act of kindness.

Mistress Thornton bustled into the room, bullying the servants in her usual manner. "Another log for the fire, you fool-born, loggerheaded pignut."

The rawboned youth tossed the huge logs as though they were sticks, then lumbered from the room.

"You there, you flap-mouthed flirt-gill." She tugged the ear of a slow-moving servant whose wheat-colored hair stuck out in stiff tufts. "Set that platter down and be quick about it."

Perspiring freely, she glanced at Quenton, who watched and listened in stony silence. "Everything is in readiness, yer lordship."

"Thank you, Mistress Thornton."

He led the way to the table, and stood sipping his ale while his brother was placed in a chair to his left, and Olivia and Liat took their places at his right.

"You may begin serving, Mistress Thornton."

When all the platters had been passed, he glanced at the housekeeper. "Tell Cook that the goose was an excellent choice."

"Aye, my lord. I told that craven, clay-brained baggage that if she even thought about mutton, I'd be boiling her hide."

He caught sight of Liat and his nursemaid choking back giggles. His own lips twitched ever so slightly before he dismissed the housekeeper with a stern nod of approval.

"So, Minerva." He turned to the servant. "How has my brother fared while I was away?"

"Fine, my lord."

"Has he been in the gardens?"

The servant nodded. "Whenever the weather has permitted, my lord."

"And has he…?" He turned a withering look on Olivia when she touched a hand to his sleeve. "What is it?"

Her voice was a whisper, for his ears alone. "Why don't you direct your questions to Bennett? There is nothing wrong with his hearing. And he would so like it if you would speak to him as you once did."

He glanced from her to his brother. Through gritted teeth he muttered, "Tell me, Bennett. Do you think the fresh air has improved your sleep?"

For a moment the young man seemed too stunned to do more than gape at his brother. Around the table, the others fell silent. Even Pembroke, usually so composed, stiffened and looked from one brother to the other.

With great effort Bennett pulled himself together and slowly nodded.

"Then you agree with Miss St. John that the hours spent in the gardens are beneficial?"

Again Bennett nodded, and this time he smiled as well. It was the first time that Olivia had seen him smile fully. It occurred to her that, despite the painfully thin arms and legs, he was a very handsome young man. Almost as handsome as his elder brother.

Quenton returned the smile. Then, as the others ate, he sipped his ale and stared around contentedly. Minerva was smiling and coaxing as she helped Bennett eat. Pembroke's stern countenance was wreathed in smiles as he refilled the lord's glass.

Quenton had believed he would never again know a moment's peace in this house. But the smile on his brother's lips had just erased years of pain. Of course, it didn't hurt to have a fire at his back, and a fine ale warming his blood. These were reasons enough to be glad to be here. The fact that the strong-willed nursemaid sat close enough that he could inhale her essence of lavender didn't hurt either.

There was a loud knock and Pembroke hurried to open the double doors. For long moments he held a whispered conversation with the housekeeper, who was looking even more flustered than usual. Then he straightened and crossed to the head of the table.

"My lord." He handed Quenton a scroll. "There is a messenger, awaiting a reply."

Quenton read the message, then said, "See that Cook provides him with a meal and some ale. Since the hour is so late, I suggest that he spend the night before returning with my reply."

"Aye, my lord."

Pembroke strode away and Quenton picked up his ale and drank. Aware that the others were watching him he said almost casually, "The king will be visiting Blackthorne."

"King Charles?" Olivia's fork stopped halfway to her lips. "Here?"

Quenton nodded, enjoying her reaction.

"But why?" Olivia shook her head, unable to fathom such an honor. "Why would the king come here?"

Quenton glanced across the table at his brother. "In our misspent youth, Bennett and I often spent our hol-

idays with the royals at Greenwich Park and at White-
hall.''

"You...spent holidays with the royal family?"

He nodded, slightly amused at the dazed look in her
eyes. Did she have any idea how expressive her face
was? "When their father, the first King Charles was
executed, the family scattered. Young Charles spent
much of his time in Paris and The Hague, and I visited
him frequently to cheer him. He has had a long and
unpleasant time of it, awaiting his chance to be king.
And now that he is, he seems to be enjoying himself
immensely. He has decided to take a holiday here at
Blackthorne.''

Olivia's cheeks were suffused with color as she recalled her remarks that day in the garden. No wonder
Quenton had looked at her with such amusement. Not
only did he know of the king's butterfly collection; he
had probably seen it for himself many times.

How foolish she must look in his eyes. The realization that she had tried to look and sound important
had the flush on her cheeks deepening. Her cousin
Catherine had been right. She was nothing more than
a country bumpkin.

"Will we be permitted to peer at the king over the
balcony?" Liat asked timidly. "Or perhaps watch
from the windows while he tours the gardens?"

"Hush, Liat." Olivia touched a finger to her lips to
still his questions. "What right would we have—"

Before she could say more Quenton interrupted.
"Peer at him? I should say not, lad." He pushed away
from the table and stood. "You'll all be expected to
join the king in his tour of the gardens. And everywhere else he goes.''

This was simply too much for Olivia to grasp. Her voice was choked. "Join the king?"

Quenton strolled toward the fire, with the others following suit. At once the stable lad was summoned to carry Bennett to a comfortable chair.

"Of course, Miss St. John." Quenton turned, and shot her a dangerous smile. "Did you expect to hide away until he departs Blackthorne?"

"I thought…" For a moment she was too overcome to speak. "He is the king. We cannot simply walk along beside him and speak and act as we always do."

"And why not?"

"Whatever would we have to say to the king? How would we act?"

"In public, you speak only when he speaks to you first. In private, you would be expected to carry your share of the conversation. Something, I might add, that you've had no trouble doing since your arrival here at Blackthorne."

She shot him a look. "I can see that you are making sport of me." She caught Liat's hand. "Come. It's time for your bed."

As they turned away Quenton called, "A word of caution, Miss St. John. When in the company of the king, never turn your back. And don't even think of leaving a room until the king takes his departure first. No one leaves the king's side until he gives his permission."

She paused. "I'll remember that, my lord. And I hope you'll remember that you are not the king. I need no one's permission to go to my room."

He shot her a dark look as she flounced away with Liat's hand firmly in hers. Then he turned to his brother, who was stifling a yawn. The anger was gone from his tone. "Would you like to go upstairs now, Bennett?"

The young man nodded. Without waiting for help, Quenton bent and lifted him from the chair, carrying him from the room and up the stairs, with Minerva following.

When he had left Bennett in the care of his young servant, he went in search of Liat. Entering the boy's suite, he could hear the drone of voices in the inner chamber.

"I could show the king my drawing of the butterfly."

The lad's eagerness had Olivia smiling gently. "I know the king would greatly appreciate your drawing. But I suspect that he has far more important things to do."

"Not at all." Quenton paused in the doorway and winked at the boy when he turned to him. "After all, I should think the king would enjoy talking to someone who shares his love of butterflies."

"Did you come up to see my sketches?" Liat asked eagerly.

"Aye, lad." In truth, he'd merely wanted to prolong his time spent with the nursemaid. How he loved teasing her. Or just looking at her. The sketches were as good an excuse as any.

Liat, dressed in a long nightshirt, raced to the other room and returned carrying a sheaf of drawings. He scattered them on the floor and Quenton was forced to kneel in order to study them.

These weren't the childish stick-figures he'd been expecting. Even without Olivia's neatly lettered titles, he could identify various species of butterflies and insects, as well as several carefully executed flowers.

He gave Liat a long, measured look. "These are very good, boy."

A shy smile bloomed. "Thank you, sir."

"Now that I've seen them, I must insist that you show them to the king."

"Truly?"

"Aye. He is quite knowledgeable about painting and the arts and sciences. I think he will find in you a kindred spirit." He glanced up. "And in you, Miss St. John."

She nodded, unwilling to trust her voice. The sight of man and boy, kneeling side by side, heads bent as they studied the drawings, had brought an unexpected lump to her throat. How was he able to turn her anger upside down so easily?

"All right now, lad." Quenton helped him gather up the sketches. "I think you'd best climb into your bed, or Miss St. John will have both our heads."

The boy placed the papers on his little writing table, then crossed to the big bed. Quenton remained where he was as Olivia tucked the linens around the boy's shoulders.

"Will you hear my prayers, sir?" Liat asked.

"Aye." Quenton took a step closer.

"Bless my mama who is with the angels. And bless Lord Stamford, who has given me this bed. And bless Miss St. John, who gives me kisses."

"She gives you kisses, does she?" Quenton couldn't help smiling as he ruffled the boy's hair. "I'll have to speak to your governess about that."

"She only kisses me good-night. Or when I'm afraid. Or sometimes just because she feels like it."

"Well, that's all right then. Good night, lad."

"Good night, sir. Ma'am."

Olivia bent and brushed her lips over Liat's cheek, then followed Quenton from the room. In the sitting chamber she turned toward her bedchamber and paused at the door.

"It was kind of you to include me in your plans to entertain King Charles. But it wouldn't be right for me to accept."

She was so solemn, he nearly smiled. "And why is that?"

"I am little more than a servant in your home, Lord Stamford. I have no right to be in the company of the king."

He couldn't resist a taunt. "If you believe yourself a lowly servant, why is your tongue always so sharp, especially with the lord of the manor?"

Her eyes flashed. "Are you so accustomed to women with soft words and empty brains?"

The warmth he'd been feeling only minutes before was now wiped away. "God in heaven, woman, you try my patience. You would be well advised to remember that you are here at my pleasure. If I so desire, I can have you sent back to London on the morrow."

He saw the flicker of emotion in her eyes before she tossed her head and stiffened her spine. "Are you ordering me to pack my valise?"

"Don't tempt me." He caught her by the chin, holding her firmly when she tried to turn away. Under his breath he muttered, "And you do tempt me. More often than I care to admit."

She felt the little thrill that always followed his touch. For a moment she was certain he would kiss her. His gaze burned over her lips and her pulse began to race in anticipation.

Just as quickly he took a step back and looked her

up and down in a measured way that had her blood heating.

"I'll have Mistress Thornton summon a dressmaker from the village. You'll need a wardrobe."

She blinked. "A...wardrobe?"

"So you'll be fit company for the king."

He strode away quickly, leaving her feeling oddly deflated because he hadn't kissed her. Still, she was happy at the knowledge that, instead of sending her packing, he had just guaranteed that she would remain a while longer. At least until the king's visit came to an end.

As she turned away, she caught the flicker of a shadow some distance along the hallway. Surely it was her imagination that she was being watched. Any number of servants might be upstairs, lighting candles, retrieving bed linens to stave off the chill of the night.

Still, it was hard to dismiss the feeling, like fingers along her spine. And the prickling of the hair at her nape.

She hurried inside her room and leaned against the closed door, listening for the sound of footsteps. But all she heard was the pounding of her own heart. And the silence of the old house as night settled in.

Chapter Nine

"**P**embroke." Quenton stood at the library windows watching as Olivia and Liat skipped along the garden path. He seemed to spend an inordinate amount of time lately standing at these windows instead of hunching over the ledgers. But as pressing as the muddled accounts were, the scene below was far more important to him. "How is Mistress Thornton holding up under the strain of the king's impending visit?"

"As you might expect, my lord, she's a bit on edge."

Quenton's lips curved into a grin. That was like saying the ocean was a bit damp. "I spotted her earlier haranguing a group of village girls who'd been brought in to help with the extra chores. By the time she left them, the air was blue with her highly imaginative curses."

"Aye, my lord. She does have a way with a word."

Quenton glanced at the older man. His features, always so bland, hadn't altered. But there had been the slightest note of admiration in his tone.

He returned his attention to the scene in the garden. A stable lad had just settled Bennett into his chair, and

Minerva was tucking a blanket around his shoulders. "Do you think I should bring in more women from the village to ease our housekeeper's burden?"

"Nay, my lord. That might give Mistress Thornton the idea that you don't think her capable of handling the king's visit."

"Is she capable of it, Pembroke?"

"Aye, my lord. If necessary, Mistress Thornton could manage Blackthorne and everyone in it all by herself. She just gets a bit worked up. Makes even the simple look difficult. But she's a most competent woman. And despite those curses, she has a good heart."

He glanced over Quenton's shoulder. "Shall I tell her to have your tea served in the garden, my lord?"

"Aye." Seeing Pembroke's gaze centered on him he felt it necessary to add, "I believe it is my duty to see how my brother fares on this fine day."

When he strolled away, with his hound at his side, the butler allowed himself a smile. How convenient that Master Bennett and Miss St. John were both in the garden at the same time.

"Look what I drew." Seeing Quenton, Liat raced along the garden path and skidded to a halt. He held up a drawing of a butterfly.

"Ah. A *Brintesia circe*. Did you draw this for the king?"

"Aye, sir. Miss St. John said it may be my best one yet."

"Quite right." Quenton glanced around. "Where is your nursemaid?"

"Over there. Talking to Master Bennett."

"Would you care to walk with me?"

"Nay, sir. If you don't mind, I'd like to search for more butterflies."

Quenton smiled as the boy scampered off. The king's visit, it would seem, had excited more than just the housekeeper. Everyone at Blackthorne was, as Pembroke had so aptly put it, on edge.

As he followed the garden path and approached his brother he could hear Olivia's voice, chattering happily.

"...was about ten or so and we were on holiday. I was wearing a new dress. Lemon yellow, with a wide yellow sash. I'll never forget it. My papa called me his little daisy. Oh, I was so proud of that dress. We were meeting a group of his fellow instructors from Oxford in a nearby park. On the way Papa pointed out a rare *Apatura ilia,* a lovely bronze and orange butterfly, and I went chasing off after it, determined to catch it in my hand when it landed."

Quenton paused, not wanting to interrupt her story. Beside him, the dog went very still. With her back to him, she had no idea that he was near. It was the perfect opportunity to observe and listen. How much more relaxed and animated she seemed in the company of his brother and the little servant. If only she could be that relaxed with him. But there was a tension between them. Perhaps it would always be there. Or perhaps they could somehow find a way around it.

He could think of one way to ease the tension. A way that had his hands clenching at his sides. He wouldn't have thought of himself as a patient man. But in this instance, he was determined to be as patient, as careful, as he could manage. Else he would surely drive her from Blackthorne, and out of his life forever.

Her laughter drifted, clear as a bell, on the breeze. "I was so busy watching the butterfly, I didn't bother to look where I was headed. The next thing I knew I had raced right into a bog and was in mud up to my waist."

"Oh, miss." Caught up in the tale, Minerva clapped a hand over her mouth. "What did you do?"

"What could I do? It was too late to salvage my dress or my pride. But I did manage to catch the butterfly. And when I showed off my catch, expecting both Papa and Mum to be angry, they laughed so hard they fell to the grass."

"They laughed?" Minerva's voice was tinged with disbelief. "Even though you ruined your new dress?"

"Aye." Just thinking about it had Olivia laughing again. "Mum told me not to fear, the mud would wash out. And Papa told me I had just proved once again that I was certainly his daughter. He said he'd often done much the same thing himself. And was none the worse for it."

"It sounds as though you had a warm and loving family, miss."

"Aye. We couldn't have been happier. Even now, I find it hard to believe they're really gone."

At the thread of pain in her voice Minerva glanced up at her, then, seeing Quenton just behind her, gave a little gasp of recognition and got to her feet, dusting off her skirt. "Oh, Lord Stamford. Begging your pardon. I didn't see you there."

"It's quite all right, Minerva. Stay where you are." He stepped forward. "I was just enjoying Miss St. John's story."

Olivia flushed. "I'd better go look for Liat."

"Don't bother. The lad's fine. He's doing what you

just described. Searching for butterflies. Hopefully, there are no bogs in the garden," he added dryly. He turned to his brother. "How are you feeling today, Bennett? Did you sleep well last night?"

Bennett nodded.

"Good. I thought as much. You're getting some color from all this fresh air. Do you think the king will enjoy our gardens?"

Again Bennett nodded.

"I quite agree."

Olivia studied him more closely. She'd never seen him quite so relaxed. Or so easy in his brother's company.

Getting to her feet, she said, "I think I'll just go in search of Liat and see for myself that he's all right."

"I'll join you, Miss St. John." As he turned to go he said to Minerva, "I'm having tea brought out. Mistress Thornton should be along with it shortly. Please don't wait for us. I know Bennett likes his tea hot."

"Aye, my lord."

Olivia wasn't the only one to notice Quenton's good spirits. Both Minerva and Bennett stared after him as he and Thor walked away beside the nursemaid.

When they had crossed the garden Quenton pointed. "You see? There's the lad. In the rose garden. Sketching another butterfly."

Olivia smiled as she watched the little boy diligently drawing. On the sketch pad was the long, spiky arm of a rosebush. And perched on the rose was an *Anthocharis belia,* its delicate wings beginning to take shape.

The dog padded closer and Liat paused to pet him before continuing on with the sketch.

Quenton led Olivia toward a stone bench. "Let's sit

here a moment while we wait for the lad to finish his drawing.''

He waited until she was seated, then settled himself beside her. The sun filtered through the branches overhead, making lacy patterns on her skirt. Her hands were folded primly in her lap. A wisp of hair had slipped from her neat knot, teasing her cheek.

''Your brother is eager to see the king,'' she said.

''How do you know?''

''I can sense the excitement in him. His color is high. And his eyes more lively than I've ever seen.''

He looked away. ''I wish there were some way to include him in everything we do while the king is here. But it could prove awkward. Especially if Charles should wish to go hunting.''

''Oh.'' Without thinking, she touched a hand to his arm. ''You can't exclude Bennett. It would break his heart.''

He closed his hand over hers. ''Do you think I don't know that? The last thing I want is to hurt him. But with all the extra work this visit will entail, I'm not certain we can spare a lad just to carry Bennett everywhere. And a day of hunting, especially with a vigorous monarch like Charles, could prove too exhausting for my frail brother.'' His voice lowered ominously. ''I don't think I could bear to have him slip back into that pale wasted shadow of himself.''

''He won't. We won't let him.'' Whenever Quenton exposed this tender side of his nature, her heart melted. She squeezed his hand. ''We'll just have to find a way....'' Her gaze lifted to the hay wagon rolling across a distant hill. ''Of course. There's our answer.''

He followed her direction, then gave a snort of disgust. "You expect me to send my brother along with the king in a crude wagon?"

"Couldn't someone in the village make a smaller version, just big enough to accommodate Bennett? If the wheels are small enough, and the wood light enough, a lad could probably push him without too much effort."

She could see that Quenton was mulling it over. "It should be deep enough that he can lean back and rest when he's feeling weary. And large enough to hold some bed linens, possibly a shawl, a pillow for his head."

"Aye." His eyes narrowed as he considered. "And while we're at it, a chair with wheels for the house."

"Oh, yes." In her eagerness she forgot herself. "Quenton, think of the freedom it would give him. And the pleasure."

For the space of a heartbeat he merely stared at her. "Say that again."

"I said think of the freedom..."

"Nay. Before that."

She merely stared at him in confusion.

"You spoke my name."

"Did I? Forgive me...."

"Olivia." He touched a finger to her lips to stop her apology. "I want to hear you say it again. Say my name."

She took a breath, still reeling from the sound of her own name on his lips. At last she whispered, "Quenton."

"Again. Please."

Her voice quavered. "Quenton."

For long silent moments he merely stared down into her eyes. Then he reached a hand to brush the hair from her cheek, allowing the silken strands to sift through his fingers. And all the while he was studying her with a look that had her breath hitching, her heart pounding.

With his hand caressing her cheek he lowered his head. His lips hovered over hers. "Do you know how very special you've become to me?"

She was afraid to speak. Afraid to even breathe, for fear of spoiling the moment.

"I must kiss you, Olivia." He bent to her and brushed his lips over hers. It was the merest whisper of mouth to mouth. And yet it sent heat pouring through her veins. Her heart swelled with so much love she feared it would burst.

His lips remained on hers while his hand moved around to cup the back of her head. He heard her little intake of breath. His fingers tangled in her hair and he crushed her mouth with his.

She wound her arms around his neck and returned his kiss with a fervor that caught them both by surprise.

On a moan of pleasure he dragged her close, thrilling to the press of her body to his. Despite the barrier of clothes he could feel the thrust of her breasts against his chest. His hands moved along her sides, his thumbs skimming the soft curves, stroking nipples already rigid.

On a gasp she started to pull away. He changed the angle of the kiss and moved his hands along her back, soothing, arousing. He could feel her relax against him. His hands dipped lower, to the flare of her hips, and he drew her firmly against him.

"Quenton." She lifted troubled eyes to his.

"Shh. A minute more." He pressed soft, moist

kisses to her temple, her cheek, the tip of her nose. His mouth followed the line of her jaw, teasing the corner of her lips until, unable to wait any longer, she turned her face and felt his lips cover hers once more.

The kiss was no longer gentle. With a guttural sound they came together in a fierce heat that threatened to consume them both.

His hands were in her hair, his mouth moving over hers as if to devour her.

Her arms slid around his waist, holding on with a strength that matched his.

"Miss St. John." At the sound of Liat's voice, their movements stilled. Two heads came up at once.

"Come quickly. I think this is my best drawing yet."

"I..." Olivia swallowed and tried to speak. Her breath was coming so hard and fast, the effort burned her throat. "I'll be right there, Liat."

She looked up at Quenton, who was watching her with the wariness of a hunter. Slowly, the darkness in his eyes gave way to mirth.

He pressed his forehead to hers. His laughter rumbled up from his chest. It was the most glorious sound she had ever heard.

It was contagious. Within seconds she had joined him, laughing until her eyes were wet from the effort.

He took a handkerchief from his pocket and touched it to her eyes. "Remind me to find a more private place the next time I'm feeling amorous."

"Aye, my lord." She motioned toward the branches of the tree. "We can be grateful for what little cover they provide. Else I'm sure we'd have given the servants a great deal to talk about as well."

"Let them whisper. It's just one more rumor they'll

delight in spreading.'' He took his time replacing his handkerchief and willing his heart to return to normal before getting to his feet. He offered her a hand, then walked beside her toward the little boy.

''Look, ma'am.'' Liat held up his sketch. ''Do you think this is fit for the king to see?''

''Indeed.'' Olivia passed it to Quenton, who examined it closely before passing it back to the lad. ''Well done, Liat. Now let's join the others for tea.''

As they walked along the garden path, Olivia felt a lightness in her heart that had never been there before.

What a remarkable day this had become. Quenton had again called Liat by his name. They had found a solution to the problem of including Bennett in the king's activities. And most remarkable of all, Quenton Stamford had stirred feelings in her she'd never even known she possessed.

Her heart was overflowing with so much happiness, she was certain that nothing could possibly spoil it. In fact, she was feeling so confident, she was actually beginning to lose her fear of meeting the king.

''Hold still, Miss St. John.'' The village seamstress wore an odd sort of apron, with many deep pockets containing needles, thread, scissors, pins. The bed was piled high with bright colored fabrics, fancy shawls, bonnets, feathers, lace.

Two village lasses huffed and puffed around the room, holding up fabrics, matching gowns to bonnets and accessories.

Olivia had been ordered to stand on a stool while the woman pinned and measured, and ordered her to straighten her shoulders, stop twitching and turn. She would not have needed any of those orders if she had been alone. But knowing that Quenton was in the next room, waiting to approve each fashion, had her feeling jittery. She had never modeled her gowns for a man before, except for her father, who didn't count.

"That's fine, Miss St. John. Come." The seamstress held out her hand and helped Olivia from the stool. "Let's see what Lord Stamford thinks of this one."

Olivia trailed the woman to the sitting chamber and stood quietly as she did her best to impress the wealthy lord of the manor.

"It is the finest satin, my lord. See how it shimmers in the light? And the ruby red is a definite contrast to the lady's dark hair. I believe I shall add inserts of lace here at the bodice."

Olivia felt her face flame as she saw Quenton's gaze fixed on her bosom. The scene in the garden flashed into her mind and her flush deepened.

"And more lace at the sleeves. The lady will look as fine as any queen, my lord."

"Indeed." He nodded and waved a hand. "I approve. What else?"

"A moment, my lord." The seamstress took Olivia by the arm and steered her back to the sleeping chamber, calling out orders to the two village girls. Half an hour later they returned to Quenton, this time to model a deep blue velvet.

When that had been approved, he ordered half a dozen more gowns, a riding outfit, a traveling cloak and the softest kid boots Olivia had ever had the good fortune of slipping on her feet.

When she finally emerged from her room, the seamstress was shoving coins into one of her pockets.

"Have no fear, my lord. The clothes will be ready in time. I trained my two nieces, who will work alongside me. Their stitches are fine and even, and I will personally examine every seam. If we have to, we shall do without sleep to have the lady's gowns ready for the king's visit.''

"Thank you, Mistress Smeed. Mistress Thornton assured me I would be happy with your work.''

At that precise moment the housekeeper came around the corner, curls drooping over her eye, sweat beading her forehead.

Quenton gave her a smile. "You may show Mistress Smeed to the door.''

"Aye, m'lord.''

The two women hurried away, with the two lasses trailing behind, their arms laden with fabric.

Quenton turned to see Olivia standing hesitantly in the doorway of her bedroom.

"What am I to do with all the frippery Mistress Smeed has left behind?''

"Frippery?''

"There are ribbons, combs, lace handkerchiefs, even a lovely shawl.''

"They are yours, Olivia.''

She shook her head. "I cannot accept all this. Papa once told me to never accept more than what I earned.''

He crossed the distance between them and took her hand in his. It was trembling, he noted. "You've earned all this and more.''

"I'm already being paid a fair wage. I have a lovely suite of rooms in a beautiful home. That is what I've earned. That and no more. Why should I accept such beautiful things?''

"Because it makes me happy to give you something.'' When she started to protest he said gruffly,

"Then you will do it because I insist. Because the king is coming to Blackthorne, and it is important to me that we all look our best."

He saw the hurt in her eyes and hated himself for it. But, he told himself, it was for her own good.

"And I promise you this. Once the king is gone," he said more gently, "you will no longer be obliged to wear them. The choice will be yours. Is that fair enough?"

She slowly nodded.

"Good." He tucked a stray curl behind her ear and thought about kissing her. Wanted to desperately. But here in the privacy of her chambers, once he started there would be no way he could stop.

He thought his wisest course of action was retreat. As quickly as possible.

When he let himself out of her room and started along the hallway, he had the strange sensation that he was being followed. He turned. The hallway was empty. But a shadow flickered, then disappeared.

He looked around for the hound. Now where had Thor wandered off to? As he passed a linen closet he heard a scratching. When he opened the door, Thor bounded out. Peering inside, he found the remains of a leg of mutton.

"Stealing, are you Thor? That's beneath you. If Cook finds you, she'll have your hide."

He picked up the bone and tucked it into his pocket. At least, he mused, they wouldn't be having mutton tonight.

Chapter Ten

The day dawned bright and glorious. A warm sun burned off the mist that had rolled in overnight from the sea. A gentle breeze set the leaves of trees swaying softly.

A fitting day for the king's arrival at Blackthorne, Olivia thought as she directed a servant to lay out Liat's clothes and prepare his bath.

Already a troop of the king's Household Cavalry Yeomen of the Guard, bearing the royal standard, had galloped through the village and up the curving driveway of the estate. As soon as King Charles set foot on Blackthorne land, the flag would be hoisted, to alert the populace to their royal guest.

For miles around the people had made the trek to the little village, some resting in carts, others lying under trees or lining the roads for a glimpse of the king. Village women sold pastries. Minstrels and mimes played the crowd, hoping for coins of appreciation. Young women flirted with strangers. Children chased one another through hedges and climbed trees, securing spots from which to view their monarch.

Amid the crowd, pickpockets and thieves plied their trade as well. It was a rowdy, festive throng.

Quenton had ridden out early that morning to join the king's procession. In the late afternoon Bennett and Minerva joined Olivia and Liat on their balcony to view the festivities.

Bennett was the first to spot something in the distance. Agitated, he pointed and the others turned to stare.

"Oh, my." Olivia squinted and lifted a hand to shield the sun from her eyes. "I see them." She dropped an arm around the lad's shoulders and pointed. "Look, Liat. There. That flash of light is sunlight glinting off the arms of the king's honor guard. Do you see?"

"Aye." He gripped the balcony railing, his eyes round and unblinking.

Now, after all the days of panic and preparation, it was about to happen.

"Minerva." Olivia turned to the servant. "You'll see to getting Bennett below stairs?"

"Aye, miss. There's a stable lad awaiting my summons."

"Liat and I will warn Pembroke and Mistress Thornton that their royal guest is almost here."

Catching Liat's hand, Olivia dashed down the stairs in search of the housekeeper. She found her in the huge refectory, dashing about like a whirlwind, overseeing the contingent of villagers who had been brought in to assist the cook.

"The king has reached the village," Olivia announced breathlessly.

Mistress Thornton let out a screech and turned on Pembroke. "We must get these fly-bitten, motley-minded wagtails assembled in the courtyard at once or we'll bring shame to 'is lordship.''

Pembroke remained perfectly composed. ''I'll see to it, Mistress. I suggest you retire to your room for a moment and take stock of your appearance.''

''My…appearance?''

Mistress Thornton looked like a cat that had been tossed, hissing and spitting, into a tub of water. Her hair, damp with sweat, stuck out in little tufts around her face. Her apron, which had originally been tied at her waist, now hung somewhere between her hips and knees. There was a dusting of flour on her chin, another on her cheek.

Olivia stepped forward. ''You'll want to look your best for His Majesty.''

''Aye, miss.'' The housekeeper seemed a bit dazed, as though just beginning to realize the importance of the occasion. ''I…wouldn't know where to begin.''

''Come with me.'' Olivia laid a hand on her arm. ''I'll help you.''

''You will?'' Mistress Thornton turned to Pembroke. ''You'll…see to the staff?''

''I'll see that they do his lordship and you proud.''

''Aye.'' She allowed Olivia to lead her toward her room off the kitchen. Inside, the room was so clean it sparkled. It was quite a contrast to the woman who occupied it.

''Here.'' Olivia led her to a chair and began to brush the tufts of hair. ''Oh, Mistress Thornton, what lovely hair.''

''Is it?'' The housekeeper sat in a daze as Olivia brushed and combed and fussed.

''Indeed.'' With deft strokes Olivia twisted flax-colored hair into a neat knot, then secured it with a comb. "Now to that apron. Do you have a clean one?"

"Aye." The housekeeper went to a small wardrobe and removed a clean white apron, edged with lace, that looked as though it had never been worn.

"For special occasions," she explained.

"It's perfect." Olivia slipped it into place and turned her around to tie a neat bow.

"What do you think?" She offered the housekeeper a small looking glass.

"Oh, my. I look..." She laughed self-consciously. "I look almost pretty."

"You look very pretty, Mistress Thornton. Now I'd better hurry back to find Liat."

She left the housekeeper still staring at her reflection in the looking glass.

In the kitchen Olivia caught Liat's hand. "Come. I think it's time we made our way outside to await the king."

Though she kept her smile in place, Olivia's heart was beating wildly. Perhaps, she thought, like Mistress Thornton, the enormity of the situation had only now begun to hit her as well.

It was a dazzling display. The royal carriage rolled into the courtyard, all white and gilt, with its set of six matched white horses, flanked by the royal honor guard in their crimson and gold uniforms. More of the king's brigade followed, in blue and gold. Behind them trailed a dozen carriages, carrying the royal staff and the king's baggage.

The soldiers dismounted and stood at rigid attention, while trumpets blared. A liveried footman leapt from the back of the carriage and opened the door.

Quenton was the first to step down. He cast a glance at his brother, seated in his new wheeled chair, then smiled at Olivia, who was holding Liat's hand. She gave him a tremulous smile in return and felt her heart begin to throb painfully. Dear heaven. Would all this pomp and circumstance cause her to faint? Ridiculous, she reminded herself. She had never fainted in her life. She wasn't about to do so now. She squeezed Liat's hand and straightened her shoulders, forcing in several deep draughts of air.

Quenton glanced toward his housekeeper and houseman and was pleasantly surprised. Mistress Thornton had somehow managed to tame her hair, freshen her apron, and compose herself as much as was possible under the circumstances.

Under Pembroke's watchful eye, the staff of Black-thorne, from cook and scullery maid to liveryman and stable master, had assembled on the lawn in perfect order.

The trumpets fell silent. The entire crowd seemed to hold its collective breath. The king stepped down and stared around as men doffed their hats and women curtsied.

"Ah, Lord Stamford. Blackthorne is even lovelier than I'd remembered it."

The voice was deep and rich, with a trace of an odd, lingering accent. Olivia knew that Charles had spent his youth in France and Scotland. Both countries had flavored his speech.

He was young, having just turned thirty. And darkly handsome. There was an arrogance to the lift of his chin. And a devilish glint in his eyes. He wore black satin breeches and brocaded waistcoat of brilliant scarlet and black. Over his shoulder was tossed a cloak of black satin trimmed with ermine. On his head was a wide-brimmed black hat with a feather dipped rakishly over one eye. Knowing the effect he had on the crowd, he paused for a moment, then tossed the cloak and hat into the carriage with a careless gesture.

When he turned and spotted Bennett he crossed to him and embraced him.

"How well you look, Bennett. Your brother has told me of your remarkable progress these past weeks. Are you hoping to make liars of my royal physicians?"

Bennett, enormously pleased at the king's gesture, smiled and nodded.

Quenton took Liat's hand and led him forward. "Majesty, this is the lad I told you about."

"Liat, is it?" The king bent down to look him in the eye. "Lord Stamford tells me you are fond of butterflies."

"Aye, Majesty." Despite all Olivia's coaching, the little boy forgot to bow and stared directly into his monarch's eyes.

"Perhaps you and I can spot a rare butterfly together while I'm here. Would you like that, Liat?"

The boy's lips curved into a wide smile. "Aye, Majesty."

"Good." The king glanced toward the young woman who stood slightly behind Liat. "And who is this lovely creature?"

"Olivia St. John." Quenton's tone softened. "She is Liat's governess."

Olivia curtsied and kept her gaze averted.

"A pity our nursemaids never looked like this when we were lads, isn't it, Lord Stamford?"

Quenton's lips quirked in amusement. "Aye, Majesty. A pity."

"Our childhoods could have been much more pleasant with such as Miss St. John to oversee our nurseries. I hope you will see that the lad and his governess sup with us often." The king shot him a sardonic smile. "I'd much prefer her company to yours, my friend."

Quenton bowed his head. "As you wish, Majesty."

"I do indeed wish." He studied her a minute longer, then turned his attention to the staff, who had been waiting patiently. "I see some familiar faces from my boyhood." He gave a wide smile. "Pembroke."

The houseman bowed. "Welcome to Blackthorne, Majesty."

"You don't look a day older than when I was last here. And is this pretty little thing Gwynnith?"

The housekeeper blushed clear to her toes and managed a clumsy curtsy.

"She is Mistress Thornton now, Majesty," Quenton prompted.

"Married, did you, Gwynnith?"

"Aye, Majesty. To a Londoner. Rupert Thornton." She blushed again. "Though he lived for less than a year."

"But he died a happy man, I'll wager." The king was clearly enjoying himself.

Quenton lifted a hand to encompass the entire staff. "Majesty, I present those at Blackthorne who hope to make your stay with us an enjoyable one."

The men bowed. The ladies curtsied. All kept their gazes fixed on the ground, though a few managed to glance boldly at their monarch's face before looking quickly away.

"A daunting task, I know. But I have faith that you are all equal to it." Charles lifted a hand and several of his staff hurried forward with wooden cages. "I've brought some plump hens from my country estate. And lambs from the Scottish Highlands. A gift to Cook."

"Thank you, Majesty." Quenton signaled to one of the village elders, who limped forward, aided by his son and daughter. "The people of our humble village are so honored by your visit, they wish to present you with this cask of gold."

Charles smiled broadly and spoke to all the assembled, knowing his words would be repeated throughout the village and surrounding towns. "You honor your king. And please him mightily. I accept this in the name of God and country."

Clearly moved by this honor, and brushing away tears, the elder limped back to join his people.

The king handed the cask to his valet, then followed Quenton, who was pushing Bennett's wheeled chair to the door. Pembroke held the door wide and the King preceded his hosts inside.

From the doorway he turned and waved to the people, who broke into spontaneous cheers and applause. He leaned over and said something to Quenton, who in turn whispered to Pembroke. At once the houseman hurried to Olivia's side.

"His Majesty has asked that you and the boy join his party."

For the space of a moment Olivia could only stare at him. Then, numbly, she caught Liat's hand and followed Pembroke up the steps.

With light hearts the crowd began to disperse. The villagers, except those honored guests who had been invited to sup with the king, returned to their homes and fields, to relive every precious moment of this momentous occasion. The household staff hurried inside, eager to please their honored guest. The king's soldiers headed toward the stables to see to their horses. Until the king left Blackthorne, the stables would be where they would sleep as well, in the hay beside their mounts.

The king's valet would be given a bed in a smaller room of the royal chambers.

At last the king turned away. The doors closed. Olivia and Liat followed along behind him, feeling slightly dazed by all they had witnessed.

"You're quiet, ma'am," Liat whispered as he danced along beside her.

"Aye." Actually, she was awed speechless.

"Where are we going?"

"I know not. To the dining hall, I suppose."

"Will we sup with His Majesty?"

Olivia shrugged expressively. "That is not for me to say. Until he leaves Blackthorne, all under this roof will do the king's bidding."

The king's bidding. As she made her way up the stairs to Liat's chambers, she had but one thought. She, a simple country lass, daughter of humble parents, had actually met King Charles II of England. This day, she had become part of her country's proud history.

In honor of the king's visit, the dining hall had been made even more festive with ornate wall hangings hand-sewn by the women of the village, depicting the history of his royal lineage. There were images of his now-dead father, Charles I, and his mother, French-born Henrietta Maria, and his sisters and brothers.

The women responsible for the wall hangings were

brought before the king, who made a great show of studying their handiwork before commending them for it.

These were simple peasant women, who had never journeyed beyond their own village. Only one or two had ever visited the surrounding towns or villages. When King Charles complimented them, they blushed and stammered. Several fell into fits of weeping and had to be helped from the room.

Afterward, the king was escorted to a table set on a raised dais so that it could be viewed with ease by all those seated in the dining hall. The king's chair was ornately carved of mahogany, with the arms and seat cushions upholstered in royal purple velvet. At the king's insistence, Quenton was seated on his right, and Bennett on his left.

Spotting Olivia and Liat in the crowd, Charles pointed a finger. "Bring the lad and his nursemaid to join us."

Olivia struggled to hide her shock as she and Liat were escorted to the king's own table.

Quenton got to his feet and held the chair beside his. Olivia had no choice but to accept. She watched in stunned silence as the crowd began taking their places at the various tables set around the room. The elder of the village sat, along with the lord mayor, at the table nearest the king. The others chose their places in the order of their importance. When all were seated, the servants began filling goblets with ale, and a series of toasts were offered to the king, his family, the success of his reign and his health and long life. With each toast there was a long, and often tiresome speech. Through it all the royal guest kept a cheerful smile upon his lips, and a merry twinkle in his eyes.

During one particularly long toast by the village's lord mayor, Charles leaned across Quenton to smile at Liat and his nursemaid.

"Are you enjoying yourself, lad?" he asked.

"Aye, Majesty." Liat lifted the back of his hand to his mouth to wipe away his milky mustache. "But when are they bringing the food?"

Charles winked. "A good question, lad. My journey has left me famished." He smiled at Olivia. "And how about you, Miss St. John? Are you hungry?"

She touched a hand to her stomach. "I can't really tell, Majesty. There are still too many butterflies."

At that he threw back his head and roared. "Another butterfly lover, Quenton." He nudged his host. "She is absolutely delightful. I must get to know her better."

"Aye, Majesty." Knowing how the King loved charming women, all women, Quenton's lighthearted mood vanished. He glowered at the lord mayor, hoping to hurry him along. But the old man, proud of his skilled oratory, and determined to use this rare chance to display it to advantage before the king, droned on.

Quenton's agitation only seemed to heighten, while the king's mood grew more jovial.

Once more he leaned over his host to remark, "Tell me a bit about yourself, Miss St. John. How long have you been a governess?"

"Hardly any time at all, Majesty. I fear I am learning more from Liat than I am able to teach him in return."

"Such humility." He turned to his host and, seeing the scowl on his face, couldn't resist adding, "I have always been absolutely enchanted by the combination of beauty and humility. Haven't I, Lord Stamford?"

"Aye, Majesty." Quenton's words were clipped.

"Something you wish to say, Lord Stamford? You have my permission to speak."

"Nay, Majesty." Quenton had clamped his teeth together so tightly he could barely get the words out.

Charles sat back and smiled encouragement at the pompous man who was putting half the room to sleep.

At last, when all were content that their monarch had been suitably impressed, the speeches ended. Mistress Thornton led Cook, who in turn led a procession of assistants, each holding a platter laden with their specialty, toward the head table. Each in turn bowed and presented an offering to the king. Charles nodded, smiled and praised them profusely, before accepting a portion of each food. The others around the table were served as well. But no one dared to begin eating until the king took the first bite.

He leaned over Quenton. "What do you recommend, Miss St. John?"

Olivia studied all the delicacies on her plate. "Cook's beef is superb, Majesty. She cooks it until it falls off the bone. And the salmon, I would think. Caught fresh this morning by the men of the village."

"Two of my favorites." He nudged a sharp elbow to Quenton's ribs and was rewarded with another frown. "The lass and I are of a like mind."

He turned to Bennett and took note of the little serving wench seated slightly behind him, helping to serve his plate. "What's this? Is there someone here at Blackthorne who has not yet been presented to me?"

Minerva's face turned several shades of red while Bennett dropped his fork with a clatter.

"Majesty." Quenton hurriedly handled the introduction. "This is Minerva, a village lass who sees to my brother's needs."

"Sees to his needs?" There was a long pause. "How generous." The king glanced from the girl to Bennett and back again. "I've always thought red hair was a sign of a very warm heart."

The poor servant's face grew even redder.

"Aye, Majesty." Quenton was determined to spare her further humiliation. "Minerva has a very warm and generous heart."

"Then you are indeed fortunate, Bennett." He cast a sideways glance at Quenton. "Perhaps I will have to insist on my right to share the good fortune of my loyal subjects."

Quenton grew silent. Olivia noted that he barely tasted his food. And such food. The meat and fish course was followed by roasted fowl, followed by bowls of summer vegetables and a clear broth. Servants passed among the tables with enormous platters of bread and rolls, while other servants continued filling goblets with mead or ale. By the time the servants offered fruit tarts and brandy-soaked currant cakes, most of the revelers had no appetite left.

Little Liat struggled bravely to stay still. He knew it was most important that he sit quietly and behave like those around him. But the excitement pulsing through his little body had him twitching with nervous energy. When the juice from the meat trickled down his new shirtfront, he mopped at it with his hand, spreading the stain around until it looked as though he were bleeding.

At the moment Olivia was engaged in a lively conversation with the king. "It wouldn't be fair of me to try to compare Oxford with London, Majesty. You see, I spent little time in London. But I..."

"Then we must rectify that situation, Miss St. John. Perhaps when I return to London, I shall order you to accompany me. That way you will have a basis for comparison."

Beside her, she felt Quenton stiffen. He shot a dark glance at the king, then his head turned in her direction and their faces were almost touching. She felt the hot sting of his breath on her cheek and started to smile at him. Catching sight of his deepening frown, she was puzzled. Though she didn't understand why, she could sense a tension simmering just below the surface. Apparently, she mused, she was not the only one to be suffering a case of nerves over their royal houseguest.

"I'm not overly fond of London, Majes..."

She paused at Quenton's little hiss of disgust. Following the direction of his gaze, she realized what he was looking at.

"Oh dear. Forgive me, Majesty. I've been neglecting my duties."

Liat had spilled his milk, and it was now dripping all over his lap.

She leaped to her feet and began to mop at the spill, which only made it worse. Soon it ran in sodden rivers across the table, threatening to overflow even onto the king's lap.

Annoyed, Quenton signaled for a servant, who hurried over with an armload of linen to clean up the mess.

"Please forgive me, Majesty. He's just a little boy and..."

Seeing her distress, the king reached in front of Quenton and laid a hand over hers. "There is no harm done, Miss St. John. It has been a long evening for the lad. Perhaps you should take him up to his room."

"But it wouldn't be right to leave before you, Majesty."

"Forget protocol, Miss St. John."

"I couldn't possibly."

"Then I shall make it simple. I order you, Miss St. John, to take the lad and leave us now."

"Aye, Majesty." She shot him a grateful smile before lifting the soiled little boy from his place at the table.

He wrapped his chubby arms around her neck and bestowed a cherubic smile on the others.

"Good night, Liat," the King called.

"G'night, Majesty. I'm sorry about the milk."

"It's fine, lad. No harm was done." Charles was laughing as he added, "Good night, Miss St. John."

She turned, managed a half curtsy and walked from the dining hall.

The king watched until she was out of sight, aware that the man beside him was also watching.

"They make a beautiful picture, don't they, Lord Stamford? Like a Madonna and Child that once hung in our royal chapel." He turned, and seeing the deepening scowl on Quenton's face, burst into a rumble of laughter. "Oh, I am so delighted to be here at Blackthorne. I do believe it is going to be a most... entertaining visit."

Chapter Eleven

"I didn't mean to spill my milk, ma'am." Liat danced up the stairs beside her, still twitching with an excess of nerves.

"Of course you didn't."

"I ate with the king of England, didn't I?"

She smiled. "Indeed you did."

"Was he ever a little boy?"

"He most certainly was." Though she couldn't possibly imagine such a thing.

"Do you think he spilled his milk?"

"It is quite possible." She opened the door to their chambers and followed him inside.

He raced to the window and climbed up on his trunk to stare at the gathering darkness below. The glow from candles flickered here and there as villagers, far from their homes, made ready to sleep in carts and wagons before beginning the long trek back. "Yesterday, while you had tea with the servants in the refectory, Thor and I explored the cowshed."

"It's fun to explore, isn't it?"

"Aye, ma'am." He turned to watch as she laid out his nightshirt. "I've been exploring the rooms of

Blackthorne. Did you know that Lord Stamford has a big room just filled with dusty books?''

She nodded and beckoned him over. While she helped him out of his wet shirt she said, ''That would be the library. It's a very important room. It's where he spends most of his time, going over his ledgers.''

''What are ledgers?'' He was racing across the room again, leaping onto the trunk, staring out the window.

''Books in which he keeps the accounts of all his holdings.'' She turned away and poured water into a basin, then rummaged through a stack of linens, selecting a soft one for the lad's soft skin. ''Now, Liat, let's get you washed and make you ready for bed.''

''What holdings?''

While she washed and dried his face and arms and milk-stained chest she explained, ''There are farms, homes, entire villages and shires that are part of the Stamford family estate. He must see that a fair portion of everything grown or raised is given in payment for use of the land.''

''He must be very rich.'' Too excited to settle down, he climbed into the bed and began jumping up and down.

She shrugged. ''I suppose. But there is an obligation on his part as well. Lord Stamford is responsible for the safety and well-being of everyone on his lands. If their crops fail, he must see that they and their stock are fed. When he hunts, he must see that a portion of the kill is given to the people. And when they are ill, they look to him for care.''

The boy's eyes rounded. He climbed off the bed and began twirling. ''Is he like a king?''

''I suppose he is.'' She picked up his nightshirt, turned and found him gone. ''Liat?''

She glanced around the empty room, then made her way to the sitting chamber. It, too, was empty. Puzzled, she made her way to her own suite of rooms, thinking perhaps the boy had gone in there for something. But he was nowhere to be found.

The door leading to the hallway was standing open. She hurried out. "Liat, if you're hiding, this isn't amusing."

The hallway was empty. She raced to the top of the stairs and could just see him disappearing below. Still clutching his little nightshirt, she raced down the stairs and saw him dart into the library. She gritted her teeth as she followed.

And to think that when she'd first arrived she had actually despaired of ever getting this boy to leave his room.

Inside she found him with his arms around Thor's neck. The dog's whole body wiggled with joy at having company after his long exile.

"Thor and I are friends," Liat said with a laugh.

"It's good to have a friend." She scratched the dog's ears, then held up the nightshirt. "Now, young man, it's time to put this on and say good-night to your friend."

She pulled it over his head and slipped his arms through, then looked up at the sound of someone approaching. "Oh, sweet heaven. We shouldn't be here."

"Come with me, ma'am." Liat caught her hand and dragged her toward a wardrobe. "We'll just hide in here until they leave."

Before she could argue he had the door open. She had no time to think or to reason over the foolishness of her actions. And though she had never done anything like that before in her life, she found herself crouching down and gathering him onto her lap, then pulling the door closed.

Village minstrels had been invited to play for the king. During their overlong performance, Charles smiled and applauded politely. When at last he waved a hand, signaling an end to his interest in them, Quenton gave a sigh of relief. Now perhaps this interminable evening would come to an end.

"Would you like to retire to your chambers, Majesty?"

Charles grinned. "You would like that, wouldn't you, Lord Stamford?"

Aware that the servants could overhear, Quenton kept his tone low. "I desire only your comfort, Majesty."

"I'm gratified to hear that. Bring your brother along." Charles stood, and at once everyone in the dining hall shuffled to their feet.

Inclining his head slightly, the king graced the throng with the benediction of his smile, then turned and made his way to the door.

As he passed each row of guests, the men bowed, the ladies curtsied. Trailing behind, Quenton pushed Bennett's wheeled chair, and signaled for Pembroke to follow, all the while wondering what mischief his guest was up to now.

When they were alone in the hallway, Charles started forward at a quickened pace. "As I recall, your grandfather's library is this way."

"The library?"

"Aye. All day I have been looking forward to a

private room, a comfortable chaise and a glass of ale without a score of eyes watching me.''

When they reached the room they were seeking, Quenton pushed his brother's chair forward, leading the way inside. Thor, pacing beside the wardrobe, bounded over, slathering a welcome on his master. At the king's coaxing, he allowed himself to be petted.

Charles glanced around. ''Have you something to drink?''

At a signal from Quenton, Pembroke scurried away and returned carrying a tray on which rested a brimming decanter and several crystal goblets. He poured, then discreetly disappeared, to stand guard outside.

Once the three were alone, all pretense of formality fell away.

''Well, old friend, this is what I've been thinking about all day.'' The king clapped Quenton on the back. Laughing delightedly, he turned to Bennett and embraced him. Then he tossed his brocaded jacket aside and rolled the billowing sleeves of his shirt. Quenton did the same and handed around the filled goblets.

Charles took several long swallows of ale and gave an exaggerated sigh. ''You have no idea how relieved I am to finally be here at Blackthorne. During this damnable journey we could hardly move, what with the throngs of people slowing the carriage to a crawl.''

''The people love you, Majesty.'' Quenton perched on the edge of the desk.

''Aye. So you are fond of saying. I hope 'tis true. But sometimes I think back to our lives when we were boys. It all seemed so much simpler then.''

''Indeed it was.'' Quenton laughed. ''As I recall, our biggest worry was how to outsmart those who were charged with our care. Now we have grown up. We're the ones charged with the care of others. We're the ones with the grown-up problems to deal with.''

Charles lounged in a chaise and unfastened the buttons at his throat. ''Aye. Man-sized problems. Or in my case, king-sized problems. Do you have any idea how vexing it is to have to put up with all this pomp and pageantry every minute of my life?''

Quenton shot a glance at his brother, and the two grinned.

Charles frowned. ''What's so funny?''

''You forget that we've known you for a lifetime. You may complain about it now, but when you were a boy, you once said you'd kill anyone who tried to keep you from your rightful place on the throne.''

''A figure of speech. Besides, I am the rightful heir. And the throne is rightfully mine, even if I did have to wait a lifetime to ascend.''

''Exactly. Now, would you like us to feel sorry for you because you must bear a little pomp and pageantry?''

Charles started to chuckle, that deep, rich laugh for which he was famous. ''If you were true friends you would have permitted me to wallow in self-pity for at least a little while longer.''

''If you want to shed some tears, shed them for the poor villagers, who will probably go without warm cloaks this winter in order to fill that cask with gold.''

''You said yourself they love me. And I love my people.''

''Aye.'' Quenton couldn't help laughing. ''And the fact that they present you with gold makes it a little easier to love them.''

''I think, Bennett, your brother has become jaded.''

Bennett drained his glass and grinned from ear to ear as his brother lifted the decanter to refill it.

"I'll have some of that." Charles held out his goblet. He tasted, smiled. "Blackthorne still has some of the finest ales, my friends. Do you recall the time we hid ourselves in that wardrobe?" He pointed a finger at the closet along the far wall where Thor was once more pacing and whining.

"Aye." Quenton settled himself in a chaise across from the king. "We waited until Grandfather went below stairs, then we helped ourselves to his whiskey."

"It was either very strong whiskey, or we had very weak constitutions. I had to help the two of you to your beds." Charles belched into his handkerchief.

"Your memory is a bit faulty." Quenton shot him a knowing smile. "Perhaps a sign of your doddering age. It was I who helped you to bed."

"Well, perhaps," he conceded. "But only after I'd carried poor old Bennett down a flight of stairs and held his head while he christened Cook's garden."

At the memory, Bennett grinned foolishly.

"Do you remember what we called each other?" Charles emptied his glass and reached for the decanter. "I was Chills."

"Because you were always cold." Quenton said with a trace of sarcasm.

"Nay. Because I had already perfected a cool look that would wither grown men. Don't deny it. You know that for a fact."

"Perhaps. I still say it was because you were always cold." Quenton glanced at his brother. "Bennett, you were Baby, though you hated the name. That's probably why you became such a fighter in your youth. I've never known a tougher lad."

Bennett seemed inordinately pleased at that description.

The King turned to Quenton. "And in all our games you were always Q, a spy for the crown." The two shared a conspiratorial laugh before the king said to Bennett, "Did you know your brother had a chance to live out his fantasy?"

At Bennett's arched brow Charles said, "When Q went to sea, he went with my blessing. And he performed a great service for his country. He made a name for himself as a fearless privateer, waging war on foreign vessels, keeping the waters safe for English ships. But what the rest of England didn't know is that he was also sending coded messages to me so that our warships always knew where the enemy was sailing."

At Bennett's stunned look he gave a delighted laugh. "You didn't know? Why, Q, you sly fox. You never even confided in your own brother?"

Quenton stared down into his glass. "Old habits die hard. I became so accustomed to working alone, in secret, I forgot how to share things with anyone. Even my brother."

"Then it's a good thing I came to visit. We're going to share everything, just as we did when we were lads. Hunting, riding, wenching, games of chance. I want to do it all before I leave Blackthorne. And when we're alone, I don't want to be called Your Majesty. I want to be called Chills. And you shall once more be Baby and Q."

The three men grinned at one another, feeling as warm, as comfortable with one another as though they'd never been apart. And for a little while, as the ale flowed freely and they talked of boyhood escapades, they were no longer a king and his subjects, but boyhood friends who had shared a common history.

Olivia was stunned at what she had overheard. It shamed her to be eavesdropping on such an intimate conversation. But she could see no way out of it. To reveal herself would be to incur the wrath of the king. She would be immediately dismissed as governess, and she would be sent back to London in disgrace.

Liat's nervous energy had faded, leaving him exhausted. He had fallen asleep in her arms. In the cramped, stuffy confines of the wardrobe, she was forced to sit with her knees bent, her back stiff. She had long ago lost all feeling in her arms.

Worst of all, each time she started to relax and convince herself that they would go undetected, Thor would begin sniffing around the wardrobe, scratching and whining, until his master would summon him to his side.

Her nerves were stretched to the breaking point. She had begun to believe she would rather be caught than have to stay here another minute, heart pounding, palms sweating, while in the room beyond this closet, three old friends caught up on the years that had separated them.

"Exile in France was horrid. They pointed to Cromwell, running our country without a crown, and I, the true heir to the throne living hand to mouth, and said that English monarchy was no monarchy at all."

The candles guttered in pools of wax, and the three friends had managed to empty several decanters of fine whiskey. Thor lay dozing by the fire.

"I was in Holland." Charles gave a short laugh.

"Playing tennis, of all things, when I received the news that Cromwell was dead. I fell on my knees in gratitude that my father's executioner had finally met his fate."

"You had to be devastated when you heard that he had named his son, Richard, to succeed him."

"Aye. At first. But from the reports I was getting, I knew that Richard was a weakling. 'Twas really his father, ruling from the grave. I knew that sooner or later I would return home in triumph." He stared broodingly into his glass. "The triumph was short-lived. There is more, I've discovered, to being a ruler than pleasing the people. I have no problem there. But pleasing Parliament. Now that's another thing."

"You have friends in Parliament, Chills."

"Aye. And more than a few enemies. Some who hated my father, and hate me for being his son. They're accusing me of bankrupting the treasury."

Quenton studied his old friend. "Are you in trouble?"

Charles shrugged. "England's finances are in shambles. Parliament fell short of its collection of taxes by hundreds of thousands of pounds."

"What will you do?" Quenton topped off the king's goblet yet again.

Charles stood and began to pace. "Perhaps I should go through all the villages allowing them to pay me homage by giving me casks of gold."

Quenton and Bennett exchanged smiles. "Considering the effort it took to get here, I doubt you'd want to do it all over England. Even if the reward be gold."

Charles glanced at his friend and nodded. "Aye. But there may yet be a way. I have been approached by some powerful people in London." His eyes darkened for a moment. "I'm not certain I trust them. There are whispers that they were close to Cromwell. But others suggest they were merely being expedient, in order to hold on to their wealth. Whatever their political affiliations, they are extremely wealthy. They have offered to share their wealth in exchange for...certain political favors."

"Such as?"

Charles paused, ran his hand over the head of a cane resting in the corner of the room, testing its strength. "I remember your grandfather using this, not only to walk, but to reach out and rap us when we were impertinent."

Quenton smiled, as much at the memory as at the knowledge that his old friend was avoiding the issue. "What political favors, Chills?"

"The father has his eye on a title and estates. The son wishes only to be admitted to my inner circle, perhaps as royal adviser or grand counsel."

"That would make him privy to state secrets, my friend."

"Aye. But I would have the money I need to impress Parliament. My father's downfall was war, or rather, the lack of funds with which to wage war. I can't afford to make the same mistake."

He looked so sad that Quenton crossed the room and draped an arm over his shoulder. "Just don't act in haste, Chills. Perhaps I could ask around and find out a few things about this family and its money."

The king's grin was quick. "You just can't resist being Q, can you?"

"I told you. Old habits die hard. Now tell me their names, and I'll see what I can learn about them."

The king considered, then shrugged. "I'll think on

it. Perhaps I'll give you a chance to meet them at the end of the week.''

''And where, may I ask, would I be meeting these mysterious people?''

''Here at Blackthorne.'' The king drained his goblet, then looked up to see his friend's blank stare. ''Ah. I see I forgot to mention the fact that I've decided to have a royal ball at Blackthorne in honor of my visit with my good friends.''

Quenton shook his head. ''Chills, you'll be the death of my housekeeper yet.''

''Nonsense. I'll charm her and she'll be delighted to take on the burden of a royal ball.''

He looked annoyed as Thor once again shuffled to his feet and began to sniff around the wardrobe. ''I do believe you have a rodent, Q. Why not open the door and let the hound have his fun?''

Quenton crossed the room. ''What is it, old boy? A mouse? You'd enjoy a good chase, wouldn't you?''

He pulled open the door and the hound lunged, tail wagging, tongue lolling. The three men stared in openmouthed surprise at the sight that greeted them.

Olivia, hair curling damply around her face, got stiffly to her feet and climbed out, still holding the sleeping boy to her chest.

''What the…?'' For a moment Quenton seemed to have lost his voice. Then, through gritted teeth he demanded, ''Miss St. John, you will explain yourself at once.''

''Aye, my lord.'' She glanced at the king, who was staring at her with a bemused expression. ''I was…getting Liat ready for bed. But then he was gone. So I followed him in here…but then when we were about to leave we heard footsteps…and…''

"And you just thought you'd jump into the wardrobe and spy on us?"

"Well, my lord, it wasn't quite like..."

"Did you mean to reveal yourself, Miss St. John?"

"Nay, my lord. But we didn't mean to spy. We just..."

Liat awoke. Rubbing his eyes, he glanced around, then smiled. "Hello, Majesty. I ran in here to say good-night to Thor. He's my friend. And when we heard somebody coming, I pulled Miss St. John into my new hiding place. Isn't it grand?"

The king returned his smile. "Aye. I've hid in there a time or two myself."

"You have?" The boy's eyes grew big. "Were you ever caught?"

"Aye. Lord Stamford's grandfather once found us in there. As I recall, we couldn't sit for a week."

Liat glanced at Quenton. "Are you going to spank us?"

"I ought to." If he weren't so angry, he might find the thought of spanking the nursemaid's bottom appealing. At the moment, however, he thought it wise to get rid of this troublesome duo as quickly as possible.

"I suggest you go to your room, Miss St. John."

"Aye, my lord." She turned toward the door.

"And this time, see that you make no stops along the way."

As she started out, the little boy, clinging to her neck, gave them another of his angelic smiles.

"Good night, Liat," the king called.

"G'night, Majesty."

They waited until the door closed and Olivia's footsteps receded. For several minutes there was complete silence. Then all three burst into roars of laughter.

"By heaven, they're a bit of a handful, aren't they, Q? Here. Pour me another. Let's drink to grown-up responsibilities."

"I'm so happy to be here. Always loved Cornwall, even though most of its inhabitants don't even consider themselves Englishmen."

Quenton bit back a smile at the king's slurred words. He glanced over at his brother, whose glass was empty, and whose eyes were slowly closing.

"Aye. We're an independent lot. But I think we'd better debate the finer points of life in this splendid wilderness at some other time. Right now we'd better hie ourselves off to bed. Or we won't have a shred of energy for all that hunting, riding, dancing and wenching you've planned."

"Speaking of wenching...." The king dropped down in the high-backed chair behind the desk. Without the support, he would more than likely have fallen over. "I saw the way you and the pretty little nursemaid were making eyes at each other."

Quenton made an attempt at dignity, setting his goblet on the mantel and leaning an arm along its polished surface. "I don't know what you're talking about."

Charles hiccuped. "Not that I blame you, Q. If I had something that fresh and innocent living a stone's throw from my bed, I'd be hard-pressed to ignore it either. But I should think you could make an effort to hide your feelings."

"I'm hiding them very well, thank you."

The minute the words were out of his mouth, he realized what he'd said. The king threw back his head and roared. Even Bennett, nearly asleep in his chair, perked up and began grinning.

"And you, Baby." The king pointed their grandfather's cane at his young friend. "You're fooling nobody with that helpless act."

At Bennett's arched brow he bellowed, "You've had no trouble lifting ale to your lips all night. But you let that pretty little village lass feed you like a helpless infant and—" he sneered "—see to all your other needs. I wager I know what those other needs are."

Bennett's eyes grew stormy. He made a sound of disgust in his throat.

"Ah. I see I've touched a nerve." Charles launched himself out of the chair and wielded the cane in the air like a sword. "How about a little wager, my friends, to make my stay here even more interesting."

Quenton glanced at Bennett, then at the king. "What sort of wager?"

"A thousand pounds each says that before I leave Blackthorne and return to London, the two of you will admit your feelings for the ladies in question."

The two brothers exchanged knowing glances. A slow smile spread across Quenton's features. "You're on, Chills. A thousand pounds each. You may as well pay us now. You can take it out of the village cask if you wish."

"I was just about to suggest that the two of you pay up. 'Twill be easier than the alternative."

"Alternative?" Quenton's goblet of ale was forgotten.

"Ah. I see I neglected to mention the rest of the wager." Charles jabbed the tip of the cane against his old friend's shoulder, enjoying the game he was playing. "Unless you and Baby declare these two women to be under your…special protection, I shall order the two lovely ladies to accompany me when I return to London. Where, as you well know, they will soon be devoured by the preening peacocks at court."

He saw the banked fury in his friends' eyes and nearly laughed aloud. Oh, this was going to be such fun.

He tossed the cane and grinned with satisfaction when it landed neatly in a tall vase in the corner of the room. Then he threw an arm around Quenton's shoulders. "Now Q, my loyal spy, take your king to his chambers. And tuck him into his royal bed. And that is a royal command."

Quenton and the king had wrestled and stumbled their way up the stairs, balancing poor Bennett between them. Fortunately, his brother had been too drunk to have any fear. By the time they'd turned him over to Minerva's tender ministrations, he'd been sound asleep.

The king had been another matter. He had insisted upon dragging his old friend into his suite of rooms for one more tankard of ale. Fortunately for Quenton, Charles fell asleep before he was able to take more than a sip. Quenton had left the king sprawled on his bed, still dressed in his frilly shirt and breeches. The king's valet, asleep in the other room, would taste the royal temper in the morning.

As he stumbled past the door to Olivia's chambers he paused. The thought of her, lying in that big soft bed, was too great a temptation to ignore. Without a thought to what he was doing, he let himself in. The hound trailed behind.

The sitting chamber was cool. The fire had burned to embers. In the sleeping chamber, however, a log still burned on the grate. The flickering flames cast eerie shadows on the walls and ceiling.

Quenton stumbled his way to the bed and stood staring down at the vision that greeted him.

Dark hair spilled over the pillow and framed a face that always caught him by surprise with its sweetness. He watched the steady rise and fall of her chest and experienced a rush of heat that left him weak with desire.

Suddenly he was reminded of the king's wager. He'd be damned if he'd let anyone force him to declare his intentions. Especially since he hadn't a clue what his intentions were.

Was it love he was feeling for this woman? Admiration for her feisty spirit? Or mere lust?

He clenched a hand at his side. What did it matter? He'd lusted and loved before. And what had it brought him except a broken heart and shattered dreams? For the Stamfords, dreams had a way of becoming nightmares.

"Damn you, Chills," he muttered aloud.

"What? Who?" Confused, Olivia sat up, shoving tangles from her eyes. At the shadowy figures of man and beast, she shrank back and let out a cry. Then, recognizing Quenton, she covered her mouth with her hand to stifle the sound. "Why are you...what are you doing here?"

Feeling more than a little silly he reacted with a show of bravado. "Looking at you. And it's a very pretty sight indeed."

"You've come about that little incident in the library."

"Not at all. The entire inci…inci…thing is forgotten."

She knelt up in the middle of the bed. Her eyes darkened to stormclouds. "You're drunk."

"Aye. So I am. What of it?"

"I'll thank you to leave my chambers at once."

He gave her a silly grin. "You'd thank me a whole lot more if I stayed."

"Oh." She scrambled out of bed and headed across the room. Thor pranced at her side.

"Where are you going?"

"I'm taking you to your bed."

His smile grew. "Now there's a good lass. I never dreamed this would be so easy." He followed, draping an arm lazily over her shoulder.

She pushed his arm away and strode through the sitting chamber and into the hall, closing the door behind her, taking care not to make a sound. The last thing she needed was to have someone hear them. The whole household would be buzzing with gossip and rumors by morning.

With a silly grin he draped an arm around her shoulders and leaned heavily against her. He was like a deadweight, as he pushed his face close to hers. "I suppose I should have asked you weeks ago."

"Asked me what?"

"To come to my bed. Had I known you'd be so agreeable…" He paused to nibble her neck.

"Stop that." She slapped him away. "We have to get to your room."

He blinked, then grinned. "Oh. Aye. You're in a hurry, I see. Well then…" He tried to walk faster and succeeded in weaving, dragging her with him as he bumped into a wall.

He gave a muttered oath before squaring his shoulders and plunging forward. They rounded a corner and paused at the door to his chambers, where Thor stood, his tail swishing, tongue lolling.

"Here we are, my sweet thing. And not a minute too soon."

As she paused to nudge open the door he pulled her back against him and pressed his mouth to her ear. "Oh, the things I'll show you." His lips nuzzled her neck while his hands closed around her, resting just below the fullness of her breasts. "Treasure beyond belief, my lady. A garden of delight."

For a moment Olivia went very still, feeling her bones turn to liquid, her blood turn to fire. Then, reminding herself that he was very drunk, and probably wouldn't remember a thing about this in the morning, she disengaged herself from his arms and firmly opened the door.

"Come, my lord." With a crook of her finger she beckoned him across the room toward the bed.

"Aye. Willingly. I can't wait to taste the nectar of your lips."

"I believe you've tasted enough nectar for one night." She paused beside the bed and, while the hound curled up before the fire, considered whether or not to relieve Quenton of his clothes and boots.

He drew her into his arms and buried his lips in a tangle of hair at her temple. "Oh, you smell so good. Like a summer garden. Have I told you how much I love the smell of lavender?"

"And you reek of ale, my lord." She decided her best course of action was to dispose of him as quickly as possible.

"Let me help you with your night shift, my lady."

As he released her and reached for the buttons of her gown, she pressed both hands against his chest and pushed with all her might.

He tumbled backward into the bed and thrashed among the linens, looking for all the world like a turtle trapped on its back.

"Are you...ready to join me, my lady?" he managed finally.

All he heard in answer was the slamming of his door. And the sound of footsteps retreating along the hall.

And then the room spun dangerously out of control. And he knew that on the morrow he would pay a dear price for tonight's momentary lapse.

Chapter Twelve

"Good morrow, miss." Scowling, Edlyn entered Liat's chambers and stood watching as the nursemaid helped her young charge work on his letters. "Mistress Thornton sent me to fetch you. You and the lad have been summoned by His Majesty to the dining hall."

Olivia looked up in alarm. "Did she say why?"

The servant nearly smiled, then caught herself. "Nay."

"Thank you, Edlyn." Olivia tried to shake off the feeling that the surly servant was studying her a little too carefully.

She had seen a shadow in the hallway when she'd taken leave of Quenton's chambers, and had the feeling that someone had been watching. If it had been a servant, the scandal of the nursemaid and the lord of the manor would be all over the household by now. But there was something much worse to fret over. Last night she had overheard secrets not intended for her ears.

She ran a brush through Liat's hair and gave him a glance of approval before catching his hand and heading toward the door.

"Do you think the king is going to punish us for what we did last night?"

"If he does, it is because we deserve it. What we did was very wrong."

Though she spoke firmly, her heart was pounding. Liat was certainly safe, since he had fallen asleep and had heard nothing of importance. She, on the other hand, knew that Quenton had been a spy for his country. Knew also, that the king was considering accepting help from certain individuals in exchange for favors. Dangerous knowledge indeed.

Perhaps it would be even worse if the king heard about Quenton's drunken display, and had somehow learned that she had been in Quenton's chambers. Would such an indiscretion offend King Charles? Would she be publicly humiliated? Would her actions bring shame upon Quenton and his family?

By the time she arrived at the great hall she had worked herself up into a case of nerves that had her pulse hammering in her temples.

Pembroke announced them. "Majesty, Miss St. John and young Master Liat."

"Thank you, Pembroke." The king looked up from his platter, which was heaped with thinly sliced beef, a joint of fowl and several slices of bread still warm from the oven. In his hand was a tankard of hot mulled wine.

To his one side sat Bennett, whose skin was the color of wax. Beside him was Minerva, whose pleas that he eat something were being ignored.

On the other side of the king sat Quenton, toying with a goblet of water.

Both brothers looked so miserable, Olivia felt certain her fears were correct. Had she brought shame upon all of them?

"Ah, Miss St. John. Liat. Come closer, so that I can better see you."

Olivia felt heat rush to her cheeks and cursed this weakness that had her blushing so easily.

"Will you join me for some meat and fowl?"

"Join you...?" She caught herself before she started to babble. "We have already broken our fast, Majesty."

"Then sit and watch me eat. I crave some pleasant company." He pointed his tankard at Bennett and Quenton. "My two hosts are extremely unpleasant company this morrow."

"Perhaps it is something they drank," Olivia muttered as she took a seat beside Quenton.

He shot her an angry look before glancing away.

"There was a time," Charles said between bites, "when I envied these two their strong Stamford constitutions. But they've obviously grown old and weak. Very soon now, I'm afraid, they're going to need someone to cut their food and tuck them into bed each night." He waited a beat before adding, "Perhaps what each of them needs is a wife."

Quenton's jaw clenched, and for a moment it looked as though he might counter with an equally cutting remark of his own.

Charles quirked a brow. "Something you care to say to your king, Lord Stamford?"

"Nay, Majesty," he managed through his teeth.

Charles chuckled. "I thought not. Ah well. Perhaps later tonight you'll find your voice."

"Aye, Majesty. You can depend upon it."

The king glanced beyond him to Olivia. "Lord

Stamford has been kind enough to plan a day of hunting. I hope you and the lad will join us again.''

"Of course, Majesty." She would have agreed to almost anything, as long as it meant she was not to be publicly humiliated by the king.

"Good." He pushed aside his platter and called, "Mistress Thornton. My compliments to Cook. That was excellent. I can't wait to sample her next meal."

Quenton and Bennett groaned. And longed for their beds.

"Come on, boy." Quenton opened the door and Thor raced ahead of him to the garden.

Quenton knew he needed this late-night walk as much as the hound, to work off his energy, to settle his mind. Once again he'd been forced to play the part of host, drinking with Charles, reminiscing with him about their boyhood pranks.

What dreams they'd had. What grand plans. Charles had been so determined to ascend to the throne. He had spent his life in single-minded pursuit of the crown. Yet, now that it was his, he wore it grudgingly.

Bennett, the baby of the group, had wanted so badly to be treated as a grown-up. He'd kicked, fought and scrapped his way to acceptance by the others. And here he was, being carried about like an infant.

Even his own dreams of spying for the monarchy had only come about because of family tragedy. And though the work had given him a measure of satisfaction and had helped him put his personal problems aside, it had solved nothing. For all his cleverness, he had no answers to the mystery surrounding the death of Antonia and the disastrous injury to his brother.

He walked along the path briskly, keeping pace with

the hound. Tonight he'd been a little wiser, switching
to water when he'd had enough ale, and carrying his
brother to bed at his first yawn. After a day spent in
the saddle, the king had followed willingly.

Quenton breathed deeply, enjoying the familiar tang
of the ocean. He had expected to miss the pitch and
roll of his ship, the keen edge of danger that was a
constant companion on the seas. Instead, he found
himself settling into life at Blackthorne with unexpected ease.

Because of Olivia.

The thought came without warning.

He glanced toward her window and saw a light
burning. She was clearly silhouetted, head bent over a
task at her desk. What was she doing while the rest
of the household slept? Perhaps writing to relatives
about her strange experiences here at Blackthorne.
Perhaps she kept a journal. His lips curved into a
smile. Wouldn't he love to read it, and discover all
her secrets? He had already learned that there was
much more to her than the prim and proper image she
showed the world. She had a kind heart. He'd heard
it from all the staff. How she put them at ease and
genuinely seemed to care about all of them. He'd seen
for himself how she could spot a need and find a way
to answer it.

She was gentle yet firm with Liat. And, if truth be
told, more mother to the lad than mere tutor. She had
found a way to draw Bennett out of himself and bring
him back to the land of the living. A true miracle, in
Quenton's mind. The physicians had suggested Bennett be put away, a suggestion that Quenton and his
grandfather had adamantly refused. But until the arrival of Olivia, nobody had found a way to bring Ben-

nett out of the terror locked inside his mind. Nobody but Olivia. With simple charm and an amazing determination, she had done what no one else could. Perhaps that was why he loved her.

He stopped in his tracks, stunned by the enormity of such a thought. Love? It wasn't possible. After Antonia he'd vowed to never love again. But there it was. The moment the word had formed in his mind, he realized it was true.

God in heaven. He loved her. But what to do about it?

Though her kisses were chaste, he could sense a simmering sensuality just beneath the surface. There were secrets there. Dark, deep secrets. Aye, there was passion in Olivia St. John. He clenched his hand into a fist at his side. And he wanted, more than anything in this world, to be the one to unleash it.

By day, the sight of her taunted him. By night her image played in his dreams. He hadn't wanted to admit to Charles just how much she affected him. But the king had been right. That impertinent little nursemaid was driving him mad. And all because she had somehow tricked him into falling in love.

Olivia labored over the contents of the letter to her aunt and uncle. She wanted it to be concise, yet polite. She would thank them for taking her in after the death of her parents. She would assure them that her current employment suited her and that, even when she was no longer needed at Blackthorne, she would seek a position as nursemaid or governess elsewhere. That way they would be relieved of the burden of having to care for her in the future. And lastly, since she would have no further contact with them, she would ask that the balance of her mother's estate, provided there was anything left, be sent to her here at Blackthorne.

Though her aunt had made it sound as though she might be penniless, Olivia had seen their lavish lifestyle in London. Grand furniture. A household staff that rivaled the staff at Blackthorne. Food and clothing fit for royalty. Old Letty had said that her mother's family had enjoyed both wealth and title. If that were true, then there ought to be some small pittance left in her mother's estate. The fact that Wyatt had been so determined that she sign over whatever inheritance she might have nagged at her mind.

How she wished she could talk to someone who was knowledgeable about such things. But the only one she knew was Quenton, and the thought of sharing such information with him was unimaginable.

Quenton. She lifted her head to look out at the darkened sky. What was she going to do about these feelings for Quenton? She knew very well that he was a worldly man who would be completely unsuitable for the likes of her. What was she, after all, but a penniless nursemaid, with no knowledge of the world beyond her door?

Yet she had feelings. Strange, unsettling feelings that seemed to ebb and flow whenever she was around Quenton. And if those feelings weren't bad enough, there was more. A strange yearning of her heart. A rare sort of joy whenever she saw him speak kindly to his brother, or encourage Liat. A sense of pride whenever one of the staff said something flattering about their very own Lord Stamford. As though his goodness, his kindness reflected upon her.

In the secret recesses of her heart, she thought she

loved him. Truly loved him. But it frightened her to think that she could be nothing more than a little fool.

Oh, how she wished her wise mother were here to advise her. Was it love she was feeling?

Seeing the path of a shooting star, she squeezed her eyes shut and made a wish. And found herself blushing because of the things she'd wished for.

Quenton moved soundlessly up the stairs, with the hound at his heels. For the space of a heartbeat he paused outside Olivia's chambers, debating the wisdom of what he was about to do. Without bothering to knock he tore open the door and entered the sitting room. At a signal, Thor settled himself in front of the fireplace to await his master. Quenton crossed to the bedroom, opened the door and peered inside.

She was seated at her desk in a little alcove, her face lifted to the sky. Her feet were bare, and peeking out from the hem of a night shift that was made of some delicate fabric that could have been spun by angels. She had brushed her hair long and loose, and it fell in darkened tendrils around her shoulders.

Feeling a dryness in his throat, he crossed his arms and leaned a shoulder against the doorway, enjoying the view.

She turned and caught sight of him. For a moment all she could do was stare. He looked every bit like the seagoing privateer the servants whispered about. The pirate who, in her dreams, carried her off to his ship and sailed with her to distant, exotic shores.

The quill slipped from her fingers and fell, unnoticed, to the desk. She pushed back her chair and got to her feet.

"I didn't hear you knock."

"That's because I didn't bother with such formalities."

His tone, as much as the narrowed eyes, alerted her to his dangerous mood.

"Well." She started toward him, intending to escort him to the door. "If you think you can just walk in here…"

"I can." He caught her roughly by the arm and dragged her close. "I can do anything I want here at Blackthorne. Here, just as at sea, I make the rules. This is my own little kingdom."

She tried to brush him aside and was caught in a grip of steel. "Then find yourself some pliant subjects."

"I don't want pliant, Olivia." He closed a hand over her other arm and pinned her against him. "I want strong, willful, defiant. I want a woman who will stand up to me. And stand with me."

"You want." She hoped her attempt at a sneer didn't sound as weak to him as it did to her own ears. But the nearness of him had her heart doing strange fluttering things. "And what about what I want?"

"What do you want, Olivia?" He lowered his mouth to hers. "This?"

The kiss was rough. Sharp-edged with need. He wasn't so much kissing her as devouring. His lips plundering hers, and demanding more.

When he lifted his head she pushed against his chest and dragged air into her lungs. His breathing was as harsh, as ragged as hers. She could feel his heartbeat thundering. "How dare you?"

But as she lifted a hand to strike out at him he caught hold of her wrist and held her fast.

He saw the look of surprise in her eyes as he lifted

both her wrists, locking them around his neck. "I dare because it's what I want. What you want." His hands slid down her arms, and along her sides, his thumbs stroking her nipples. He swallowed the little gasp of indignation that rose in her throat and kissed her with a thoroughness that had her trembling.

Heat engulfed her, searing her lungs, turning her blood to molten lava. Her bones seemed to have melted. She felt soft, pliant. His to mold as he wished. Even her mind had deserted her. She hadn't the will to stop him.

He tasted like the sea. All dark, swirling waters and swift, compelling waves. Pulling her to him. Carrying her along with the tide of his passion.

He lingered over her mouth, drawing out all the sweet, exotic flavors. Against her lips he whispered, "Now tell me you don't want this."

Just moments ago she'd been determined to send him packing by any means necessary. Even if it meant resorting to shouting down the household. Now she couldn't manage a single word.

When she didn't answer he lifted his head. "Tell me, Olivia."

In reply she stood on tiptoe to offer more. With a growl of pleasure he took, feeding all the hunger, all the loneliness.

He changed the angle of the kiss and took it deeper. His hands stroked and kneaded, adding to the pleasure until it was almost more than she could bear.

She was exciting to watch. All that sweetness, that innocence, masking a fire smoldering just below the surface until it suddenly ignited. She wrapped herself around him, returning kiss for kiss, touch for touch.

"You see." He brought his lips to her throat and

felt her shuddering response. "You want what I want, Olivia. The pleasure, the release, is ours for the taking."

Somewhere in the distant recesses of her mind a warning bell sounded. It was something about the words he'd just spoken. She fought her way up through the layers of pleasure, struggling for the strength of will she had always possessed. The common sense to determine just what it was he was offering.

"So." She took in a long, calming breath, then another. "What you're saying is, we can pleasure each other."

"Aye." He pressed kisses across her forehead, her temple, her cheek. His mind was still clouded with her. His lungs still filled with the taste, the scent of her.

"But you've said nothing about love, Quenton. Or happiness ever after."

He gave a short laugh and was surprised at how difficult it was to speak. Or even breathe. "You make it sound like a fairy tale. I can tell you from experience that there is no ever after."

"For you, perhaps. And if that's true, then I'm sorry. But I will not settle for less."

He smoothed the damp hair from her face and framed it with his hands. "You're much too sensible for such nonsense."

"Nay, my lord. You are the one who's much too sensible. As for me, I prefer to hold out for fairy tales. Or nonsense as you call it."

She took a step back, breaking contact. He would never know how difficult it was. As she looked into those dark, troubled eyes, she felt her heart breaking into little pieces. Even now she wanted what he was offering. And would never accept it.

"Now leave my chambers. And don't come back unless you're invited."

Olivia stood at the window, staring at the midnight sky. There was no point in trying to sleep. She was so agitated, she couldn't even stand still. She turned, paced restlessly, then returned to the window.

What was wrong with her, that she could be attracted to a rogue? A blackhearted villain? When had her common sense deserted her? Her parents would be shocked and disappointed at her lapse.

She remembered the girl from her little town of Oxford who had returned to her parents' home with a baby. Mum and Papa had clucked their tongues like all the other neighbors, and Mum had said that there were two kinds of men. Those who would honor their women and those who would take a maiden's innocence and leave her with nothing but shame. And that poor neighbor lass had settled for the latter.

When Olivia asked her how to tell the difference, Mum had sighed. "Oh, Livvy. When you're old enough, you'll just know."

"Did you know right away that Papa was honorable?"

"I don't know about honorable." Mum's eyes had burned with a strange, girlish light. "But from the moment we met, I couldn't think about another man. Even my sister's strong disapproval wouldn't deter me. I had to have him. And he had to have me."

I have to have you, Olivia.

Sweet heaven, what was the matter with her? She felt the sudden rush of tears and was caught completely by surprise. She would not cry over that man. She would not.

But despite her determination, the tears fell. She threw herself down on the bed and wallowed in misery.

Chapter Thirteen

Olivia made her way to the kitchen. Her eyes were still swollen from the tears and the lack of sleep. Across the room, huddled beside the ovens, stood the butler, the housekeeper and the cook.

"Ye'd best stay out of his lordship's way this morrow," Mistress Thornton was saying. "I don't know when I've seen him so surly."

"He was in a fine mood when I retired last night." Pembroke sipped his tea while arranging breakfast on a tray. "Now he looks like he'd be happy to tear off a hide or two."

"Well I don't want it to be mine." Cook looked up from the biscuits she'd just removed from the oven. "Good morrow, Miss St. John."

"Good morrow." Olivia struggled to paste a smile on her lips.

"Here's yer tea, miss." Cook set a pot of tea on Olivia's tray. "Biscuits, miss?"

"Thank you. Just one this morning. Liat does love your biscuits."

"And you don't?"

Olivia was quick to soothe. "Oh, it isn't that, Cook.

I do like your biscuits. But I'm just not hungry this morning. I've lost my appetite."

"From what I hear, you'll lose more than yer appetite if you go near his lordship."

"I'll remember that." She crossed the room and spooned fruit conserve onto a plate. As she worked she could hear the muted conversation.

"There's talk His Majesty is so pleased with Lord Quenton's...work for him that he'd gladly send him back to sea." Pembroke added a flagon of mulled wine to the tray in hopes it would soothe the lord's temper.

"Then 'tis true? His lordship did report directly to the king?" Mistress Thornton's voice lifted in excitement. "Was he a pirate then?"

"Privateer," Pembroke corrected gently. "From what I've heard, the best that ever sailed the seas. There wasn't a sea captain alive who didn't fear falling into the hands of Captain Quenton Stamford and his cutthroats. Though from what I've overheard recently, it was all done to protect his king and his country. He was fearless in battle. And heartless when protecting the king's navy."

"He looks the part." Cook giggled like a girl. "I'd let him plunder my ship anytime."

All three looked up when Olivia picked up her tray with a clatter and beat a hasty exit.

The housekeeper watched her leave, then said softly, "Maybe whatever got to his lordship got to Miss St. John as well."

"Aye." Pembroke nodded. "You may have something there, Mistress Thornton." He'd seen the way those two looked at each other when they thought no one would notice. He frowned, deep in thought. "You may indeed have something there."

Upstairs, Olivia hurried along the hallway, eager for the sanctuary of Liat's chambers. At least there she wouldn't have to listen to any more of the staff singing the praises of Quenton the sailor, Quenton the privateer, Quenton the king's hero.

"Ah, Miss St. John." The king's booming voice sounded overloud in the morning silence.

She froze in her tracks as Charles stepped into the hallway directly in front of her. Behind him, looking perfectly composed, stood Quenton.

"The very person I was hoping to see."

"Good morrow, Majesty. My lord." She managed to curtsy while balancing the tray, all the while cursing herself for lingering in the kitchen below. A minute sooner and she would have been safely inside Liat's room and away from prying eyes.

"You're looking especially fetching this morrow." He turned to Quenton. "Don't you agree, Lord Stamford?"

Quenton forced himself to look at her without expression. "Aye, Majesty."

She hated the blush that crept up her neck and colored her cheeks. "Thank you."

"I've just told Lord Stamford..." Charles paused, smiled broadly. "Though he seems a bit rough today. Perhaps too much ale. Or not enough excitement in his life here at Blackthorne. At any rate, I told him I wish to go sailing today. And I'd like you and the lad to join us."

"Sailing?" She was trying to keep her smile in place, but it was impossible, with Quenton standing so close, watching her with that bored, distant expression.

"Do you sail, Miss St. John?"

"I don't know, Majesty."

"You mean you've never been aboard Lord Stamford's ship?"

"Nay, Majesty. I've never been aboard anyone's ship."

He turned to Quenton. "Then the lass is in for a treat. Don't you agree, old friend?"

"Aye, Majesty."

At his lackluster response Charles threw back his head and laughed. "Oh, we'll have a fine time. Tell Cook we'll have a midday meal aboard ship." He turned to Olivia. "Bring the lad down as soon as he's broken his fast. We'll take my carriage to the docks."

As Olivia started away he called after her, "And Miss St. John?"

She paused, turned.

"I promise you Lord Stamford's disposition will improve as the day progresses. I've never known him to be anything but cheerful aboard ship."

Olivia hurried to Liat's room. While the boy ate, she paced. How could she bear to spend an entire day under that cool, dispassionate gaze of Quenton's? Perhaps she should feign illness. It seemed the coward's way, but what other choice was there?

"What will we do today, ma'am?" Liat broke the biscuit into pieces and slathered them with fruit conserve.

Since it wasn't in her nature to hide the truth, she was forced to admit, "King Charles has invited us to sail with him. But perhaps..." She turned to him hopefully as a thought struck. "Perhaps you get violently sick in boats?"

"Nay, ma'am. I sailed all the way here from my

island with Lord Stamford. Never was I sick. Oh, I do
so like the ocean and the feel of the boat.''

"You…do?'' Her heart sank. So much for that idea.

"I miss being on the water, ma'am.''

"But you're so young, Liat. Did you go out in a
boat often?''

"Almost every day.''

"With your…father?'' Her heart nearly stopped.

This was the first time that the lad had volunteered
anything about his life in Jamaica. Though Quenton
had discouraged her from initiating the discussion, he
had said nothing about allowing the boy to speak his
mind.

"With my mother.'' Liat's smile grew dreamy.
"She caught fish, and sold them in the square. And I
went with her every day.''

Would Quenton have allowed his lover to work at
such a humble task as fishmonger? "Do you remember anything else? Your father, perhaps?''

His smile faded. He raced across the room and
climbed up onto the trunk in the alcove, staring out to
sea.

Had he been warned not to speak of his father? she
wondered. Was that the reason for such a reaction?

When he turned, his sunny smile was back in place.
"Let's go, ma'am. I can hardly wait until we're aboard
ship.''

She swallowed back her disappointment. Liat's life
in Jamaica, it would seem, was as much a mystery as
Bennett's fall from the cliffs.

Like everything the king did, their day of sailing
entailed dozens of servants and a caravan of carriages
and wagons to transport people and supplies to the

docks. Along the way, the road was lined with villagers, eager for a glimpse of their monarch. Charles waved to and acknowledged them, keeping his famous smile in place until they reached the docks.

By the time Charles and his party arrived, the chaos had been smoothed, the supplies stowed aboard ship and the servants dispatched.

At the docks Quenton glanced around. "Where are your servants, Majesty?"

"I had them sent back to Blackthorne."

"You would do without your servants? What about your Yeomen of the Guard?"

"Dispatched to follow in a second boat. I want this day to be a private one, spent among friends."

"I see." Quenton understood his old friend's need for freedom from the restraints of the throne, even if he didn't always agree. Still, with the soldiers close behind, the king's safety was ensured. He had earned the right to a day of leisure.

Quenton pointed to the gleaming boat anchored just offshore. "There is the *Prodigal,* Majesty."

"Ah, Lord Stamford. Your grandfather's ship. We spent many an afternoon sailing these waters. She looks none the worse for wear."

"Aye. She ages gracefully." Quenton directed a muscular lad to lift Bennett from the carriage, then led their party toward a boat manned by several oarsmen. Pembroke helped them aboard and they were rowed across the narrow channel to the *Prodigal.*

As they climbed aboard, Bennett was seated in a comfortable chair, with Minerva beside him to see to his needs. Quenton went to the helm, leaving Pembroke to make them comfortable.

The craft was a small, beautifully appointed sailing

vessel, with a covered deck to shelter guests from the sun and wind. Below was a cozy cabin with padded benches suitable for sleeping and a table and chairs anchored to the floor.

As soon as he was aboard, the king removed his brocaded jacket and wide-brimmed hat and handed them to Pembroke. Seeing the surprised looks on the faces of Olivia and Minerva, he gave them a boyish grin. "I am among friends now, my ladies. I hope you will not be disappointed if I insist on removing some vestige of ceremony."

"Nay, Majesty," Olivia managed to say. "All we desire is your comfort."

He chuckled. "You see, Lord Stamford? There are some loyal subjects who still care about their king. You, Miss St. John, are a source of constant delight to your king."

With an economy of movement Quenton tossed aside his jacket and hat and unfurled the sails. Olivia marveled at the sight of the breeze filling them. Even more of a marvel was the sight of his broad shoulders and muscled arms, his strong, capable fingers. The wind ruffled his dark hair, sending it spilling across his forehead.

With his hand at the wheel Quenton guided the boat from its mooring and into the open water.

"May I steer?" Liat asked.

Much to Olivia's surprise, Quenton agreed. "Let's see what your governess has been teaching you. Come, lad. Put your hands here." Standing behind him, Quenton watched as the boy took the wheel.

"Every good sailor knows how to read a compass," he said softly. "Here are your headings. Do you know what they mean?"

"Aye, sir. Miss St. John said *N* is north, *S* is south, *E* is east and *W* is west."

Quenton arched a brow, and the king, listening, gave a nod of approval.

"Now, Liat, you can see from the billowing sails just which way the wind is blowing. Which way do you think we ought to turn the boat in order to use the wind to our advantage?"

With great concentration Liat studied the sails and compass, then said, "The wind is coming out of the south." He turned the boat until the compass heading showed north, away from the wind. "With the wind behind us, we ought to move smartly through the water."

Quenton smiled his pleasure. "Quite right, lad. Why, you're a natural sailor." He allowed the boy to keep his hands on the wheel, while he deftly assisted in keeping the boat on an even keel. When he could feel Liat's strength ebbing, he said, "I'll take over now, if you'd like to join the others."

"Aye. Thank you, sir."

The boy beamed with pride as he danced over to take a seat beside Olivia. Pleased, she ruffled his hair.

Charles, watching Olivia's face, had seen the look of appreciation as she'd studied the man at the wheel. "How about giving his nursemaid a lesson now, Lord Stamford?"

"That isn't necessary, Majesty."

She blushed when he dismissed her objections with a wave of the hand. "I insist, Miss St. John." He turned to Quenton. "Come on, Lord Stamford. Let her have a feel of the ship beneath her own hands."

She squared her shoulders and walked to the helm. Quenton moved back a step, allowing her to stand directly in front of him. When she placed her hands on the wheel, she was startled by the tug of the waves. Even with both hands firmly grasping the wheel, she could barely hold it steady.

"It feels...alive," she said with a trace of awe.

"Aye. The sea is a living, breathing thing. With a mind of her own." He leaned against her and closed his hands over hers to steady the wheel. He became achingly aware of everything about her. The dark curls tied back with a simple white ribbon. The high color on her cheeks. The intoxicating scent of lavender that seemed as much a part of her as the soft voice and warm laughter. "Sometimes she's as gentle as a woman in love. And sometimes as violent as a woman betrayed."

"Why do you refer to the sea as she?"

"She's a woman. Every sailor knows that. Everywhere you look, she nurtures an abundance of life. There, just ahead, is a school of marlin. See how sleek they are. They can cut through the water faster than any ship. Faster even than the wind."

Olivia caught a glimpse of their silvery-blue fins as they sliced the water. And became aware of his strength as he kept the ship on a steady course through the choppy waves.

"Over there is a dolphin."

Olivia glanced over and saw the creature, as frisky as any puppy, keeping pace with the boat.

"Sailors consider them good luck. No matter where we are, no matter how far from land, we see their smiling faces and feel less lonely."

"With all the danger and excitement you faced on those exotic shores, I can't imagine you feeling lonely, Quenton."

"Aye, there was plenty of danger and excitement. And many an opportunity to visit foreign shores that were lovely." His tone lowered with feeling. "But none of them was England." And none of the exotic women he'd met had matched the rare beauty of this woman.

She shivered. Unconsciously her hands tightened on the wheel.

"The water will be smoother when we leave this channel behind and reach open sea." He lifted a hand to point. "You see how the water changes color? Here below us it's almost the color of the sky. But up ahead it's more green than blue. And far out there, to the west, it's so deep blue it's almost black."

She followed his direction and nodded. "I've never been at sea. It's not at all what I'd expected. It's like being thrust into another world."

"Are you afraid?" He returned his hand to the wheel, his fingers warm and strong as they covered hers, as if to reassure her.

She turned her face slightly to answer him. "Nay. I'm not afraid. Just enchanted. I never dreamed it could be so beautiful."

Nothing could have pleased him more. He was elated to know that she loved the sea as he did.

His earlier temper dissolved. His mood lightened. Pressing his lips to her temple he murmured, "The beauty of this ocean pales beside yours, Olivia."

She felt the familiar little jolt to her system and stood very still, wishing this moment could go on and on and never end. It felt so good to be standing here, the wind in her hair, Quenton's strong hands on hers.

She knew, with absolute certainty, that she was safe in the circle of his arms.

"Look," he called, pointing.

Everyone turned.

"Land's End."

"Truly?"

He returned his lips to her temple. "It is, quite literally, land's end. We've passed the westernmost tip of Britain."

Olivia was charmed by the wild, primitive beauty of the spot. And enchanted by the name. But she was even more enchanted by the man who called this place home.

From his position on the deck, Charles watched his old friend and began to smile. It would seem that his little plan was working.

Oh, the royal spy thought he'd mastered the art of keeping his thoughts to himself. But when it came to the pretty little nursemaid, he was as transparent as these azure waters. The fool was in love. And Charles intended to point out that fact to his old friend. In his own good time.

"Lord Stamford." Charles shaded the sun from his eyes and pointed off the bow. "Why don't we drop anchor in that little cove?"

"Aye. It would give us a good chance to see what Cook prepared for our midday meal." Quenton guided the boat into the shallows, then dropped anchor a short distance from shore and set about lowering the sails.

Pembroke went below deck and returned with a tray of drinks. Bennett and Minerva sat in the shade of the canopy, while Olivia and Liat joined Charles and Quenton in the sunlight.

The king breathed deeply. "I do so love being out of London. Though I often cruise along the Thames, the air isn't half as sweet as it is here." He turned to Olivia. "Have you been to London, my dear?"

She thought about her brief visit to her aunt's house, and a shadow seemed to pass over her happiness. "Aye, Majesty."

"And what did you think of it?"

"I much prefer the country."

He gave Quenton a meaningful glance. "Perhaps you just haven't seen it in the company of the right people. I was thinking of inviting you to court."

"To…court?" She glanced at Quenton and saw the scowl. Was it something she had said?

Just then Pembroke crossed the deck and paused beside the king. "Majesty, your meal is ready below deck."

"Ah, thank you, Pembroke. This sea air has given me quite an appetite." He caught Olivia's hand and tucked it through the crook of his arm. "Come, my dear. Let's lead the way, shall we?"

He led her down the stairs and held her chair at table, while Quenton carried Bennett, and Minerva and Liat followed.

The king picked up a goblet of ale and watched as Pembroke filled his plate with tender biscuits, thin slices of poached salmon and beef and kidney pie.

After the first bite he gave a sigh of contentment. "Lord Stamford, Cook has outdone herself."

"Aye, Majesty." Quenton smiled. "Of course, it could be that the sea air has invigorated your appetite."

"Perhaps. But if you're not careful, old friend, I may have to steal her away to London as well. Perhaps, by the time I leave Blackthorne, you and Bennett could find yourselves all alone. And I will have all the lovely, tempting females who make your lives so comfortable at Blackthorne, surrounding me at court. ''

Instead of his usual scowl, Quenton smiled. "You may find yourself having to deal with insurrection if you should try."

Olivia allowed the friendly banter to flow around her while she enjoyed her meal. She couldn't remember when she'd had such a lovely day. She glanced at Quenton from beneath lowered lashes. And all because it was spent in the company of this mysterious, fascinating man.

After lunch they took their drinks on deck, enjoying the sunshine.

Liat pointed to the rock-strewn beach, where driftwood lay like beached whales and gnarled trees spread their misshapen branches to the ground. "Could we swim to shore, sir?"

"Swim?" Olivia looked thunderstruck.

"I take it you don't swim, Miss St. John."

She glanced at Quenton. "Nay. Do you?"

"I had no choice. It was learn to swim, or sink like a stone."

"You mean you were simply tossed into the water and left to manage on your own?"

"That's exactly what I mean."

She made a sound of distress. "Who would do such a cruel thing?"

"A couple of drunken sailors."

Charles winked at Bennett. "I hope you made them pay for their prank."

"I was a little preoccupied with saving my life. After thrashing around and drinking several gallons of seawater, I managed to learn the rudiments of swimming.''

''And then did you go after your assailants?'' Charles asked.

Quenton shook his head. ''Unfortunately their ship had already left port.''

Charles leaned his arms along the rail. ''A pity.''

Quenton grinned. ''Fortunately it was a Dutch ship.''

As Bennett smiled broadly and the king chuckled, Olivia was puzzled. ''Why was that fortunate?''

''Because they made the mistake of sailing into English waters. And as a loyal subject of King Charles II, I was forced to make an example of them.''

''Their gold, as I recall, was a welcome addition to our coffers.'' Charles gave him a broad smile. ''And once again my loyal friend had served his king and country with distinction.''

''And those sailors who taught me to swim regretted their rude behavior.'' Quenton abruptly lowered himself over the side of the boat and called, ''Come, Liat. The water here is shallow. You can swim to shore.''

''I'll go with him.'' Charles removed his fine kid boots and, without a care about his elegant satin breeches, jumped into the water and began to wade to shore.

''Are you coming, Olivia?'' Quenton called. ''Or do you wish to wait here with my brother?''

Olivia looked at him in surprise. ''And how am I supposed to get to shore?''

''You can jump in and swim along with Liat.'' Quenton lifted his arms. ''Or you can trust me to catch you and carry you to shore.''

She glanced around. The gentle rocking of the boat

seemed to be lulling Bennett into a stupor. Beside him, Minerva's head bobbed. Pembroke had gone below deck to clear away the remains of their meal.

She eased herself over the railing, taking care to keep her billowing skirts modestly in place. "You won't drop me?"

Quenton gauged the distance, then lifted his arms. "I give you my word."

What in the world was she getting herself into? Trusting that he would keep his promise, she took a deep breath and jumped.

He caught her easily.

She was forced to wrap her arms around his neck. That brought her face dangerously close to his. For the space of several seconds he stared into her eyes. She felt her cheeks grow hot, and knew that he had to be aware of her discomfort.

As he started through the shallows he said, "I'm going to have to speak to Cook. She needs to see that you eat more. Why, you hardly weigh more than a flower petal."

"I doubt you'd say that if you had to carry me any great distance."

He paused. His lips were mere inches from hers. "If you asked, my lady, I'd carry you clear across England."

"What's taking you two so long?" Charles had already reached shore and was seated on the warm sand.

Liat was running along shore, dodging the waves that rolled up, washing away his little footprints.

"Don't forget, I have this heavy burden to tote." Quenton laughed as he deposited Olivia beside the king.

"Oh, now I'm a burden. Just minutes ago he tried

to flatter me by saying I weighed no more than a flower."

"You must never believe what a man tells you." Charles winked. "Believe instead what his friends tell you behind his back." He turned to Quenton. "I believe the lad wants you to help him climb that tree, Q."

"Aye. He needs a hand." Quenton sauntered off.

Olivia turned to Charles. "I heard you call him that the other night."

"You mean, when you were hiding in the wardrobe?"

Her cheeks flamed. "Aye. I hope I am forgiven, Majesty."

Charles couldn't help laughing. "It will make for an interesting story in years to come. I thought you most delightful, my dear. Since you overheard, you know that we call Bennett Baby, and they call me Chills."

She seemed distinctly uncomfortable, which had him laughing louder. "Don't be too shocked, my dear. Childhood habits die hard. Only when I am alone with Baby and Q can I truly be myself. Now remember, I have just told you that in strictest confidence. If a word of it is ever repeated, it will be denied. And I shall have your head."

He patted her hand, lowered his voice. "While we have these few minutes of privacy, I'd like to tell you an interesting tale about an old friend of mine. When he was just a youngster, not much older than Liat, he lost his parents in a tragic accident and was taken in by a very stern but loving grandfather. When he grew up he fell in love with a beautiful lady who loved him in return. But something went terribly wrong with their love. And he was left alone to bear the pain of the loss of his wife, of his brother's infirmity and the vicious gossip that followed him everywhere. And when my loyal friend went to sea he risked his own life many times out of loyalty to his king."

She listened in stunned silence and realized, when the tale ended, that the king had just given her a most precious gift. Now, finally, she was able to see Quenton as a child, as a young man and as a true friend to his monarch and hero to the country.

She grieved with him over the loss of his wife and the suffering of his beloved brother, but she no longer cared about the rumors and the gossip. None of it mattered. The only thing that did matter was the fact that she was hopelessly, desperately, in love with the king's old, dear friend.

She turned to him with tears in her eyes. "Thank you, Majesty."

"For what?" He stood and helped her to her feet.

"For telling me what I needed to know."

He squeezed her hands. "Your heart already knew, my dear."

"Am I so easy to read?"

He smiled. "I knew what the two of you were feeling before you did. I'm not certain Q knows yet just how deep his feelings are. But I warn you. He is a man of very great passion. Once that door is unlocked, prepare your heart for a siege."

She looked away. "I'm not certain that I am ready for any of this."

His voice was kind. "What does your heart tell you?"

She gave a shaky laugh. "My foolish, fickle heart

has been behaving badly for some time now, whenever I am around your friend Q.''

He caught her chin and stared deeply into her eyes. ''My dear Miss St. John. Always trust your heart.''

Chapter Fourteen

"Ah, my friend." Charles stood at the rail, staring heavenward. The setting sun was a crimson fireball reflected in the crest of the waves. The *Prodigal* sliced neatly through the water, its snowy sails a brilliant contrast to the darkening sky. "I wish this day would never end."

Quenton guided the sleek boat through the channel. "There will be other days."

Charles glanced down at his sodden breeches, his bare feet planted wide. He wiggled his toes, loving the sense of freedom. "None so fine as this, I fear. Once I set foot on those docks, I shall be forced to become, once more, the king. And on the morrow, even more so."

"Why is that?"

"Did I not tell you? My guests will begin arriving for the ball. They will expect me to behave as a monarch. I cannot disappoint them."

"Have you given their names to Mistress Thornton, so she can prepare their chambers?"

"Aye. She and I went over the list as soon as I gave her the good news about my little ball."

Quenton knew there would be nothing little about it. It would take all of his housekeeper's skills to prepare it in the lavish style for which their king was famous. "How did she take the news?"

Charles smiled. "She is as eager as I. I told you, my friend. No one can resist my charm."

"Aye. So you've said. It wouldn't have anything to do with the fact that you are king, would it?"

Charles's laughter rang through the gathering dusk. "Relax, Lord Stamford. You will enjoy my ball as much as I. And you will find yourself entertaining some of England's most interesting people."

Quenton kept his thoughts to himself. He'd had his share of the fawning peacocks and jealous lackeys who surrounded the king at court. These were creatures who would say or do whatever it took to curry favor with the one in charge. Should the king's fortunes shift, they would attach themselves to the next ruler, and spare Charles not a thought.

He dropped anchor and lowered the sails. While he worked he glanced toward Olivia, seated beside Bennett and Minerva. Liat was stretched out beside her, his head in her lap, his breathing slow and easy.

They made such a picture. The beautiful woman. The innocent lad. The sight of them caused an unexpected ache around his heart.

"A lovely view, is it not, Q?"

Quenton was startled by the king's voice, so close beside him. "I didn't see you approaching."

"Aye. You seem to have eyes only for the lass. Quite understandable." He winked. "London will fall in love with her. I have no doubt she'll be the most popular lady at court. Ah." He glanced toward the small boat heading toward them. "Time to go ashore."

As Quenton turned away, Charles saw the little muscle working in his friend's jaw and nearly laughed aloud. How he loved to tease. Especially since the poor fool was so blinded by love, he had lost his sense of humor.

Their little party was escorted to the docks, where the king's soldiers and servants awaited him. Then they were helped into a waiting carriage and began the ride back to Blackthorne. Along the way the roads were once again lined with cheering villagers. Charles continued to smile and wave until the crowds were left behind. When they finally arrived at Blackthorne, he stifled a yawn. "I believe I will take my evening meal in my chambers. Perhaps even in bed. Will you tell Mistress Thornton, Pembroke?"

"Aye, Majesty." The butler assisted him from the carriage.

The king glanced back at Liat, asleep on Olivia's lap. "I see I'm not the only one to be done in by the sea air."

As she started to rise Quenton took the lad from her arms. "He's much too heavy for you. I'll carry him up to bed."

"Thank you." She struggled to ignore the little jolt of pleasure when their hands touched.

She accepted Pembroke's hand as she stepped from the carriage.

With Quenton beside her, carrying the boy in his arms, she led the way inside and up the stairs to their rooms. And all the while she was achingly aware of the man beside her.

In the boy's chambers Olivia turned down the linens

and stood aside as Quenton lowered Liat to his bed and brushed a kiss over his cheek. It was such a sweet moment she felt as though a dagger had pierced her heart.

"I'll take off his boots," she whispered.

That done, she pulled the covers over him and blew out the candle on the nightstand, then made her way to the outer room, with Quenton following.

When she stepped into her own suite, Quenton paused on the threshold.

"If you're too weary to sup in the dining hall, I could have one of the servants fetch you a meal."

"Nay. I'm not weary, my lord. In fact, I feel invigorated by the sea air."

"Then I'll expect you below stairs shortly."

"Aye. I'll just freshen up."

When she was alone Olivia stripped off the simple white shirtwaist and long dark skirt. After washing, she pulled on a pale yellow gown and fastened up her hair with gilded combs.

She was dressing carefully, she realized. She paused and studied her reflection in the looking glass. Like a woman dressing for her lover. Sweet heaven. The thought made her heart beat faster.

As she made her way to the dining hall she thought about all the things King Charles had told her about his oldest and dearest friend. Had the king merely wished to unburden himself? Or had there been some other reason for telling her?

It mattered not. Her heart was lighter for it. He had given her a glimpse of a lonely, frightened boy, who had grown into a man who kept his own counsel. A fiercely protective firstborn who would do anything for a younger brother. A highly principled man willing to give his life for king and country.

This wasn't a man who would harm his wife and brother in a fit of rage. Nor was he a man who would father a son and refuse to give the lad his name. Whatever gossip was being spread about Lord Quenton Stamford, she had no doubt that it was false.

And she had no doubt that she wanted, more than anything in the world, to show him how she felt.

At the foot of the stairs she was approached by Pembroke. "Lord Stamford requests that you join him in the library, Miss St. John."

As she followed the butler down a long hallway, she felt the sting of disappointment. Quenton was sending her a clear signal that he would rather work than spend his time with her. The lovely evening she had envisioned was already fading from her mind. Her chance to offer Quenton her love was slipping away.

Quenton stared at the rows of figures that had become a blur. He'd locked himself away, determined to work. It was imperative that he make some sense of his grandfather's finances. But the truth was, all he could see, all he could think about, was Olivia. How she looked aboard the *Prodigal,* her hair wind-tossed, her skin glowing. How she felt pressed against him, her hands under his at the helm.

What would he do if Charles took her off to London? He tried to imagine Blackthorne as it had been before she had arrived. Cold. Bleak. A prison. And he had been a prisoner, every bit as much as Bennett.

Since her arrival, everything had changed. He still wasn't quite certain just how she'd managed it. With innocence, and impertinence and good humor she had plunged in, coaxing Bennett out of his room and out of his torment, and throwing open the windows of this musty old fortress to fresh air and sunlight.

He closed the ledger and stared down at the desktop. He couldn't bear it if she left. Couldn't bear to go back to the darkness and the despair. He needed a plan. A plan to keep her here at Blackthorne.

There was a way. He could admit his feelings for her and hope that she shared those feelings. But that was something he could never do. She was, after all, a maiden in his employ. He had no right to cross that line. And so he would have to see to it that he tread very carefully. He could enjoy her company, as long as he kept a respectable distance.

For tonight, he would walk a fine line between the man who employed her and the man who secretly loved her.

Pembroke knocked, then opened the library door and allowed Olivia to precede him.

"My lord, Miss St. John is here."

Quenton looked up and caught his breath. She was wearing a yellow gown, much like the one she'd described in her tale of the mud hole. He would forever think of her as a bright yellow daisy.

"Thank you, Pembroke." He got to his feet and came around the desk.

Olivia found herself staring. He was dressed all in black. Black breeches tucked into tall black boots, black jacket and shirt. In the firelight his dark hair looked blue-black. His handsome face was cast in light and shadow. It occurred to Olivia that this was how she would always see him. A proud, haughty, dangerous pirate. A man of such mystery. A strange mixture of light and darkness.

"I hope you don't mind. I took the liberty of ordering Mistress Thornton to serve our meal in here tonight, since you and I are the only ones eating."

"What about Bennett?"

"He's as done in by the fresh air as Liat and the king. Minerva is serving his meal in his room." He poured two glasses of pale wine and offered one to her.

She sipped, then took a few moments to look around. Her only other time here had been a blur of embarrassment.

A fire blazed in a massive fireplace. On either side of the hearth, sculpted lions stood guard. Above the mantel hung an enormous coat of arms showing a pair of fierce lions, a sword, a shield and a crown, in tribute to the close friendship between the Stamford family and the Stuarts. To one side were crossed swords with jeweled hilts that gleamed in the firelight. Two walls held shelves of books from floor to ceiling. On a fourth wall, gracefully curved cathedral windows offered a wonderful view of the gardens and the cliffs and the ocean beyond.

"I like this room. I think perhaps it suits you more than any other room I've seen at Blackthorne."

He looked around, trying to see it as she did. "Why is that?"

"I'm not sure. The books perhaps. I've heard that you work on your grandfather's ledgers far into the night."

"I do. Too often." His voice held a trace of weariness.

"The swords over the fireplace." She turned to him. "I assume you know how to use them."

He nodded gravely. "I won't apologize for that. A privateer who doesn't know how to use his weapons is a dead man."

"I didn't mean it as an insult, my lord. Merely as a fact." She turned, pointed. "And the windows, because they offer you a view of the sea that you love."

"You're a most observant woman, Miss St. John."

There was a knock on the door and Mistress Thornton entered, followed by several servants. The housekeeper's bullying began at once.

"Straighten that linen cloth, you spongy mammet. Put the candles to one side, you reeky nuthook, so his lordship can see to feed himself. No. No. Not the ale, you plume-plucked miscreant. The wine."

By this time the housekeeper was sweating profusely and using the edge of her apron to mop moisture from her face. "Will I leave one of these qualling mumble-mews here to serve the table, my lord?"

"Thank you, no, Mistress Thornton. When we're ready to sup, I'll summon Pembroke."

"Aye, my lord." She tugged on the arm of one of the servants, dragging her along as she herded the rest from the room.

When the door closed, Olivia bit her lip to keep from laughing aloud. When she glanced over, she realized that Quenton was doing the same. That was all she needed to burst into peals of laughter, with Quenton following.

At that, all attempts at formality fell away.

"You realize, don't you," he said, "that for all her harsh words, she truly has a good heart?"

"Aye. I've come to realize that. Looks can be deceiving." To keep from staring at him she took a turn around the room, studying the many shelves of books. "For instance, Papa used to point out that in nature, sometimes the prettiest berries and seeds could tempt a child to eat something that could make him violently ill."

"Have you ever been tempted?" Quenton filled her glass and carried it to her.

"Many times." She accepted the glass from his hands and felt the warmth of his touch. "Even with my father's words of caution, I had to learn for myself."

"And did you ever eat the pretty berries?"

"Oh, I admit I tasted a time or two. Not enough to be sick, but enough to know that they were bitter indeed." She gave him a wry smile. "I am, after all, human."

"Are you? That's a comfort to know. I'd begun to think..." He stared down into her eyes and cautioned himself. There was danger here. He was playing with fire.

"Think what?"

He caught a strand of hair, watched it sift through his fingers. "That there was simply no way to tempt a woman of your superior breeding and intelligence."

"And did you wish to tempt me?"

He caught the sparkle in her eye. Why, she was flirting. Shamelessly. And thoroughly enjoying herself. "Aye. Without a shred of success, I might add."

"Perhaps you should save your charm for someone with wealth and title. Why waste it on a commoner?"

He tugged on her hair, drawing her face closer. Their lips were mere inches apart. The heat began to rise to his loins. "There is nothing common about you, Olivia."

"Ah, but I am. Of course, Papa also used to tell me that the leaves from a common plant can be the most soothing."

"I think nothing could soothe the burning in this heart." He caught her hand, pressing her palm against his chest. "Feel what you do to me."

She felt the thundering of his heartbeat. It matched her own. She looked up. "What's to be done, then?"

"There's no cure that I know of. But there are things we can do to slow the process."

"Such as?"

His lips curved into a smile. "First a little more wine."

Following his lead she lifted the glass to her lips and drank.

As she lowered the glass he surprised her by kissing the corner of her lips. The jolt was quick and potent.

He had to take a step back, before he did something he would regret.

Unaware of the battle he was waging, she moved closer, leaning toward him. "And then?"

"Food."

She blinked. "Food?"

"Aye." At her look of bewilderment, he forced a smile to his lips. The trick was to keep his wits about him, at least for a little while longer. If he were to relax his guard, for even a moment, all would be lost, for the touch of her, the taste of her, did strange things to his senses. Already his hand was trembling.

He walked to the door and called, "I believe we'll eat now, Pembroke."

"Very good, my lord."

When the butler entered the library, Quenton held a chair for Olivia.

Still puzzled by his behavior, she crossed to the table and accepted the seat he offered.

When they were seated the butler began serving their food.

There were tender quail, glazed with cherries and stuffed with chestnuts, served on a bed of fresh vegetables. There was hot crusty bread still warm from the ovens.

"I've placed the rum cake and pear tarts on the sideboard, my lord. Along with brandy." Pembroke topped off their wine. "Will there be anything else?"

Quenton shook his head. "Nothing more. Thank you, Pembroke. I'll summon you if I need you."

The butler let himself out.

Olivia picked at her food, determined to follow his lead and keep the evening light. "I had a fine time today, sailing with the king."

"Charles has always been pleasant company."

"He is charming. I didn't realize what close friends you are."

"It isn't something I like to talk about. Once it is known that he and I are close, there are those who would use my friendship for their own gain."

"That wouldn't occur to you, would it, Quenton? To use your friendship with the king for your own good?"

When he said nothing she went on, "The king truly loves you."

"How can you be so certain?"

"I heard the respect and love in his voice today when he spoke of you."

"And when would that be?"

"While we were ashore."

He remembered seeing Charles and Olivia sitting together in the sand, their heads bent close, in quiet, earnest conversation.

"He told me about your childhood here at Blackthorne, and about your stern grandfather."

"Aye, he was a stern man. But he was fair. And he was an anchor to two frightened little boys who had been cast adrift in a stormy sea."

"The king also told me about your loyalty while you were a privateer."

At that Quenton arched a brow. "He told you?"

She nodded. "It doesn't seem fair that such a thing should be kept a secret. While you were risking your life for your country, there are those who scorned you as carefree and heartless."

With a smile, Quenton covered her hand with his. At once he realized his mistake. The mere touch of her had him wanting things he had no right to. And thinking things that would make her blush.

"Had I but known you would become my fierce defender, my lady, I would have told you myself, long ago."

"You're teasing me. How can you make light of this? Don't you know that there are people who spread vicious lies and rumors about you? They believe you to be a blackhearted villain."

"Do you think that matters to me?" Restless, needing to put some space between them, he scraped back his chair and walked to the fireplace, staring into the flames.

She followed him, placing a hand on his arm. "How can you bear to be so vilified?"

He felt the heat and closed his hand over hers, intending to remove it. Instead, his fingers curled over hers. "I care not what others say or think about me." He turned and grasped her by the shoulders, staring deeply into her eyes. "I care only what you think."

"I think..." She prayed for courage. As much courage as he had shown when facing a challenge. She swallowed and tried again. "I think you are the bravest, finest man I have ever known."

Something flickered in his eyes. Then he managed a dangerous smile.

"Again, Quenton, I sense you are laughing at me."

His smile grew. "I could never laugh at you, Olivia." His hands moved slowly, lazily along the tops of her arms, drawing her ever closer. "It is not my noble soul I am concerned with at the moment."

"What then?"

He lowered his head. His lips found hers, moved over them with a thoroughness that had them both gasping.

"This." His lips covered hers again, and the jolt of passion was hot and swift. "Only this. It's all I can think of. You are all I can think of."

He poured all his feelings into that single kiss, lingering over her mouth as though it held him in its thrall. A kiss so hot, so hungry, it left her trembling, and begging for more.

The hands that moved over her, the lips that drove her ever higher, spoke of all the years of loneliness and desperation. It was a kiss that drained her even as it filled her.

She returned his kiss with a passion that caught them both by surprise. Boldly she wrapped her arms around his neck and offered her lips. What had been a fire deep inside erupted into a blazing inferno.

"Quenton." She swayed and clutched blindly at his waist. "I want…" She pressed her mouth to his and murmured against his lips, "I want what you want."

He froze.

Coming up for air, he held her a little away from him and took deep draughts of air, filling his lungs, clearing his mind.

He was staggered by the enormity of his feelings. The thought of taking her here, now, had him fighting desperately for control.

"Quenton…"

"Shhh." He touched a finger to her lips, then withdrew it when he felt the heat. "A moment, Olivia. I need to think."

"I don't want to think." She lifted her face, offering her lips. "I've had enough thinking. I want to feel."

"God in heaven. Do you know what you're saying?"

She smiled and lifted herself on tiptoe to brush her lips over his. "I'm saying I want this. I want you."

His eyes were hot and fierce and dangerous.

He covered her mouth in a searing kiss. Against her lips he muttered, "I ought to know better. Haven't I fought against this very thing? But God help me, I have neither the strength nor the will to resist."

When she lifted her face for another drugging kiss he held her a little away and forced himself to breathe deeply.

"Not now, Olivia. Not yet. If I dare to kiss you one more time, we'll never make it up the stairs."

Chapter Fifteen

The door to the library was abruptly yanked open. Pembroke, chatting with the housekeeper, was startled as Lord Stamford and Miss St. John stepped into the hall.

"We're finished, Pembroke. Mistress Thornton, you may have a servant clean up now."

"Aye, my lord. Will there be anything else?"

"Nothing. Miss St. John and I will be retiring for the night. You two may do the same."

"Very good, my lord." Pembroke watched as they made their way to the stairs. Then he entered the library to bank the fire, while the housekeeper turned to the table.

"Odd," she remarked. "They didn't touch a bit of their food."

"Perhaps it was cold."

She cut off a bite of quail, tasted. "'Tis perfect."

He crossed the room and glanced at the two plates, filled with food, just as he'd served them, the wineglasses still brimming. "Quite right. They haven't eaten a thing." He glanced up. "Did you happen to notice Miss St. John's cheeks?"

"Her cheeks?"

He nodded. "Very high color. And her hair had been mussed."

"Her hair?"

"Aye. And Lord Stamford had the look of a wild thing about him. A panther perhaps, about to pounce."

"You think they've had words then? You know how quick they are to lose their tempers. Perhaps that got them into a tangle."

He shook his head. "They may have tangled. But I'd wager it wasn't temper."

As the truth dawned, the housekeeper put a hand to her heart. "Oh my. Lord Stamford? And dear little Miss St. John?"

A slow smile lit Pembroke's eyes. "They'd be evenly matched, I'd say."

"Not a chance of it. Why, you said yourself he was like a wild thing. He'd devour her."

"Don't count our little governess out. She has a tart tongue and a sharp wit. There's steel beneath that slender frame. I'm betting she can hold her own against Lord Stamford." Pembroke glanced at the filled plates and brimming goblets. "Seems a shame to waste this fine meal. And a cozy fire." He rounded the table, gave an uncharacteristic wink and held out a chair. "How about sharing it with me, Gwynnith?"

Careful to avoid touching, Quenton and Olivia climbed the stairs and moved along the dim hallway. Though they tried to appear casual, their movements were stiff, hurried.

With each step, Olivia waged a war with herself. She knew that this was what she wanted. But she had no idea just what she'd gotten herself into. Would a worldly man like Quenton be put off by her lack of experience in such matters? Worse, would he find her ignorance laughable?

When they reached the door to her chambers, she paused, thinking he would open the door and lead her inside. Instead, without a word Quenton scooped her into his arms and stormed down the hall until he reached his own door.

Once inside he nudged it closed and set her on her feet.

She felt a wave of panic. "I think…"

"Don't think. Just feel." He touched his mouth to hers. The merest brush of lips to lips, but they both felt the rush of heat and were staggered by it.

She knew that he was trying to be gentle, for her sake. And she loved him for it.

"You're soft. So soft," he murmured against her mouth.

"And you're so strong it frightens me."

"Don't be afraid." He framed her face, staring deeply into her eyes. "I'd never hurt you."

"I know that."

"Do you? Do you know that I'd kill for you, Olivia? I'd die for you. Or beg or crawl for you. But I'd never hurt you."

She closed her hands around his wrists. Her eyes were huge, her tone solemn. "Don't say that. Not even at a time like this."

"That I'd die for you? Kill for you? It's the truth." He lifted his hands to remove the combs from her hair. "Do you know how long I've wanted to do this?" He watched as it tumbled in heavy dark waves around her face. "God in heaven, you're so lovely."

He nuzzled her lips and felt the rush of heat that

nearly overwhelmed him. He wanted to go slowly, to give her the time she needed. But already the needs were beginning to clutch and claw at him, and he had to struggle to hold them at bay.

He plunged his hands into the tangles and covered her mouth with his, tasting all the sweetness, the innocence. It only served to make him hungry for more. With a guttural sound deep in his throat he kissed her until she was breathless. When she tried to catch a breath, he kissed her again and again, feasting on her lips like a man who'd been starved.

She pushed a little away, dragging air into her lungs. "I was certain I'd thought all this through."

He pressed kisses to her temple, her cheek, her ear. "And now?"

She shivered as his breath tickled her ear. "I don't know anymore. I can't think when you kiss me."

"Good. That's part of my plan. To keep you off stride." He plunged his tongue into her ear and heard her little moan of pleasure.

A dangerous smile curved his lips as he dragged his mouth down the smooth column of her throat. He could feel the wild rhythm of her pulse. Could taste the softness of her flesh. He filled his lungs with the fragrance of lavender as he feasted.

Her breath was ragged as her head fell back, allowing him easier access. For a moment, for just a moment, he was able to be gentle as he nibbled wet kisses down her throat and across her shoulder.

She shivered, trembled and felt her breath shudder. But just as she relaxed against him, he lowered his mouth to her breast, nibbling and suckling even as he cursed the barrier of her clothes.

This was a new sensation. One she hadn't anticipated. Deep inside a liquid fire began to flow and ebb with hot, wet contractions.

She felt him reach for the buttons of her gown. Heard his muttered oath when he wasn't quick enough.

She lifted eager hands to his. "Here, I'll help...."

The fabric shredded as he tore it in his haste.

"Quenton. My new gown..."

"I'll order you a dozen to replace it. Two dozen." He watched as it fell to the floor, pooling at her feet.

And then his hands were on her flesh, teasing, tormenting, arousing, and his mouth, his lips, his tongue, followed.

Her skin was softer than he could have ever dreamed. Flesh so pale it gleamed like alabaster in the firelight. He felt the way she trembled at his touch and thrilled to it.

His hands moved to the lace of her petticoats. With a simple tug the ribbons untied and the lace fell away to join the rest of her clothes.

She had always thought that such a moment, when a lover first glimpsed her naked body, would bring a flush of embarrassment. But when she saw the way his dark eyes gleamed in approval, she felt unbearably aroused.

"Olivia, you are so beautiful."

"I never cared before. But now I want to be. For you, Quenton. Only for you." With a moan she moved against him, pressing her lips to his throat.

The feel of her lips on his flesh was exquisite torture. He knew that he could take her here, now. Release was his for the asking. Release from the hard, grinding need that was building inside him. But it wasn't mere release that he wanted. He wanted it all.

To pleasure her beyond her wildest dreams. To offer her a banquet of delights. A feast of fantasies.

He took a step back, needing to see her.

"I've dreamed of seeing you like this. Of feeling you like this." He lifted his hands to her small, firm breasts, his work-roughened thumbs teasing her nipples until she thought she would go mad from the pleasure. But that was just the beginning. When he bent his lips to her breast and began to nibble and suckle, she sighed and moaned before tangling her hands in his hair. Wild with need she tore at his shirt, eager to feel him the way he was feeling her.

She was surprised at her own strength when she heard the fabric tear in her hands. And then his shirt was gone and she could feel him, heated flesh to heated flesh. Heartbeat to heartbeat. His was thundering, she realized. And the knowledge that she was the cause of it made her bolder.

Caught up in the frenzy, she tugged at his breeches. With a sigh of impatience he released her long enough to kick off his boots, step out of his clothes. Then they came together in a firestorm that had them both quaking.

"Touch me, Olivia. I need you to touch me."

Her hands skimmed his flesh, touching him the way he'd touched her. Tentatively at first, then, hearing his moan of pleasure, she grew bolder, touching him everywhere. She thrilled to the muscles of his back and shoulders, the flat planes of his stomach. It excited her to feel such incredible strength in his arms and hands. Hands that moved over her as gently as though she were made of fragile glass.

She had lost all ability to think. Now there was only this wild, primitive need that drove her. She felt the heat from the fire, but it was no match for the fire that raged inside her. Heat clogged her lungs, burned her flesh, leapt along her nerves, leaving her quivering with need. Unbearable need.

She was lost in a world of dark, delicious pleasure.

Too weak to stand, they dropped to their knees, still locked in a kiss. When his lips left hers she made a little sound of protest. But as he laid her down amid their strewed clothing and his lips began a lazy exploration of her body, she could only sigh with pleasure.

Through eyes heavy-lidded with passion she saw him. Dark hair. Dark eyes gleaming with pleasure. Sun-darkened skin, all sinew and muscle, glistening with sweat. Her dark angel.

This dark side of him both frightened and excited her. And unlocked a similar dark side of herself she'd never known.

Steeped in sensations, she felt as if she were floating above her body, watching, listening. Were those her nerves strung to the breaking point? Her sighs and whispered words that were unintelligible? Her heartbeat roaring in her temples?

Outside a night bird cried to the moon and the ocean roared as it broke over the jagged rocks at the base of the cliffs. But inside, the room was silent except for the hiss and snap of the fire. And the sighs and moans, the unintelligible words of love. The world beyond these walls no longer mattered. The only thing that mattered was this man, this woman, this moment.

And then Olivia heard his ragged, muttered oath. Felt the roughness of his hands as he brought her pleasure beyond belief.

He watched her face as he drove her to the first peak. She was lovely to watch. Those wide, expressive eyes that seemed to glaze over with surprise and disbelief.

He gave her no time to recover as he took her again and again on a dizzying ride. This was how he'd wanted her. Not just soft and pliant but wild, and raging, and writhing with reckless abandon.

His woman. Only his.

He felt himself teetering on the very brink of madness. And still he held back, keeping release just out of reach. He wanted, needed, to give her more. To give her everything. To make this a night that would live forever in her mind, as he knew it would in his.

She was hot. So hot she wondered that her flesh didn't melt, her bones dissolve. Her body was damp with sheen. Her hair wet and plastered to her cheeks and neck.

At last, when he knew he would have to take her or go mad, he skimmed his lips along her body until they found hers.

He entered her then and swallowed her little gasp. "It may hurt, but only for a moment."

She tensed, expecting pain. Instead she felt only pleasure. Wave after wave of intense pleasure. She had thought it impossible to absorb any more. But as he began to move, she moved with him, experiencing an incredible strength she hadn't known she possessed.

Hers, she thought as she wrapped herself around him and began to climb once more. He was hers. Only hers.

And then all thought fled as they climbed higher, and higher still, until they broke free and erupted into a blaze of firelight that shattered into a million tiny sparks.

* * *

They lay, still joined, their breathing ragged, their heartbeats thundering. Their skin was damp, slick with sheen.

Quenton levered himself on his elbows and stared down at her. There were tears in her eyes. Tears? His heart nearly stopped. He clutched her to him with such bone-crushing ferocity it left her gasping. "God in heaven. I've hurt you."

"No. Oh, no, Quenton. These are happy tears."

"Truly? You're certain?"

She nodded. "Aye."

He felt his heart begin to beat once more as he wiped her tears with his thumbs. "Do you know how long I've wanted to hold you like this? Love you like this?"

"How long?" Even those two words were difficult with a throat so clogged with love.

"I think since that first night I saw you. You were so haughty. So afraid."

Her tone was aggrieved. "I was not afraid."

"Liar. You trembled when I touched you."

"Well, maybe a little. You looked so fierce."

He chuckled. "And you looked completely untouchable. I knew, there and then, that I wanted very much to touch. To muss this hair," he muttered, brushing the damp hair from her face.

"Then why did it take you so long?"

His lips curved into a smile. "If you'll recall, you weren't very cooperative."

"I felt shy."

"I know. I found that very appealing."

"Did you? I didn't think you liked me very much."

"Oh, Miss St. John, I do like you." He brushed his lips over hers. "Very much." He rolled to one side and drew her into the circle of his arms. "And I intend to show you just how much, as often as possible. Oh, Livvy, there's so much I want to show you."

He noticed that she'd gone very still. He leaned up on one elbow. "What is it? Is it something I said?"

"You called me Livvy."

"Did I?" He smiled, relaxed again beside her. "It just seemed to fit. Do you mind?"

She shook her head. "That's what my parents always called me."

"You see? I was right. It fits. And when we're alone, I intend to call you Livvy. Of course, you'll still be Miss St. John when we're with others. The very prim and proper governess, Olivia St. John."

"Is that how you see me? Prim and proper?"

"Aye. And how do you see me?"

"A dark, dangerous pirate," she said without hesitation. "Who would sail to exotic lands and engage his enemies in battle without fear."

He smiled and twisted one of her curls around his finger. "This dark, dangerous pirate is laid flat by a single touch from you, little nursemaid."

"Be careful, my lord. 'Twould be dangerous for you if I should believe I hold such power." Just then she touched a hand to his chest and felt him tremble at her touch. Tremble? She gave a little cat smile and moved her hand lower.

He flinched. His voice was a low growl of pleasure. "If you don't stop, my lady, you may discover just how much power you wield."

"Is it possible...? I mean, could you...? Could we...?" She smiled. "Again?"

He gave a mock sigh of impatience. "One moment you are a sweet, untouched maiden. Now a wanton."

"Aye." She sat up, unselfconscious about her nakedness. Her dark hair tumbled about her face and shoulders in a most beguiling way. She bent over him, pressing her lips to his throat. "I believe you said there were things you wanted to show me."

"And you wish to see them all now, little one?"

"Aye." She moved her mouth lower, to his muscled, hair-roughened chest, then lower still across the flat planes of his stomach, and heard his quick intake of breath.

Drunk with power she gave a delighted laugh.

He dragged her fully on top of him. "I see I have no choice but to give you another lesson in the art of love."

"Aye, my lord."

Her little laugh was cut short by a hot, hungry kiss.

Quenton and Olivia lay tangled among his sumptuous bed linens. Dawn light was just painting the horizon. Some time during the night he had carried her to his big bed in the sleeping chamber. The fire had long ago died to embers, but neither of them had any wish to leave the warmth of the bed to add another log. And so they lay, arms and legs entwined, bodies touching.

All night they had loved, then slept, then awakened to love again. The depth of their passion caught them both by surprise. At times the loving had been as fierce as any storm, battering their senses, leaving them feeling oddly bruised and breathless. At other times it had been as sweet, as gentle as though they had loved forever.

Quenton brushed an errant curl from her eye and

smiled. But who had been the teacher? The worldly sailor? Or the shy governess?

She had opened to him like a flower. She had given generously. And had been greedy as well. She was, he realized, a source of constant delight.

She blinked. "What are you thinking?"

"How pleasant it is to wake with you. How did I bear it all these years without you?"

She'd been thinking the same thing. She stretched, snuggled closer. "I feel so..." She paused, wondering just how honest she ought to be.

"You feel so what?"

It was on the tip of her tongue to say she felt as contented as a well-fed cat. Instead she finished simply, "Safe with you, Quenton."

"You are, my love. I give you my word, no harm will ever come to you." The words were a fierce whisper as his arms closed around her and he dragged her against him.

"My bold, brave pirate." She traced a finger over one of the many raised scars that laced his shoulders and back. "I hate that you bear the scars of battle."

"They are only scars, my lady."

"But they were once a source of pain. And I hate to think of you in pain."

"The pain is gone, love. You've kissed it all away. Now come and kiss me again. Drive all the pain from my heart."

And then his mouth was on hers, and his hands, those wonderful, clever hands, were once more working their magic.

The sky outside the windows lightened. Birds began their morning chorus. Inside, two people felt as alone as two others must have felt at the dawn of creation.

"I went to sleep last night at Blackthorne," he murmured against her mouth. "And awoke this morrow in paradise."

With soft sighs and whispered words of love, they drifted once more into their own enchanted Garden of Eden.

Chapter Sixteen

"**M**y lord." Edlyn's muffled voice outside his chambers, and the sharp rap on the door, had Quenton and Olivia sitting up, sleepy-eyed and confused, among the tangled linens.

Olivia gasped, then covered her mouth and whispered, "It cannot be morning already."

The heavy coverings at the windows prevented them from seeing outside. But a tiny stream of sunlight filtered through a gap in the draperies.

Quenton shot her a wicked smile. "It would appear that we have overslept, my love."

"How will I get to my chambers? My gown…" She cast a horrified glance at the tatters still lying in a heap where she'd left them. "Quenton, everyone at Blackthorne will know."

There was another sharp rap, followed by a more urgent call. "My lord. Mistress Thornton has sent me to build your fire."

"Thank you, Edlyn." He glanced at the lovely young woman beside him and saw the flush of embarrassment on her cheeks. He swallowed back a chuckle. "I'll see to it myself."

"And what of your tray, my lord? There's tea and biscuits."

Olivia groaned aloud.

"Leave it outside the door. I'll fetch it in when I'm dressed."

There was a moment's hesitation. Then a muffled "Aye, my lord."

Quenton waited until he heard her receding footsteps. Then he fell back among the pillows and roared with laughter. "Oh, Livvy. You should see your face."

"How will I ever face the staff? And poor little Liat. He must be frantically searching for his errant governess." She turned to him. "Oh, Quenton, what will we do?"

"Well." He traced his fingers up her arm, across the slope of her shoulder, loving the way she reacted to his simple touch. "You could fetch that tray while I build a fire. Then you'll be all cozy and warm while you sip your tea and nibble your biscuits. And while you're doing that, I could...nibble something else."

She shot him a look. "How can you lie here and make sport of this situation while I'm sitting here worrying myself sick?"

"You're right. It isn't fair." He reached up and pulled her down on top of him, then began nibbling his way along her throat. "If you're going to worry, the least I can do is make you comfortable." His mouth dipped lower, to the swell of her breast. He heard her little gasp of pleasure and smiled. "There now. Doesn't that make you feel much better?"

She thought of several tart replies. Thought, too, about fighting him. But as always, she was beginning to lose herself in the wonder of his touch.

She would give voice to her clever responses later. Right now, she decided her best course of action was to simply enjoy the pleasure he was offering. And face what was to come later.

"Ah. Lord Stamford. Miss St. John." The king looked up from his meal to study the couple as they advanced toward the table. Bennett and Minerva were already there, as was Liat.

Servants bustled about the room, casting furtive glances at the arriving couple. Pembroke, standing at attention by the door, never altered his expression as he watched them enter. Mistress Thornton, frazzled as always, bumped into the table at the first sound of the king's greeting, then hurriedly backed away and busied herself with a platter.

"You're looking especially fine, my old friend." Charles patted the chair beside him. "Sit here, Miss St. John."

Quenton held her chair and she settled herself beside the king. When Quenton took the seat next to her, their fingers brushed, clasped.

"I must say, Miss St. John, that the sea air certainly agrees with you. Why, you're positively glowing."

She blushed furiously while he glanced beyond her to his old friend. "Don't you agree, Lord Stamford?"

"Aye, Majesty." What had he been thinking of, bringing her down to break their fast with the king? He should have simply barred his door and kept her to himself for the entire day. Even now, just sitting beside her, he wanted her. Wanted to be alone with her.

"Have you two been walking in the gardens?"

"In the...gardens?" Olivia glanced from the king to Quenton. "Why do you ask, Majesty?"

"Because I met young Liat outside his chambers. He said he'd been searching in vain for you all morning, Miss St. John." He shot her a knowing smile. "I assured the lad that you were probably walking with Lord Stamford. After all, there are few hiding places here at Blackthorne." His smile grew. "And even fewer secrets."

Olivia wished she could sink under the table and disappear. But since that wasn't possible, she retreated into silence while her face flamed.

Taking pity on her, the housekeeper paused behind her and said gently, "Here's some tea, miss. And a little hot mulled wine. 'Tis said to be most relaxing."

Olivia offered a weak smile. "Thank you, Mistress Thornton."

When a servant approached with a platter of meats and breads, Olivia helped herself to a single biscuit, while Quenton filled his plate.

"I see you have a hearty appetite this morrow, my friend." The king drained his goblet and nodded his approval when a serving wench refilled it. "Nothing like a refreshing day at sea to sharpen...all sorts of hungers."

Quenton saw the light of merriment in the king's eyes and understood it. At any other time he would have thoroughly enjoyed his old friend's gibes, and given them right back. Perhaps even preened a bit, pumped up his manhood with a few boasts of his own. But he was aware of Olivia's acute embarrassment and was determined to shield her. Since she couldn't take leave of this room until the king did, he had to find a way to hurry Charles along.

"I thought you might desire a visit to the stables, Majesty."

"I saw the horses just two days ago when we went hunting."

"Aye. But we didn't get a chance to race our steeds." At the king's bored expression he added, "I'll willingly wager a thousand pounds that my horse will take yours."

The king brightened. "You wouldn't be trying to distract me, would you, old friend?"

"I don't know what you mean."

Charles threw back his head and laughed. "Oh, you know exactly what I mean. And I just may accept your wager, since you know how much I would enjoy taking your gold. But for now I wish to walk in your gardens."

He got to his feet and the others followed.

Relieved, Quenton leaned close to Olivia and muttered, "You would be wise to take Liat to his chambers now and get started on his lessons."

"Aye." She couldn't wait to escape the king's merciless taunts.

But as they followed Charles from the room, he turned to Olivia. "You will accompany us, Miss St. John. Liat has been telling me how knowledgeable you are about plants and insects. I should like to see for myself."

She groaned inwardly, while keeping her smile firmly in place. "Aye, Majesty. It would be my pleasure."

At the sight of Quenton's face, a wicked gleam came into the king's eyes. "Was there something you wished to say, old friend?"

"Nay, Majesty." He would say it later, when he

got his old friend Chills alone. And this time, the air would be blue with his curses.

"Good. Come along then."

They stepped outside into glorious sunshine and moved slowly along the grassy path.

"If you'd like to run ahead of us, lad, you can search for butterflies."

"Thank you, Majesty." Feeling frisky and free, Liat veered from the path and danced eagerly among the roses.

The others strolled more slowly, pausing to admire the carefully tended hedges, and to breathe in the lovely fragrance of roses, bluebells and buttercups that wafted on the breeze. The king walked in front, demanding that Olivia walk beside him, with Quenton walking behind. Bennett, pushed in his wheeled chair by Minerva, brought up the rear.

The king turned his head. "I do believe Blackthorne has some of the loveliest gardens I've ever seen, Lord Stamford."

"Thank you, Majesty. I shall convey your praise to our gardeners."

Charles caught Olivia's hand. "And you, my dear, are the loveliest flower of all."

Behind them, Quenton's hand curled into a fist by his side. Charles knew exactly how to get to his old friend. And he was doing a splendid job of it.

"I fear you mistake me for one of your titled ladies at court, Majesty."

Seeing the color that came to her cheeks he turned to his host. "Can this be? A beautiful woman who is unaware of her beauty?"

Quenton's eyes softened as he nodded. "Aye, Majesty. She is a rare treasure, is she not?"

"A rare treasure indeed."

They looked up at Liat's excited cry. Following the sound of his voice they found him pointing to a butterfly perched on a pale pink rose. "Look, Majesty. It is a *Celastrina argiolus*. Miss St. John said they are very rare here in Cornwall."

"This is wonderful." Catching the lad's hand, the king moved in for a closer look. "You see these lovely colors?"

Liat nodded. "Miss St. John said they look like the windows of a cathedral."

"An apt description, Liat. Ah, see how gracefully it flits from flower to flower."

They darted about the garden, keeping the butterfly in sight, while the others followed behind. It was the perfect opportunity for Quenton to take Olivia's hand and pretend to help her over the rough paving.

"I wish we were alone," he whispered. "I want to hold you. Kiss you."

"Hush, Quenton. Someone will hear."

"I care not if the whole world knows." He paused beside a bed of ferns and skimmed a hand over her cheek. "Let's run away."

"Where would we run?"

"I know not. To sea perhaps. Aboard the *Prodigal*."

She shared his smile. "Oh, wouldn't that be lovely?"

"Ah. Here you are." The king's voice sounded just behind them, causing them both to step apart. "The *Celastrina* has flown off across the meadow."

He gave Quenton and Olivia a long, knowing look, then broke into an impish grin. "Let's sit right here, lad, and see if we can spot another."

Olivia could hear Quenton's little hiss of impatience when the king and Liat dropped down on a stone bench to discuss in detail what they had just seen.

Charles gave them a wide smile. ''This has been quite a morning. Two rare beauties.''

''Two?'' Liat looked puzzled.

''Aye. The *Celastrina argiolus* and your governess.'' With a rumble of laughter at his little joke he caught the boy's hand. ''Let's walk some more, Liat, and see if we can find more rare treasures.'' He turned and said in his most imperious tone, ''Lord Stamford, I expect you and Miss St. John to join us. And this time, try to keep up.''

''Lord Stamford, the number and variety of butterflies in your garden leaves me dazzled.'' The king was in high spirits after several hours in the company of Liat and Olivia. ''The lad is being very well tutored. I can't say enough about his governess. The depth of her knowledge is much more than I'd expected.''

Hearing such praise, Olivia found herself blushing again.

Quenton loved the color that leapt to her cheeks whenever she found herself the center of attention. It was just one more of her endearing qualities.

As they neared the courtyard Charles said, ''You must tell me more about the source of your knowledge.''

''I was tutored by my father, James St. John. He was a shy, humble teacher of botany at Oxford.''

The king paused and turned to study her. ''James St. John? This is amazing, Miss St. John. I know of your father.''

Her eyes widened.

"We corresponded after I read several of his papers. I was enormously impressed by the range of his knowledge and interest. He sent me several specimens for my collection. And in return I awarded him a title and a very generous stipend."

"A...title and stipend?"

"As the newest addition to my circle of royal advisers I thought it only fitting that he be given the title of Lord. And with the title, a modest estate in Oxfordshire." He studied her more closely. "You seem surprised, my dear."

She nodded, too stunned for words. "Why would my parents have kept such a thing from me?"

"You did not know?" Quenton asked.

"Nay."

He took her hand. "You declared them to be humble people. Perhaps they thought such a revelation would sound as though they were boasting."

"Perhaps. But wouldn't they have wanted to share such an honor with their own daughter?" She was clearly shaken. "And what could they have done with the estate and the stipend?"

Quenton turned to the king. "You say this was given to Olivia's father, Majesty?"

"I did not personally meet with him. The decision was made at court and an emissary dispatched to notify them."

Quenton turned to Olivia. "They may have died before they knew of it." He turned to the king to explain, "Olivia's parents were killed recently in a fall."

The king touched a hand to her shoulder. "My sympathies, my dear. Their death is a great loss for England. And I am certain the loss to you is painful and deep."

"Aye, Majesty." She was touched by his genuine concern. Having lost his own father, Charles I, who was publicly beheaded, he would know a great deal about pain and loss. "Thank you for your compassion."

Pembroke appeared in the doorway. "Majesty. Lord Stamford. Several carriages are approaching."

"Our guests from London." The king's eyes lit with pleasure. "You are in for a treat, my lady. You are about to meet some of the wisest and wittiest people in all of England. Isn't that right, old friend?"

Quenton tried to work up a little enthusiasm, knowing that the peace he had so recently found at Blackthorne would certainly be disrupted until his guests departed. He glanced at Liat, who was clinging wearily to Olivia's skirts. All he desired was to carry the lad to his bed, and then slip away with Olivia to his own bed. The thought had him almost dizzy with need. But one look at the king's face and he knew there was no hope for it. What little privacy they'd had was lost.

He turned to Olivia. "Perhaps you should take the lad up for a nap. You and Liat can meet our guests this evening at the king's ball."

She saw the tight line of his mouth and could guess his mood. She had hoped, foolishly, that they could slip away together. But it was not to be.

"Aye, my lord. I think that would be wise."

Even from so great a distance she could hear Mistress Thornton shouting insults to the servants as the carriages rolled up to the courtyard. There would be dozens of guests, along with their personal servants, to be escorted to their rooms. Dozens more trunks to be hauled up several flights of stairs and unpacked. For the next hours, chaos would reign at Blackthorne.

Though she wished with all her might that Quenton could be with her, Olivia was grateful to escape.

As she walked away, holding Liat's hand, Quenton stared after her with a smoldering look.

"She is a beautiful woman, old friend." The king clapped him on the shoulder. His eyes glinted with wicked amusement. "She will be a welcome addition to the ladies at court."

Quenton kept his voice low. "When we were lads, Chills, you always used to try to best me. Do you remember?"

"Aye."

"And you never could."

"True enough. But we are grown now, and I am king."

"If you wish to live to reign for another year, you'll say no more about taking my lady to London."

"Your lady, is she?" Charles held out his hand. "I believe that will cost you one thousand pounds, old friend."

Too late, Quenton realized what he'd admitted. He gritted his teeth. "You'll get your gold."

Charles stopped in his tracks. "You concede?"

"Aye."

The king caught him in a great bear hug. "I knew it. I knew the moment I saw the two of you this morrow."

"From the looks on the servants' faces, I'd say the whole of Blackthorne knew it."

"Aye. You make a dazzling pair. By heaven, Quenton. This calls for a celebration."

"It calls for nothing of the kind. For now, I'd like to be left alone to enjoy my good fortune."

"Aye. All right. You'll have your privacy." Charles grinned. "For today."

"You mean it? You'll excuse me?"

"Not just yet, old friend. But soon. Now come. Let's greet our guests."

Grinning like conspirators, the two men strolled to the courtyard to face the noise and confusion.

Chapter Seventeen

Olivia hummed to herself as she tied the ribbons of her chemise and studied her reflection in the tall looking glass. While Liat was taking his rest, she had bathed and washed her hair and laid out a simple white woolen gown with high neck and tapered sleeves. It was the perfect attire for a governess meeting titled guests for the first time.

Outside her room the corridors of Blackthorne rang with the procession of footsteps as servants hurried about, fetching water and linens and scented soaps for the guests. The air rang with a chorus of strange voices, some cultured, some coarse. The high-pitched sounds of women's laughter competed with the deep voices of men.

She knew it was selfish of her to wish that Quenton would come to her. Still, she yearned for the sound of his voice, the touch of his hands. When she heard the outer door to her sitting room open, and the sound of hurried footsteps, her pulse began to race, but before she could turn, she caught sight of Quenton's reflection behind hers in the mirror.

"Ah. Now here's the sight that will lift my spirits."

He walked up behind her, wrapping his arms around her, drawing her against the length of him.

"Quenton." She stared at their reflected images and shivered as he bent his head to run kisses along her shoulder. "I thought you'd be busy with your guests."

"I was. But I had to see you."

"I've heard so many footsteps in the hall I was beginning to think the king had invited an army."

"It may as well be. Every room at Blackthorne is filled. Poor Mistress Thornton is slowly going mad."

She turned to face him. "And how about our gracious host? Are you going mad as well?"

"I believe I would have if I'd had to remain below stairs much longer." He kissed her, long and slow and deep, then pressed his lips to her temple and murmured, "Oh, Livvy, I needed that."

She clutched his waist. "Then I'm happy to oblige, my lord."

"I wonder what I would have done if I hadn't found you. I suppose I would have had to invent you."

"Was your life so bleak, my lord?"

"Aye. Bleak and empty. A dreary existence. With no hope for a better future. And now…" He lifted his hands to frame her face. "Now there is my beautiful, my perfect Livvy. Come to bed with me, love."

"Now?" She glanced toward the closed door. "Liat will awaken soon. He'll expect his nursemaid."

"There's time. We'll make time. I need you more than he does right now." He lifted his hands to the ribbons of her chemise.

She thought about all the reasons why they shouldn't do this now. But then the fabric parted and his lips, his hands, began to work their magic. Her blood heated and her bones dissolved, along with her common sense.

"Oh, Quenton. How can I refuse you anything?"

"No more than I can refuse you, love." He lifted her, carried her to her bed. And proceeded to show her in a thousand different ways how much he cared.

"Quenton, you must make yourself ready to sup with the king and your guests." Olivia slipped out of bed and began to dress.

"Why must I?"

"Because you are the lord of Blackthorne." She tied the ribbons of her chemise and slipped into her petticoats.

"All the more reason why I should do as I please."

She turned to glance at him. His lean, muscled body looked thoroughly relaxed, propped in her bed with the pillows mounded behind his head. His eyes were dark and stormy, but his lips were curved in a smile of pure masculine appreciation as he watched her dress. Dark hair spilled over his forehead, adding to his rakish appeal.

"You are host to the king of England and his closest friends. You cannot offend them."

"Aye. You're right. I suppose I must be sensible." He tossed aside the linens and walked unselfconsciously across the room to a basin where he began to wash.

As Quenton redressed, Olivia picked up the ivory gown and slipped it over her head.

Catching sight of her in the mirror, he turned. "What is this? Why are you wearing such a plain gown?"

"My lord, I am a simple governess."

"There is nothing simple about you, love. I have something else in mind for this night." He crossed to the wardrobe and sorted through her new clothes until he located the gown he'd been looking for. Turning, he held out a spill of green satin. "I want you to wear this."

Puzzled, she studied him for a moment, then nodded. "All right. If it pleases you."

He dragged her close and brushed his lips over hers. "You please me, Livvy. You please me very much."

The depth of his emotion caught her by surprise.

While he watched, she stripped off the ivory gown and slipped into the green one. When she had finished securing the buttons, she studied her reflection in the looking glass. The gown was deep green satin with a neckline that dipped perilously low, revealing the swell of high, firm breasts. The off-the-shoulder sleeves were huge flounces that gradually narrowed until they were tightly fitted at the wrists. The voluminous skirt was gathered here and there with matching green satin bows. Her hair fell in fat sausage curls tied to one side with matching ribbons, spilling over one breast.

The woman in the mirror had a look of polish, of sophistication, that both startled her and pleased her.

"Oh, Livvy." Quenton walked up behind her. "You are, without a doubt, the most beautiful woman ever to grace Blackthorne."

She smiled shyly. "I think you are looking with your heart instead of with your eyes."

"These eyes can see only you, love. And you grow more graceful and charming with each day." He reached into his pocket and removed a small pouch. "I brought you something."

"A gift? Quenton. What is it?"

He loved the excitement in her eyes. She looked as delighted and as curious as a child.

He opened the pouch and filled her hands. "These are the Stamford emeralds. They belonged to my grandmother. I want you to wear them tonight."

She gasped as she held up a lacy gold filigree interspersed with glittering emeralds and diamonds. "Oh, no, Quenton." Shaking her head, she started to hand them back. "I couldn't possibly wear these."

He closed his hand over hers. "I insist, love."

He took the necklace from her and secured it around her throat, then stood back to admire her.

"I was right," he muttered. "There isn't a woman in the world who could rival your beauty."

They both looked up at the timid knock on her door. She hurried over and found Liat, looking refreshed from his nap. When he caught sight of her, his eyes rounded.

"You look like a queen," he said.

"Be careful, lad." Quenton's eyes crinkled with laughter. "I wouldn't wish to give His Majesty any ideas." Then he surprised Olivia and Liat by taking the boy's hand. "Come on. You and I both need to get dressed for the ball."

"How do I look, sir?" Liat stepped into the sitting chamber and paused in front of Quenton.

"You look splendid." Quenton smiled his approval at the blue satin breeches and little blue brocaded jacket. On Liat's feet were matching hose and soft kidskin boots. Beneath the jacket was a white shirt with a lacy jabot at the throat. His raven hair had been brushed back from his face. His dark eyes were bright with excitement.

Quenton eyed the parchment in Liat's hand. "And what is this?"

"A gift for the king. Miss St. John said I may present it before we sup."

When the lad made no offer to show it, Quenton decided not to press. Even a small boy was entitled to his secrets.

"Shall we go now?"

Liat nodded.

Quenton led the way, then held the door for Olivia and the boy. As they stepped into the hallway they were assaulted by the sounds from below. The rumble of masculine voices raised in earnest conversation. The soft ripple of a woman's laughter. The tinkle of crystal. Muffled footfalls of servants moving discreetly among the guests.

At the top of the stairs Quenton offered his arm and Olivia placed her hand on his sleeve. Beside her, Liat clasped her hand and moved with her down the stairs.

When they reached the great hall the noise of the gathering reached a crescendo. A chorus of voices seemed to be all speaking at once.

Pembroke, standing guard outside the hall, caught sight of them and stepped smartly to announce them.

"Majesty. Honored guests." His announcement had the desired effect, quieting the crowd, snagging their attention. "Lord Quenton Stamford, Miss Olivia St. John and young Master Liat."

The crowd fell strangely silent. Olivia could feel every person in the room watching as they entered.

King Charles was standing on a raised dais at the front of the hall, with a dazzling young woman beside him. With them were Bennett, in his wheeled chair, and Minerva, standing behind him.

Without glancing right or left Quenton began to lead Olivia and Liat through the throngs, keeping his gaze fixed on Charles. It would not be proper to greet any other guests until he had first greeted the king.

As they passed the clusters of guests, the whispered comments could be overheard.

"Who is that beautiful creature? I don't recall meeting her in London."

"I know not. But I intend to find out before the night is over."

"Look. Are those the famous Stamford emeralds around her neck?"

"Aye. I don't believe they've been worn since Stamford's grandmother went to her grave."

"Are you saying his wife never wore them?"

"I'm not certain she was even allowed to see them. The old man swore no one but his own wife would ever wear them in his lifetime."

"The old man is gone now. And his wishes along with him. Long live the new lord of Blackthorne."

"Who is the lad?"

"No one knows. Some say he is Stamford's bastard."

"What of the mother?"

"A Jamaican. A servant at Blackthorne whispered to my servant that she met the same fate as Antonia."

Olivia knew her face was flaming. She was grateful for the voluminous skirt that hid the trembling of her legs. Liat's little hand was clutching hers so tightly she had lost the feeling in her fingers. But having Quenton's quiet strength to draw on permitted her to carry on without stumbling.

When they reached the dais, Charles stepped forward.

"Ah. Lord Stamford. Miss St. John. Liat." His booming voice could easily be heard throughout the hall. "How grateful we are to be made to feel so welcome here in your home, my friend."

"It is my honor and privilege to welcome you to Blackthorne, Majesty. I pledge to do all in my power to make your visit to our humble home as pleasant as possible."

"Thank you, Lord Stamford. Such a pledge means much to me. As does your friendship." In a voice so low only Quenton could hear, he added, "At least your brother had the good sense to be on time. You're late. Very poor manners, Q. You've ignored protocol. I ought to have you flogged."

In an equally low voice, Quenton whispered, "Sorry, old friend. Very pressing matters to see to."

The king's brows lifted. "The only thing pressing was the bed in the lady's room, I'd wager. Not that I don't understand, mind you. She's the loveliest lady in this room."

Quenton shot him a wounded look. "Now who's showing poor manners, Chills?"

Charles grinned. "There is not a thing wrong with my eyesight, old friend. And from the mutterings as you walked up here, I'd say every man in the room took notice of the same thing."

He turned to Olivia and said loudly. "Miss St. John, your beauty dazzles your king and graces this hall."

"Thank you, Majesty." She managed a sedate curtsy and was grateful that she hadn't embarrassed herself in front of this assembly.

"And young Liat. We had a fine day, did we not?"

"Aye, Majesty." The lad bowed, then offered the parchment in his hand.

"What is this?"

"A gift, Majesty. Miss St. John said I might present it to you."

"A gift. Let's have a look." Charles unrolled the parchment and studied it, then gave a solemn nod of appreciation. "Did you draw this yourself, lad?"

"Aye, Majesty. It is a *Heodes alciphron.*"

"I see that. And an excellent rendition. Miss St. John, has the boy had training in drawing and composition?"

"Nay, Majesty. What you see is the product of his own talent."

Since it was unseemly for a monarch to bend to anyone, the crowd of guests was stunned when the king got down on one knee, in order to better speak to the little boy.

"Did you know that, besides my love of butterflies, I am much interested in painting and composition?"

"Nay, Majesty." The boy's eyes rounded with surprise.

"I do greatly admire it, though I have little talent for it. You have been given a rare gift, Liat. It is my hope that you will study with the masters, in order to polish your craft. And some day, I think, you will be counted among them."

The boy beamed at the compliment.

"I thank you for this, Liat. I shall treasure it." Charles got to his feet and held the drawing aloft, so that the crowd could see and admire. They burst into polite applause, while the little boy stood flushed with pleasure.

"Come, Liat. I think they must see this as I have

seen it, so that they might appreciate your talent.''
Charles handed the parchment to his valet, then caught
Liat's hand and led him through the crowd. His valet
walked a little behind, holding the drawing out to the
admiring public.

As the titled men and women had an opportunity to
examine it more closely, their enthusiasm grew. Men
ruffled the lad's hair while women bent to kiss his
cheek. For a shy boy who'd had little contact with
such people, it was a heady experience. By the time
he and the king returned to the dais, Liat's smile was
beaming.

Charles was thoroughly enjoying the role of benev-
olent monarch. He kept the boy's hand in his as he
turned to Quenton and Olivia. "You have not yet met
the other member of my party." He drew a pretty
young woman forward. "I present Louise de Keroualle."

Quenton kissed her hand and she gave him a shy
smile before turning to Olivia.

"The boy is yours?"

She spoke with a decidedly French accent.

Olivia shook her head. "How I wish he were
mine."

She didn't see the look of surprise and pleasure that
crossed Liat's face. But Quenton did. And felt his
heart stir.

"I am his governess," Olivia explained.

"You teach him?"

"Aye. And see to his care and upbringing."

"A noble endeavor. You are most fortunate," she
said in halting English.

"Come, my dear." Charles caught Louise's hand
and led her to the edge of the dais, positioning her on

his left side. Turning, he said to Olivia, "You will stand to my right, with Liat in front of you and Quenton beside you."

They did as they were told.

"Pembroke," the king called.

At once the butler hurried forward.

"You may begin the presentation now."

The older man bowed. "Aye, Majesty."

At a signal the crowd surged forward, forming a line of couples to be presented to their king and his host. The most important people were led to the front of the line, while the others were asked to step back and make room.

Olivia couldn't believe this was happening. The daughter of a simple professor was standing beside the king of England, grandly welcoming England's elite.

She barely heard the names of the sleek, handsome men and their elegant ladies as they were presented to the King.

The names droned on, and through it all Olivia behaved as was expected, smiling, nodding, saying all the right things.

As she was making polite conversation with an elderly duke, she became aware of a sudden tension in Quenton. It wasn't anything he said, but rather a stiffening of his spine, a clenching of his fist at his side.

Pembroke's voice intoned, "Lord Robert and Lady Agatha Lindsey and their son and daughter."

Olivia looked up and felt all the blood drain from her face. There was a strange ringing in her ears when she found herself staring into the cold, brittle eyes of her aunt and uncle, and behind them, her cruel cousins, Catherine and Wyatt.

Chapter Eighteen

"Lord Stamford. Niece." Robert Lindsey gave a curt nod of his head in greeting. Knowing the king was watching and listening, he was careful to say or do nothing that could be considered unfriendly toward this man who was the monarch's closest friend, or the woman who stood beside him.

Agatha was too furious to say a word. The sight of Olivia standing in the place of honor beside the king had her eyes glittering with jealousy. It had been her greatest source of pride that she and her family had been singled out for this visit. She had come to Blackthorne believing that she and her family would be treated as honored guests and that her niece would be consigned to some dreary suite of rooms with the brat she had been hired to tutor. It had never occurred to her that her sister's child would be invited to stand beside England's ruler, wearing a king's ransom in jewels.

Beside her, Catherine could do no more than stare. Her sulky look said it all. How could this plain lump of a cousin from some dreary little village have turned into this glittering, sparkling beauty? It was so unfair.

She should be the one to be favored by the king. Couldn't he see that she was far superior to her cousin?

Of the four, only Wyatt was able to compose himself. As he had waited patiently for the long procession to move, he'd had time to think through what he would say and do. It gave him such pleasure to know that Olivia had been caught unaware. He could see, by the way she was staring, by the way the color had drained from her face, that she was feeling far more shocked than he.

He gave her a long, assessing look that had her skin crawling. Enjoying her discomfort, he shot her a chilling smile and took her hand in his.

"How delightful to see you looking so well, cousin. It would seem that life in the country agrees with you."

He brushed his lips over the back of her hand and felt her shrink back from him. So, she was still afraid of him. That realization caused him to chuckle with delight.

"Oh, this will be such an enjoyable visit. I am so looking forward to many long, intimate conversations, cousin."

When he moved on Quenton leaned close to mutter, "Cousin? You are related to Lindsey?"

"Aye." Odd, how difficult it was to speak. As though she had swallowed a stone and couldn't dislodge it. Fear, as sharp and swift as a knife, sliced her heart. This was followed by a rush of such loathing, she was actually trembling.

She wiped her hand along her skirt, hoping to wipe away the touch of Wyatt. "His mother and mine were sisters. Do you know the Lindseys?"

"Nay. I know only their son." His voice was chillingly devoid of any emotion. As though waging a war within himself. "Wyatt."

Before Olivia could ask how he knew of her cousin, more couples approached and she realized she would have to put aside whatever questions she had for a later time. Despite her agitation, she fell into the easy rhythm of greetings and conversation.

Finally the interminable introductions were concluded, and the king led the way to a cluster of chairs where the guests could view him. At a signal from Mistress Thornton, a servant brought a tray of wine and ale. Other servants began to circulate among the crowd, filling tankards and goblets.

A mime and a juggler entertained, and the crowd, following the lead of their king, applauded with enthusiasm. Musicians, brought from the village, began to play, and the king eagerly led his lady, Louise, into a dance. At once the crowd was on its feet, joining in.

Quenton glanced at Olivia. She still appeared drained and shaken. He welcomed the opportunity to hold her.

"Come, my love. It is required that we dance."

"All night?"

At her stricken look he gave her a gentle smile. "Nay. Just the first dance. I promise you, as soon as the king gives us leave, we will escape to our rooms."

Escape. It was her only thought. She had to escape the evil in Wyatt's eyes. And the venom of his tongue. The mere thought of being in the same hall with him had her quaking.

As Quenton led her to the floor, she leaned into him. Oh, this was what she'd needed. The sanctuary of his arms, holding her warm and safe. As long as she was assured of his love, his quiet strength, no harm could come to her.

"I'm sorry about Bennett," she murmured. "I saw him leaving the hall right after greeting the guests."

"Aye. Apparently the time spent in all those introductions was too long and tedious for his frail health. He looked exhausted and very pale. But at least Minerva is with him. Now," he said easily. "Tell me about this aunt and uncle."

"There is little to tell. I never met them until the day I buried my parents. They arrived from London and announced that they were taking their penniless niece home with them."

"I believe you said your stay was unpleasant."

She nodded.

He placed a finger under her chin and lifted her face for his inspection. "Tell me why, my love."

She shook her head. "I can't bear to speak of it. It is enough to tell you that I was made to feel…most unwelcome in their home."

The fact that she couldn't speak of it made it all the worse in Quenton's mind. He knew of Wyatt's reputation with women. Many a father throughout England wept after his daughter had come in contact with the man known to be a brute and a bully. And now, to learn that Wyatt's parents were the people who had sent Olivia packing in the dark of night was simply one more reason to despise them.

"You are both looking far too serious."

They looked up to see Charles and Louise beside them.

"My lady." The king caught Olivia's hand. "You will dance with me." He winked at Quenton over her shoulder. "I shall soon have your lady smiling, old friend. And you have my leave to dance with the lady Louise. I daresay she will put a smile on your face as well.''

He whirled away with Olivia in his arms. True to his word, he soon had her laughing aloud with his irreverent comments about their many guests.

"You see Lady Edwards?"

Olivia glanced toward the plump woman dripping with jewels. "Aye."

"She would much rather be eating than dancing."

"How could you possibly know that, Majesty?"

"We are well acquainted. Very soon now she will manage to develop a pain in her knee, or a discomfort in her hip. Then, as soon as her husband joins the other gentlemen in a tankard of ale, she will send a servant to fetch—'' he raised his voice to a falsetto impression of the lady's voice ''—just a bit of mutton, perhaps a small bite of biscuit. And, oh yes, while you're at it, you may as well bring me a slice or two of that brandy-soaked cake.'' He joined in Olivia's laughter. "And she'll wash it all down with several goblets of wine."

"Oh, Majesty. What would the lady say if she could hear you?"

"She would try to deny it. But it would be difficult while chewing all that food."

He nodded toward the Duke and Duchess of Renfrew. "It is most fortunate that the lady was born of wealth."

"Why?" Olivia asked in all innocence.

"Because it is the only way a woman with that face would have ensnared a husband. Else she would have remained a spinster to her dying day."

"Majesty." Olivia's mouth dropped in surprise.

He shrugged. "Everyone knows the duke's fortunes were at low ebb. It was necessary for him to marry well. And he did. Very well, indeed." He whirled her around several times, then smiled at Lord and Lady Weldon. "Now there," he whispered in Olivia's ear, "is a very rare thing."

"And what is that, Majesty?"

"A true love match. They are each comely in person, and each had many suitors. They brought both wealth and love to their marriage bed. And 'tis rumored that they love each other still."

"It shows," she said. "In their eyes. In their smiles."

"I see the same in yours, my lady." He gave her a long, steady look. "I'm pleased that my old friend has found someone to give him back his smile. It has been sorely missed." His voice deepened with emotion. "Quenton's life has not been easy. Perhaps that is another reason why I love him so. We have a history of shared misery. And now we rejoice at each other's successes."

Olivia was astounded by the king's candor.

"And now, my lady, if you will excuse me, I must dance with Lady Edwards. Just to torment her, you understand. 'Twill keep her from the food for at least another few moments."

He paused beside the couple and whirled off with Lady Edwards, leaving Olivia to dance with the elderly lord.

"My wife was just complaining about her foot," Lord Edwards said as he moved with Olivia to the music. "I suppose she will be forced to suffer for a few minutes longer, now that she is dancing with His Majesty."

"Aye, my lord." Olivia had to fight to keep from laughing aloud. She saw Charles wink at her over the lady's shoulder, and she coughed quickly to cover the laughter that bubbled in her throat. "I daresay a sore foot is little price to pay for the privilege of dancing with the king."

"I quite agree."

He moved with quiet grace, despite his bulk, and Olivia found herself enjoying the dance. Then the old lord turned when he felt a hand at his shoulder.

A man's voice said, "I believe it is my turn to dance with the lady."

Lord Edwards bowed and stepped away and Olivia looked up to see her new partner. Her heart sank.

"Well, my little country cousin. How clever you are." Wyatt's hands circled her waist and he gave her a chilling smile as he pulled her close. "Who would have thought that you would make such an impression on the lord of the manor?"

"I don't know what you mean."

"Don't you?" He boldly touched a hand to the jewels at her throat and felt her reaction as she jerked away. "Ah. I see. You still refuse to allow me to touch you." He closed his fingers around her throat as though he would squeeze the breath from her. His voice lowered with feeling. "I would wager that you didn't resist when he put his hands on you."

Her eyes widened but he merely pressed his thumb against the softness of her throat and smiled at her struggle for breath. "I have no doubt he put his hands on you, dear, sweet little Olivia. Else you would not be the recipient of such largesse as this."

He saw Quenton look over at them and turned her away so that she could see only him. "Of course, you are not the first woman to be won over by the glitter of gold.''

"How dare..."

As she struggled to break free of his arms, he tightened his hold on her and whispered in her ear, "I haven't yet finished with you, cousin." He caught her chin and forced her to glance over at the laughing couple across the room. "Look at the very young, very pretty lady Louise, on the arm of our king. Is she not lovely?"

When Olivia said nothing he gave a cold, chilling laugh. "Did you know she is a gift from the king of France?"

"A...gift?" Olivia turned to him with a look of shock and surprise.

"Aye. To replace the...services of Barbara, Lady Castlemaine."

"I don't understand."

"I think you do, little cousin. I know it sounds sordid to one as sweet and unspoiled as you. But Charles has a fondness for very young, rather childish mistresses. The French king, knowing this, wishes to curry favor."

"I do not believe you."

He shrugged. "You may ask anyone. Ask Lord Stamford. If he is a truthful man, he will tell you the same."

"Has the young woman nothing to say about this...arrangement?"

Wyatt's tone was laced with sarcasm. "Why should she mind? Don't bother to waste your sympathy on her. Like all of those who have gone before her, she will be well compensated for her...tender ministrations." His voice lowered. "Lord Stamford's friends will no doubt say the same about you, when he has tired of your charms.''

"I have had enough of your cruel remarks, Wyatt. Release me.''

"In a moment, cousin. Let us circle the floor once more, so that every man and woman in the hall can get a good look at the Stamford emeralds at your throat. They are, after all, the cause of many whispers.''

When she glanced around, she felt the sting of censure. The guests were indeed staring at her.

Suddenly, the gift that had touched her so deeply now weighed as heavily as a guillotine around her neck. There was a heaviness around her heart as well. Though she didn't want to believe him, the words Wyatt had spoken rang in her mind. Could it be that she, too, was being compensated for her tender ministrations? Had she lulled herself into a false sense of security? She had, after all, been brought here for one purpose, and one purpose only. To see to the care of a little boy of dubious parentage. And for that she was being paid handsomely. But now she had moved beyond the role of mere governess.

Without any coercion on Quenton's part she had gone to his bed. And had gone willingly. This very night she had stood by his side, looking for all the world like a woman of wealth and title, wearing the Stamford emeralds and hearing the whispers from the crowd.

She couldn't blame Quenton for any of this. He had warned her that he was a mere man, with a man's appetite. He had made no promises. Had offered her no future.

What had she been thinking? She was no better than

the young Frenchwoman who was now dancing with the king. No better than the lass from her small village who had given herself to a man and had returned to be ridiculed for carrying the seed of that illicit union.

The music stopped and Wyatt bowed low. "Thank you for the dance, cousin." He glanced at Quenton, who was scowling as he approached. "I believe your lover is coming to claim what is his." He took a step back and, with a very satisfied smile, walked away.

Quenton took one look at her face, devoid of color, and caught her arm. "What is it, Livvy? What did he do to you?"

"Nothing. I just…need to sit down a moment."

Concerned, he led her to a chair beside Liat, then signaled for a servant. A moment later he handed her a glass of wine. "Perhaps this will revive you."

She sipped, knowing nothing would help. She was sick at heart. And though she wanted to blame Wyatt, she had to admit that the blame lay with her. All Wyatt had done was point out the obvious. He had forced her to see herself for what she really was. A fool hopelessly in love with a man so high above her station she was bound to have her heart broken. For in truth, a man like Quenton Stamford could never wed her.

The king was in high spirits, and kept the crowd dancing until the small hours of the morning. When he finally bade good-night and left, with Louise de Keroualle on his arm, the crowd began to disperse.

Olivia glanced at Liat, whose eyes were nearly closed. "The poor little thing. I doubt he has the energy to climb the stairs."

"I'll carry him." Quenton lifted the lad in his arms and led the way up the stairs, with Olivia beside him.

At the sight of man and boy, she felt her heart swell. If nothing else, her presence here had brought the two closer together.

In his chambers, Quenton deposited the boy in bed. As Olivia undressed him and slipped him between the covers, he stirred. "It was a grand night, wasn't it, ma'am?"

"Aye. And the king was pleased with your gift."

"He said I might become a master painter."

"Would you like that?"

He nodded. "I would paint only butterflies." His eyes closed. "Beautiful, stained-glass butterflies."

She bent and kissed him, then followed Quenton from the room. At the door to her bedroom they both halted.

Quenton touched a hand to her cheek. "Charles has asked that I meet with him."

"Now? Quenton, it is almost morning, and you haven't slept."

He gave her a gentle smile. "Charles told me that there are some matters he wishes to discuss with me."

"As his friend? Or as Q?"

He shrugged. "It would be impossible to separate the one from the other. As both his friend and his loyal subject, he knows I will do whatever he asks."

He could read the disappointment in her eyes. It mirrored his own. He wanted her. Wanted desperately to lie with her. But there was love, and there was duty. And ofttimes the two were at odds.

"I'll come to you as soon as Charles and I have resolved whatever business is between us." He brushed his mouth over hers and felt the rush of heat. Would it always be like this? Would he be reduced to a whimpering fool each time he touched her?

He took the kiss deeper, lingering over her lips as though they had been dipped in the sweetest of nectars. When he lifted his head he gave a hiss of impatience.

"Until I return, sleep, my love. For when I do, I promise you, there will be no sleep for either of us."

She watched him walk away, then let herself into the room and made ready for bed. Though it hurt to know that Wyatt was right, she was forced to admit that, no matter how late the hour, she would be eager for Quenton's return.

There was pleasure in his arms. But there was also safety. And until he was beside her, she would not feel safe.

She shivered and huddled under the covers. And cursed herself for her cowardice. All the old nightmares would be back, she knew. And she would be helpless to fight them.

She struggled to stay awake, to hold the demons at bay. But against her will she slept, unlocking all the powers of darkness.

Chapter Nineteen

"His Majesty is expecting you." The king's valet opened the door to his chambers and led Quenton toward the sumptuous parlor where a fire blazed on the hearth. "I will tell him you have arrived."

He disappeared inside the sleeping chamber and returned minutes later, followed by Charles, looking pleasantly sated, who was tying the sash of a long robe of scarlet cut velvet.

"Bring us ale." Charles took a seat by the fire and invited Quenton to sit across from him.

The valet poured two goblets and set them and the decanter on a tray, which he deposited on a table between them. "Will there be anything else, Majesty?"

"Nothing. Leave us."

The king waited until they were alone. Then he picked up the goblet and drank. Quenton did the same.

"It would seem that my generous benefactors have been touched by my invitation to Blackthornc, old friend. In an effort to impress their king, they have made me an even more generous offer than before."

"How generous?"

"They will make me a gift of two-hundred thousand pounds, which is the amount of the Treasury deficit."

"Two-hundred thousand." Quenton's eyes narrowed. "Where did they come up with such wealth?"

"I did not ask. But it would go a long way toward guaranteeing my smooth reign. Parliament would dare not question my authority when I commanded such a purse."

"They will not give up a fortune without demanding concessions in return."

"Aye." Charles raised a hand. "Don't look so wary, old friend. What are a few titles and estates, when the reward is so great? And if I must trust them with a few state secrets in return, what is the harm? There are many at court who know such secrets. And none can offer me what these people do."

"Then you have decided to accept their offer?"

"Not yet. That is where you come in. I have need of my old friend Q."

Quenton nodded, relieved that the king wasn't acting in haste. "Give me their names. I'll see what I can learn about these loyal citizens."

"This can go no further than you."

"Understood."

The king drained his goblet. "My generous benefactors are Lord and Lady Lindsey. And their son, Wyatt."

Highly agitated, Agatha Lindsey paced the floor of her son's parlor and looked up sharply when he finally emerged from the bedchamber.

"What kept you? You sent word you wanted me here more than an hour ago."

"I was busy. A...tasty little serving wench."

She gave a hiss of disgust. "Your...appetite is getting out of control. Try to curb it until you are safely back in your own bed. Now what is so vexing that I had to be roused at this hour?"

"My spy tells me that Lord Stamford has sent a rider to London."

"What is that to us?"

"His solicitors are in London. As are ours."

She arched a brow. "You think he suspects something?"

"I think," he said, pausing to stare into the fire, "that we need to move more quickly than planned."

"Aye." Her tone was low with fury. "It is just as well. It offends me to see my sister's daughter flaunting her newfound status as mistress to the king's closest friend."

"Then have no fear. I have plans for my little cousin and Lord Stamford. By the time I'm through with them, they will welcome death like the embrace of an old lover."

Olivia was caught up in the dream again. Strong hands pinning her while she struggled to break free. Feelings of shock and revulsion as her skirts were shoved aside, her modesty violated. Eyes, cold and lifeless, staring down at her as cruel laughter mocked her. Desperate to escape the horror, she fought her way up through the layers of sleep and bolted up in the bed.

"Livvy. Livvy." Quenton's arms came around her and he gathered her close, stroking her hair. "Wake up, love. You're having a bad dream."

"Aye." Her breath was coming in short gasps. She clung to him for long moments until her breathing steadied. Then she pushed away and ran a hand through her hair. "I'm all right now."

"I wish I could ease your burden." He gave a weary sigh.

"You do, Quenton. Just having you here to hold me is such comfort from my demons."

"You aren't the only one fighting demons tonight. I just left Bennett. Minerva is worried about him. This was the worst yet. For a while, we thought we wouldn't be able to bring him out of it."

"Oh, poor Bennett. He'd been doing so well. What do you think brought it on?"

"Perhaps the strain of all these strangers at Blackthorne. Minerva said that, while greeting the king's guests, he became so agitated, she feared his heart would explode inside his chest. I've told her to watch him carefully and summon me if there is any change."

Olivia glanced around the room. The tapers were lit. Quenton was fully dressed. "You're not coming to bed?"

"I must go below stairs."

"Now?"

"I'm sorry, my love. But I believe my grandfather's ledgers hold the answers to some very pressing questions. The sooner I find them, the sooner I can help Charles." At the look on her face he was quick to add, "If I'm lucky, I might find what I'm searching for soon, and we'll still have a little time to ourselves." He kissed her, hard and quick, before turning away. At the door he paused, looked back, then strode across the room and kissed her again, long and deep, until they were both gasping.

"That will have to do until I return."

This time he made it out the door without looking at her.

When the door closed she slipped out of bed and began to pace. She shivered and thought about the warmth of the covers. But her bed held no temptation for her. She would rather walk the floor until dawn than face the dream again. What was even worse than the dream was the reality. The source of all her fears was right here at Blackthorne, separated only by a few walls.

She wouldn't feel truly safe until Quenton returned. Or until their guests departed on the morrow. Until then she would watch and wait. And keep her wits about her.

"Good morrow, my lady." Minerva entered Olivia's room and paused just inside the door.

Olivia looked up from brushing Liat's hair.

"Master Bennett desires you and the lad to break your fast with him in his chambers before you join the king and his guests below stairs."

"Bennett will not be going down with us?"

"He is unwell."

"We'll come at once."

Olivia caught Liat's hand and led him out of the room and along the hallway. Just as they reached Bennett's rooms, they saw Quenton, with Thor at his heel, walking toward them. A dark growth of beard covered his cheeks and chin. His eyes were red-rimmed, his hair tousled. The sleeves of his shirt were rolled, the buttons opened.

Olivia brushed a palm over his scratchy beard. "Have you had no sleep?"

"Nay." He caught her hand, lifted it to his lips. "And you, love? Did you sleep after I left you?"

She shook her head. "I couldn't face the demons again. We were summoned here by Bennett. I am told he is not well."

They entered the room and found Bennett seated by the window, staring at the cliffs. The servant, Edlyn, was busy removing food from a heavy silver tray and arranging it on a table set up in front of the fire.

Olivia shivered when she saw the bleak look in Bennett's eyes. This was how he had looked when she'd first arrived at Blackthorne. Helplessly lost inside a prison in his mind. His failing condition seemed all the more shocking because he'd been making such progress.

"It was kind of you to invite us to share your meal, Bennett." She dropped a hand on his shoulder and he covered her hand with his. And clung.

"What is it, Bennett? What has happened to make you so ill?"

Minerva tucked a blanket around his knees. "I think perhaps Master Bennett has partaken of too many activities."

"Aye." Quenton clapped a hand on his brother's back. "You'll rest today. And take some sun in the garden."

Across the room Edlyn poured tea and filled several plates with fruit conserve.

Seeing it, Minerva said, "Thank you, Edlyn. I'll see to Master Bennett's food."

Edlyn's usual frown deepened. "Mistress Thornton said I was to remain here and serve the table."

"We can see to ourselves." Olivia crossed the room and held the door, leaving the surly servant no choice but to leave. "I'm sure Mistress Thornton could use your help below stairs."

With a negligent shrug the servant picked up the empty tray and walked from the room.

When they were alone, Minerva let out a sigh of gratitude. "Thank you, miss. I doubt she would have left if you hadn't intervened." She lowered her voice. "That woman knows everyone's business here at Blackthorne."

Olivia nodded. "Aye." Thinking back to her first night under this roof, she added, "And is willing to share it with all who will listen."

As they began to eat Quenton cast worried looks at his pale brother, who, despite Minerva's coaxing, ate less than half his biscuit and refused even a sip of tea. From the looks of him, he would soon be too weak to leave his bed. After sipping hot mulled wine to revive his spirits, Quenton pushed away from the table and touched a hand to Bennett's. It felt as cold, as lifeless, as death.

"You must try to eat something, Bennett. If not for your own sake, then for Minerva's."

Both Bennett and Minerva shot him a questioning look. He lowered his voice, as though sharing a confidence. "If Pembroke and Mistress Thornton should decide that Minerva is not doing her job well enough, they might assign her to some other duties. And assign someone else, even Edlyn, to your care."

Satisfied that he'd thrown a sufficient scare into his brother, he turned away. "Come along now, Olivia, Liat. You two must join the king and his party below stairs. And I must see about making myself presentable."

As he started toward the door, he had the satisfaction of seeing Bennett lift the cup to his lips and sip. At least it was a start.

"Ah, here is my pretty little cousin now." Wyatt was positively glowing as Olivia and Liat entered the dining hall. He and his family were seated at the king's table. Agatha and her daughter, Catherine, were smiling smugly, enjoying the fact that they were now the center of attention. Robert and Wyatt appeared supremely confident as they flanked Charles and his mistress, Louise. Their stature had definitely improved.

"Come, my dear," the king called. "We were just talking about you. I had no idea that you were related to these fine people."

Her hand tightened on Liat's as she made her way up the steps of the dais and realized that she would have to sit beside Wyatt.

Pembroke held her chair and she gave him a weak smile.

The housekeeper appeared at her side. "Tea, Miss St. John?"

"Nay. I just finished having tea with Bennett."

"I was told he is unwell." The king helped himself to a joint of fowl. "How is he faring, my lady?"

"He seems quite weak. But perhaps after a day of rest, he will find his strength."

"He merely grieves because I am leaving." Charles glanced around. "Where is his brother?"

"Lord Stamford will be down shortly, Majesty. He told me to assure you he will be here when his guests take their leave."

Beside her Wyatt sipped hot mulled wine and gave Olivia his most charming smile. "With Lord Stamford not around, it will give my family and me a chance to visit with our beloved Olivia.'' He closed a hand over hers. ''Do tell us everything you've been doing since you left our home in London.''

''There is little to tell.'' Knowing the king was watching, Olivia was forced to go along with his little charade. But the touch of him was so repugnant, she forcefully removed her hand and clenched it in her lap. ''I find my work here very satisfying.''

''I am certain you do. I would expect no less from my sister's child.'' Agatha's smile never reached her eyes. She regarded the young woman with calculating shrewdness before turning to Charles. ''We imbued in our children a sense of honor and duty to king and country. The love and loyalty Olivia feels toward Lord Stamford is the same love and loyalty we all feel toward you, Majesty.''

Charles was deeply touched. ''Your king welcomes your affection. It will not go unrewarded.'' He glanced around the table. ''I regret that our time together was so limited. But since we will now be together in London, I will see that you are all invited often to court.''

Agatha smiled. And looked down at all the titled guests watching from their tables below. She had waited a lifetime for this. It was the sweetest victory. ''And once I am settled again in my London estate, Majesty, I will arrange a festive dinner in your honor.''

''Why, thank you, kind lady. I shall be in your debt.'' Charles lifted her hand to his lips and Agatha nearly swooned in delight.

''Come.'' The king got to his feet, and the others followed. ''We must make ready for our departure.''

As Olivia stood, Wyatt closed his hand around her waist and drew her close to whisper, ''I would hope you can find it in your heart to put aside the past, cousin, and consider that we start afresh.''

She flinched at his touch and hated herself for her reaction. But it was too late to hide her feelings. He could see that she was trembling.

''It is not so easy to put aside cruelty, Wyatt.''

He held her a moment longer and enjoyed watching her flinch. ''What you perceive as cruel, another might see as bold. Forgive my bold actions, cousin. But have pity on a man who was merely…overcome by your beauty.''

She managed to pull away and turned to face him. ''Beauty? As I recall, Wyatt, you called me a little mouse.''

He gave a boyish smile. ''A term of endearment, cousin. A man would have to be blind not to see your attributes.''

She itched to slap him. But knowing the king and his party were watching, she curled her fingers into her hand and let out a long, slow breath, whispering, ''I do not forget, Wyatt. Nor do I forgive.''

Instead of the anger she expected, he surprised her by catching hold of Liat's hand and saying, ''Your governess is very pretty, boy. Especially when her cheeks get all pink.''

''Aye, sir.'' Liat turned adoring eyes to her. ''She's even prettier than a butterfly.''

''Is that what Lord Stamford told you?''

''Nay, sir. Lord Stamford said she is a rare beauty.''

Olivia felt her cheeks flush as Wyatt and the others shared a knowing laugh.

When they walked outside to the courtyard, they found Quenton there, looking refreshed and clean-shaven.

"Ah. Here you are, old friend."

Quenton turned to smile at the king. "I regret that I couldn't break my fast with you this morrow. But at least I am here in time to bid farewell to you and our guests."

The wagons, carts and carriages laden with trunks and ladies' maids were already pulling away. As each couple was presented to their king one final time, the ladies curtsied and the men bowed, then were helped into the elegant carriages that would carry them back to London.

Agatha and Robert Lindsey and their son and daughter were the last guests to bid goodbye. Still glowing from their encounter with the king, Agatha and Catherine were helped into their carriage, followed by Robert.

For a moment Olivia felt a tremor of fear. But then, seeing Wyatt pull himself into the saddle of a sleek steed, she began to relax. As she and the others looked on, the door of the carriage was closed and the driver raised his whip. The team took off smartly, with Wyatt riding along beside them.

Olivia gave a deep sigh of relief. Safe. It was the only word that kept playing through her mind. Now that these hateful people had taken their leave of Blackthorne, and of her life, she was finally, completely safe.

"Are you crying, ma'am?" Liat caught her hand and stared up at her eyes, swimming with tears.

"They are tears of joy, Liat."

"Ah. I understand. You're crying because you have met the king."

"Aye." She wiped away the moisture and hoped she would be forgiven her little lie.

They stood together, watching the spectacle of the king's departure. The carriages laden with trunks and household goods were already rolling down the long curving drive, accompanied by the king's soldiers. Once again the staff of Blackthorne was assembled on the lawn, with Pembroke and Mistress Thornton at the head of the line.

Charles was as gracious in departure as he had been upon his arrival. He personally thanked Cook, the household staff, the stable lads, the groundskeepers. Men as well as women could be seen wiping tears from their eyes as he took a moment to speak to each of them.

When he paused in front of Liat he crouched down and reached inside his cloak. Carefully rolled up was the lad's drawing. "I intend to add this to my royal collection. And when you visit the palace, I shall give you a personal tour of my butterfly collection."

"Thank you, Majesty." Without realizing what he was doing, the little boy threw his arms around the king's neck and gave him a fierce hug.

For the space of a heartbeat gasps could be heard from those assembled. Then the king stood, still holding the boy in his arms, and turned to Olivia. "Miss St. John, you are doing a splendid job with this lad. Your king thanks you for helping to raise such a loyal and loving subject."

At a loss for words she merely curtsied.

Charles set the boy down, then moved to his host. "Lord Stamford, I thank you for your warm hospitality. The beauty and peace of Blackthorne have restored my soul."

Quenton bowed. "Nothing could please me more, Majesty."

The king moved closer and lowered his voice. "I said my goodbyes to Bennett. I am worried."

"Aye. As am I."

"He seems to have completely forgotten our little wager."

"Our wager?"

"Don't pretend you've forgotten. You and he owe me a thousand pounds. Unless, of course, you would care to see Bennett's servant and Liat's governess accompany me to London."

Quenton handed the king a pouch bulging with coins. "Two thousand pounds, Chills. I hope it weighs heavily on your journey home."

Charles gave a delighted laugh. "Stay well, old friend. And send me your earliest report on…that little matter."

"Aye."

The king turned away and was helped into the carriage. He glanced at the upper window, where Bennett and Minerva were watching, and saluted them smartly. Then, as the carriage started off, he accepted the cheers and applause of the staff of Blackthorne. It was a sound that would accompany him on every step of his journey home to London.

Chapter Twenty

Olivia led Liat to the gardens and found Quenton quietly pacing along the path, deep in thought.

"Forgive me, my lord. We didn't mean to disturb you." She started to turn away but Quenton stopped her.

"Please stay."

She sat on a stone bench, while Liat raced off along the path. "I was hoping to see Bennett here with you."

"I'm worried about my brother." Quenton glanced toward the upper window. "When I left him he was as pale as death. I fear he is slipping back. If only I knew how to reach him."

Olivia laid a hand over his. "You reached him once with love. You can do it again."

He gave her a strained smile. "Oh, my lady. If only I had your faith."

They both looked up as Pembroke approached, leading a youth in a dusty traveling cloak.

"A message for you, my lord," the butler announced.

The young man stepped forward and handed Quenton a scroll. He unrolled it, then turned to the butler. "Tell Mistress Thornton to see that the lad has something to eat. And send word to have my horse saddled at once."

"Aye, my lord."

Quenton caught Olivia's hand. "Forgive me. I must leave for the village."

A short time later she heard the sound of hoofbeats as Quenton took off at a gallop.

She sat in the sun, listening to the sounds of silence settling over Blackthorne. With the guests gone, and the lord of the manor away, the servants would sneak off for a well-earned rest. Even Cook, Mistress Thornton and Pembroke would steal away to their rooms to bask in the glow of a job well done.

"You're certain these figures are correct?" In a small room of the village pub, Quenton peered over the shoulder of the white-haired solicitor from his London office.

"Aye, my lord. I personally went over every column in these ledgers myself. I'll stand behind the tally."

"You realize what this proves?"

The old man nodded. His look was grave; his tone somber. "We should have uncovered these errors sooner. But the thief was very good. You realize our firm will make good on these. It is our solemn duty to earn and to keep the trust of our good citizens. As for the scoundrel who did this, he will be found and made to pay."

"Aye. He'll pay." Quenton shook his hand and made his way to the stable where he had left his horse.

The thought of his comfortable bed awaiting him at

Blackthorne brought a twinge. He would sleep soon, after he dispatched a report to the king. Charles would be livid when he heard this news.

He barely flicked a glance at the young man pouring water from a bucket.

"Saddle my horse, lad. There's an extra coin if you can do it in the blink of an eye."

"Aye, my lord."

Quenton turned away and carefully folded the report into a leather pouch, which he shoved inside his cloak. A footstep alerted him to the return of the stable lad. As he turned he caught sight of the upraised hand holding the club.

The lack of sleep slowed his reflexes. He ducked to stave off the blow, and the club grazed his shoulder. He fell, rolled and brought both feet up, catching his attacker off guard, bringing him to his knees. As they rolled around, exchanging blows, a second man appeared and joined in the fray, brandishing a knife.

"Hold 'im still, ye fool, and I'll finish 'im."

Quenton brought his fist to the man's face and had the satisfaction of hearing bone crunch and a cry of rage before the man dropped at his feet. Before Quenton could turn to fight the second man, he felt a blow between his shoulders. A sticky warmth spurted down his back, followed by searing, white-hot pain. His knees buckled. His legs could no longer hold his weight and he sagged to the ground. While he lay, struggling for breath, he felt a hand reach inside his cloak and rip away the pouch, and heard a familiar voice that seemed to come from very far away.

"Make certain he's dead."

"We're not staying around to find out. If 'e isn't dead now, 'e soon will be. I stuck my knife clear to the hilt. Come on. We've done our job. Give us our money.''

"Take it and go. If I ever see your faces in Cornwall or London, you're dead men."

"Don't worry about us, yer lordship. We don't..." The voice was abruptly cut off. There was a low moan, and the sound of something heavy falling to the ground.

As Quenton drifted into unconsciousness, he heard a jittery laughter. And the sound of a horse's hooves setting off at a furious pace. And then there was only blackness.

Olivia and Liat had passed several pleasant hours in pursuit of butterflies in the garden. When at last they sank down onto the grass, Liat stifled a yawn.

Olivia gave him a gentle smile. "I think it's time for a nap."

"Yes, ma'am." He caught her hand and walked beside her toward the door. "Do you think Lord Stamford will be back by the time I wake up?"

"I certainly hope so." Seeing his little frown she was quick to add, "Don't fret, Liat. He'll be along soon."

"Aye." He gave her his best smile.

Upstairs Olivia slipped off Liat's kid boots and helped him climb between the covers.

"Do you think Lord Stamford will teach me to play cards tonight after we sup?"

"I think there's a good chance of it. And when Bennett is feeling better, maybe he'll join you." She pressed a kiss to his cheek. "Sleep now. And I'll be right back after I look in on Bennett."

With Thor by her side she made her way down the

hall. The quiet of the house was a soothing balm after the constant disorder of the past days. Olivia paused outside Bennett's door and knocked, then entered. He was seated at the window, staring mournfully at the cliffs.

"How are you feeling, Bennett?"

When he didn't bother to glance her way, she looked to Minerva, who shook her head sadly.

Crossing the room, Olivia paused beside him and gently touched a hand to his shoulder. "If you must sit here, why not have Minerva move you to another window, where you could have a view of the gardens? Wouldn't that be more soothing than staring at the cliffs?"

She felt him shiver.

She dropped to her knees and caught his hand in both of hers. "Oh, Bennett. What is it? What is it that you can't tell us?"

His eyes were so bleak, so filled with pain, she had to look away. Standing, she pressed a kiss to his cheek.

"I'll be in my chambers if you need me."

Outside the room she glanced around, surprised that Thor had disappeared. Cook would skin him alive if he prowled her kitchen in search of bones. As she moved along the hallway she suddenly had the prickly sensation that she was being watched. She turned, feeling at once foolish and uneasy. Why should she feel this way now, when the danger had passed? There was no one around. No footsteps sounded in the hall, except her own.

Berating herself for her nervousness, she let herself into her room. There was a chill in the air and she noted that the fire had been allowed to burn to embers. The servants had a right to be just a little neglectful after all they'd been through. She tossed a log on the hearth and watched as flames began to lick along the bark.

Still chilled, she walked to her sleeping chamber to retrieve her shawl. As she stepped through the doorway she saw a rolled parchment in the middle of her bed.

Puzzled, she unrolled it and read the words:

I told you, little cousin, that one day you would pay. Your payment is due. You will sign this document immediately and bring it to the cliffs. Come alone. If you do not obey me, Liat's death will be on your hands.

"Liat. Oh, sweet heaven." With a cry she rushed to his room. The bed was empty, the bed linens in disarray.

On the floor, beside the bed, were several drops of blood.

With her heart in her throat she picked up a quill and signed the document, noting idly that it had been dated on the day of her parents' death. It mattered not. Nothing mattered except Liat.

There was no one who could help her. The king's soldiers were far away by now. Quenton was gone. Even the servants had all disappeared.

Fear rose like bile in her throat as she raced down the stairs and started at a run across the moors, praying desperately that she wasn't too late.

Quenton wiped a bloody hand across his eyes to clear his vision. The two strangers who had attacked him lay dead. He had recognized the voice of the man who had killed them. He wasn't surprised that Wyatt Lindsey would want no witnesses left alive.

He dragged himself to his knees and shook his head to clear it. The world seemed to spin in dizzying circles and he thought for a moment he would be sick.

Most of his anger and frustration were directed at himself. He should have anticipated this. Should have seen it coming. But he'd been so intent upon finding the proof of Wyatt's guilt, he'd been blind to the danger. And now he'd left all the others at the mercy of this madman.

Olivia. Dear heaven! She was the one most in peril.

He clamped his jaw against the pain and pulled himself to his feet, holding firmly to the railing of the stall. He didn't know how he hauled himself into the saddle, but he managed it and, leaning low over his horse's head, he nudged him into a trot.

Though the pain was almost more than he could bear, one thing kept him going. The thought of Olivia at the hands of that vicious madman, Wyatt Lindsey.

Bennett sat hunched in his chair, his gaze on the distant cliffs. Out of the corner of his eye he saw the woman running, the wind tearing at her clothes and hair. For a moment the pain of remembering was so intense, he was forced to close his eyes. It was happening again. The demons were back, haunting him, tormenting him. But...he opened his eyes. He wasn't asleep. Nay. He was awake. Still the nightmare was with him. There she was. Skirts billowing. Long hair flying.

Hair. That was what was wrong. Her hair wasn't the color of buttercups. That wasn't Antonia, racing toward the cliffs, racing toward certain death.

This was even worse than a nightmare. Much worse. It was real. God in heaven, it was happening again. And this time to Olivia.

In a panic he glanced around for Minerva. What had she said to him? What had she whispered before she'd left the room? He hadn't been listening. As always, though he loved her desperately, he'd shut her out, as he'd shut everyone out. Something about going below stairs to fetch tea and biscuits. Aye, that was it. She was gone. And he was alone. All alone. And helpless to stop Olivia from the same horrible death that Antonia had faced.

In frustration he slammed a hand against the hated chair. And felt it inch forward. His head jerked up. Slamming his hand again, the chair moved again. And again and again. Slowly, inch by painful inch, he managed to get the wheeled chair across the room, down the hall.

At the top of the stairs he opened his mouth, desperate to shout a warning. But no words came out. He stared down at the wide, polished staircase and wondered how many bones he would break before he reached the bottom. It didn't matter. Nothing mattered now except alerting someone, anyone, to what was about to happen.

Gritting his teeth against the pain he knew was to come, he launched himself out of the chair and flung himself desperately down the stairs.

Olivia could see them. Even with the wind whipping her hair around her face, she could see, high on the cliffs, Wyatt, holding tightly to little Liat's hand.

When she was close enough to see more clearly,

she realized that Liat's eyes were wide and terrified. And Wyatt was laughing.

Above the roar of surf and wind he shouted, "Did you sign?"

"Aye." She held up the document, and the wind nearly snatched it out of her hands.

"Be very careful, cousin. If you should lose it, I might have to let go of the boy, and the wind would surely snatch him over the cliffs before I could save him."

"Don't…" She could barely get the words out over the fear that clogged her throat. "Please. Don't hurt him any more than you already have."

He arched a brow. "What does that mean?"

"Please. I saw the blood.…"

"The little fool bit me."

She felt an inordinate sense of pride at Liat's courage.

"Come closer." Wyatt beckoned, and she took several tentative steps along the cliffs. The rocks were slick underfoot, coated with spray from the sea.

"I saw you leave with your family, Wyatt. Why did you come back?"

His smile was chilling. "I told you. We have some unfinished business, cousin. When I discovered your letter, asking for an accounting of your estate, I realized I had badly underestimated you."

"My letter?" She looked thunderstruck. "But I never sent it. How could you know…?"

His smile grew. "I have my spies."

She nodded. Hadn't she known all along? "Edlyn. How did you get her to spy for you?"

"It was easy. She hated Quenton Stamford—" he

gave a burst of laughter ''—for killing her beloved mistress, Antonia.''

''Why do you find that so amusing?''

''Because she was wasting her hatred on the wrong man. Quenton didn't kill Antonia.'' He laughed again, a wild, nervous sound that was chillingly unreal. ''I did.''

Quenton pushed himself and his mount to the limit. He realized that now that Wyatt had nothing to lose, he had become even more dangerous. Desperate men were willing to take desperate measures.

At Blackthorne he leapt from the saddle and raced up the steps. An ominous silence greeted him. A quick check of the bedrooms revealed them to be empty. He hurried to a window to peer at the gardens. They were as empty as the rooms. Puzzled, he was about to turn away when a movement high on the cliffs caught his eye.

His heart stopped. Even from this distance he could make out Olivia and Liat. And his worst nightmare. Wyatt Lindsey.

A cold black rage seemed to settle over him as he sprinted down the stairs and out the door, heading toward the cliffs. He had no weapon. And no plan. Armed only with a desperate will to save the two people he loved, he ran headlong toward disaster.

''Oh, Lord Stamford. Thank heaven.'' Minerva, her hands raw from struggling to push Bennett's chair over rocky outcroppings, dropped to her knees. ''Master Bennett has gone mad.''

Quenton barely paused. ''Go back, Minerva. Take Bennett back to the house.''

"My lord, look at him."

Quenton did look then, and was shocked. Blood spurted from a gash on his brother's forehead to mingle with a bloody nose that had soaked the front of his shirt. "Was it Wyatt? Did that monster attack you?"

Bennett shook his head, gesturing wildly.

"My lord, he threw himself down the stairs to get my attention. And when I finally realized that he wanted to go to the cliffs, I couldn't refuse, even though it seemed impossible."

"Aye." Quenton closed a hand over his brother's shoulder. "I understand. And I'm grateful. Stay here, Bennett. I'll save her. Or die trying."

Olivia moved closer, holding out the document as bait. "Take this, Wyatt. It's what you want. I have no use for it."

"But you've figured it out, haven't you? You have a surprisingly facile mind, little mouse."

"I don't understand all of it. But I assume, since you're so desperate to control my estate, that I must not be penniless."

"Far from it, cousin. When I was first employed at your solicitor's firm, I made it my business to learn all about you." He gave her a chilling smile. "When my firm was asked to convey the king's stipend and the title of Lord to your father, I offered to be the messenger."

"But why? You have no need of another title, Wyatt. And the stipend couldn't have amounted to much more than a few hundred pounds."

"And a lovely little house in Oxfordshire." He nodded. "I had your dear parents sign it all over to me before they...met with their little fall."

As the horror of what he had just revealed began to dawn on her, she shrank back from him. "You killed them? You killed my parents for the sake of a pittance?"

"Ah, but all those pittances add up to a fortune, cousin. Did you know that I'm one of the richest men in England? And soon, thanks to our rather poor and needy monarch, I'll also be the most powerful."

He glanced beyond her and began to laugh when he caught sight of Quenton racing toward them. Far back, inching along, were Minerva and Bennett. "Well, now, isn't this cozy? It seems all the players have arrived."

"Players?" Quenton paused to catch his breath, staring first at Olivia, to assure himself that she was unharmed, and then at Liat, who was being held firmly by both wrists. "Do you consider this all a game, Wyatt?"

"Aye. All of life is a game. I learned that at my mother's knee. And the man who amasses the biggest fortune gets to play, while all the others exist only to serve him." He shot Quenton a look of triumph. "The boy served to get me what I want now."

"What do you want, Wyatt?" He could see the madness in his eyes. Could hear it in his voice.

"Everything you have, Lord Stamford. Everything."

With a jolt Quenton recalled the old seer in Jamaica who had said, "There is one who desires everything you hold dear." He had laughed at the time. Now he understood with chilling clarity.

"I'll start with this boy." Wyatt's words brought him out of his reverie.

As Wyatt dragged the boy closer to the edge of the cliffs, Quenton called, "Wait, Wyatt. There's something you should know."

Wyatt paused. "And that is?"

"There's no need to harm the boy. He isn't mine."

"Not your little bastard? Whose then?"

Quenton gritted his teeth, hating the truth. And hating himself for having to admit it. "He's your son, Wyatt. When his mother lay dying, she begged me to keep him safe."

For a moment Wyatt was too stunned to react. Then his surprise slowly turned to rage. "The Jamaican slut, Mai, meant nothing more to me than a moment's pleasure. You cannot expect me to acknowledge her spawn as my own."

Olivia was horrified. "Please, Wyatt. If what Quenton says is the truth, you would be killing your own flesh and blood."

"That matters not to me."

"Then think of this. If it is true, it makes Liat my cousin as well. If you won't spare him because he is your son, spare him because he owns my heart. I would do anything for him."

His eyes glittered with madness. "Anything?"

Olivia nodded.

He gave her a dangerous, feral smile. "Then walk here to me and take the boy's place."

"Don't do it, Livvy." Quenton's words were torn from his throat. "You know what he'll do to you. I love you too much. I couldn't bear to go through this again."

Wyatt gave a high, shrill laugh. "Oh, this is such a

sweet dilemma. Will you watch as I throw the lad to his death, dear cousin? Or will you exchange your own life for his, and know that Quenton Stamford will never again know happiness?''

Olivia turned to Quenton. ''Please understand. I love you more than life itself. But I can't stand by and allow him to harm Liat.''

As she walked to him Wyatt threw back his head in a roar of triumph. ''Now, Lord Stamford, I will have everything you ever valued. Olivia. Antonia.''

''Antonia?''

At Quenton's arched brow he said, ''You didn't know? Oh, this is such fun. I was here that summer.''

''Here?''

''I thought you knew, Lord Stamford. I own Duncan Hall. Right here in Cornwall.''

''That cannot be. It is the Earl of Lismore's estate.''

''Aye. I acquired it after his...untimely death. And then, while you were off sailing your boat and seeing to your tenant farmers, I was busy seducing your lovely, innocent young bride.''

Quenton remained as still as death. But the look in his eyes was frightening to behold.

''It took a great deal of time and patience. She was...reluctant. But when the deed was accomplished, she was so remorseful, I knew she would have to be...silenced, before she went running to you with the truth.'' He was smiling now, as though it were nothing more than a business transaction. ''Of course, young Bennett had to complicate matters. He saw us up here and tried to come to her rescue.'' Wyatt shook his head. ''I don't know how he survived. But it would have been better if he'd died. Had he been my brother,

I would have helped him out of his misery a long time ago.''

He released Liat while clamping a hand firmly around Olivia's wrist. ''And now I have it all. And no one will believe your tale. You see, I waved to the crowd along the king's route this very day. Hundreds of people will attest to it. And my family will swear that I was with them, nearing London, when this little tragedy occurred.''

He was, Quenton knew, completely, utterly mad. He wished he could comfort Liat, but there was no time. Instead he set the boy safely behind him, then turned to Wyatt. ''You forget one thing. I'll know, Wyatt. And I won't rest until you pay for this.''

''You.'' Wyatt's eyes darkened. His smile was wiped away, and in its place was a look of pure hatred. ''I should have made certain you were dead back at the village before I came here. But I will not miss again. When I finish with your lady…'' He held up a gleaming dueling pistol. ''I will permit you to join her on the rocks below. Along with yonder servant and your poor crippled brother.''

''Then do it now.'' Quenton started forward, determined to give his life rather than see Olivia die.

Out of the corner of his eye he saw Bennett pull himself from his chair, and for the space of a heartbeat he feared he would have to see his brother tumble to his death as well.

Then all his energy was focused on Olivia. He heard her cry out as he caught hold of her hand and tugged her free. Heard the terrible roar of the dueling pistol as a ball of lead hurtled through his shoulder and sent him spinning backward. Heard a shriek that sounded strangely like Bennett's cries in the night. Then heard

Wyatt's gasp of surprise as he stiffened, then tumbled over the cliffs.

Protruding from his back was the hilt of Bennett's knife.

Quenton and Olivia turned in time to see Bennett, still standing, his arm still upraised. Then, as the enormity of the miracle he had accomplished set in, he slowly sank to his knees, then slumped to the ground.

Quenton gathered Olivia and Liat into his arms. A sob escaped his lips as he muttered, "Thank heaven. Oh, thank heaven."

And then, like his brother, he slowly sank to the ground. Olivia gave a cry of distress when she realized that the back of his shirt, his breeches, his boots, were soaked with his own blood.

Chapter Twenty-One

"Mistress Thornton." Pembroke came upon the housekeeper crumpled in a chair in the library. "Here now. What's wrong?"

"Nothing." She blew her nose loudly, then tucked the handkerchief in a pocket and turned her head.

"Are those tears?" He knelt in front of her.

"Not a bit of it. Just dust in me eye." She blinked furiously.

"Go ahead. You deserve a good cry. Look what you've been through lately. Helping Miss St. John nurse Lord Stamford back to health."

"Aye. When I thought for certain he would die from the knife wound in 'is back and the pistol ball in 'is shoulder. But look at 'im now."

Pembroke nodded. "And you've been lending a hand to our Minerva while she worked with Master Bennett, teaching him how to walk and talk again."

The housekeeper nodded. "The lass is amazing. Such patience. Such love. And Master Bennett's making such progress."

"Aye. And now the king and his entourage have

returned and you have the weddings to deal with. This is all too much for you.''

She shook her head. ''Not really. Everyone's been doing their share. Especially Edlyn. Ever since she found out the truth about that scoundrel Wyatt Lindsey, and realized 'e'd lied to 'er all these years about Lord Stamford, she's been a changed person.''

Pembroke smiled. ''You could have knocked me over when she asked if she could be lady's maid to Minerva after she marries Master Bennett.''

''Aye. And a more devoted maid I've never seen. All the staff are saying how generous it is of Lord Stamford to allow 'er to stay on when 'e learned she'd been taking money from Lord Lindsey all these years to spy for 'im. Why, she even admitted to luring poor old Thor into the closet with a bone, though she didn't know Lord Lindsey's evil motives.''

The butler shook his head. ''How was she to know what to believe? Lady Antonia had been distressed, and had admitted to her maid that she had something terrible to tell her husband. Something that would cause him great pain. I suppose it was natural for Edlyn to assume Lord Stamford had flown into a rage and killed his young bride.''

''Aye. Especially when that villainous, crook-pated skainsmate Lord Lindsey continued to feed upon her hatred all these years.'' Mistress Thornton sighed. ''I'm just so glad all the bad times are behind us, and Blackthorne can be a happy place again.''

Pembroke got to his feet and drew her up with him. ''So why were you crying?''

She shrugged. ''I guess I'm just a tottering, dismal-dreaming dewberry. Weddings always make me weep.''

The butler couldn't help smiling at her descriptive words. "I love it when you get all fired up, Gwynnith."

"You do? I can't help it. The words just tumble out of me mouth."

"Aye. They do that." He cleared his throat. "Far be it from me to be the cause of any more tears. But I was thinking that I might...that you might...that we could..."

She clapped him on the shoulder. "Come on, man. Stop the mammering, fawning, mumble-news. Out with it."

At her words his grin was quick and amused. Then he sobered, swallowed and tried again. "Gwynnith, I'd be honored if you'd be my wife."

For the space of a full minute she went completely still. Her face drained of all color until it was the shade of her new apron. This wasn't at all what she'd been expecting him to say. Oh, not that she hadn't had her dreams, like any woman. And all of them spun around this very special man. But they'd seemed like so many fairy tales. And now, here he was, saying the one thing she'd always hoped she'd hear.

"I'm sorry, Gwynnith. I've made you cry again."

"Aye. Haven't you just now." Then she fell into his arms, blubbering like a fool.

"Well, old friend." King Charles sat in the small room off one side of the chapel at Blackthorne, and watched as Quenton paced. "How strange life is. Who would have believed that Q would uncover so many deep, dark secrets? How does it feel to discover that you are one of the wealthiest men in England?"

Quenton shook his head. "It still hasn't quite sunk

in, Chills. I knew that my grandfather's estates were vast. I just didn't know how wide-ranging were his interests. Tea in India. Diamonds in Africa. He had even established trading with the colonies in New Amsterdam, and it seems to be flourishing.''

The king chuckled. ''You're very wise to wed your little governess before the rest of the eligible men in England learn about her wealth. When a woman is that beautiful, and has a handsome dowry as well, she would soon find herself swamped with suitors.''

Quenton paused, smiled. ''I'm not about to let her get away. Not when I had to fight so hard to win her.''

Charles stretched his arms wide. ''Ah, it's good to be back in Cornwall. And I do so love weddings. But I wish you'd have let me bring along the archbishop from London.''

''Bennett and I both prefer the old priest from the village. Did you know he presided over our parents' wedding?''

''Aye. So you've told me now three times.'' He smiled as Quenton changed course and began to pace the other way. ''Do I sense some nerves, old friend?''

''Nay. I just want this over. I think every village and shire in Cornwall has emptied out and their citizens are now filling those pews, waiting to see if I'll stumble or forget my name.''

''It'll do you good. Give you a taste of how I must live my life every day.'' Charles filled two goblets with wine and handed one to Quenton. ''Here. Drink. 'Twill do you good.''

The two friends drank in silence.

''Tell me about Bennett's recovery. It seems quite remarkable.''

''Aye.'' Quenton smiled. ''He is determined to walk

up the aisle with his bride. He may have to lean on her arm a bit, but I think he'll make it.''

"And his speech?"

"Coming back slowly. But he'll manage to speak his vows."

"I'm happy for him. For both of you."

"Not nearly so happy as I am, Chills. I have my brother back. And the woman I cherish. When I thought I was going to lose Olivia, I realized that she was my reason for living. Without her, nothing else in life would matter."

"Then you've found something I've yet to find, Q. I'm not certain I ever will. I envy you, my friend."

Both men looked up when the door opened and Olivia, holding Liat's hand, entered. Over her arm was a small embroidered bit of cloth.

"Majesty." She curtsied, then came forward as Charles held out his hands.

"My lady." He held her a little away, to better see the gown of white gossamer shot with threads of gold. At her throat were shimmering jewels, the famed Stamford diamonds. "You are truly a vision."

She dimpled. "Thank you, Majesty. And what think you of Liat?"

The lad wore a white jacket and breeches and hose, and was looking as nervous as Quenton.

"You look splendid, lad. Do you have the rings?"

"Aye, Majesty."

"And do you know which one goes to Quenton's bride, and which to Bennett's?"

The boy patted his pockets. "The one in this pocket goes to my Aunt Minerva, and this goes to Mum."

"Mum is it? Next I suppose you'll be calling me Uncle Charles."

"And why not?" Quenton said with a smile. "I was hoping you'd offer to stand for him at his christening. It's time we welcomed our son into the faith of his king."

"I'd be honored. But only if the two of you will agree to come to London, and allow the Archbishop of Canterbury to perform the ceremony."

Olivia turned to Quenton. "Oh, my love, would you mind?"

He laughed. "Right now you could ask me anything and I'd give it. Would you like the moon, my love? 'Tis yours. The stars? Take them all. I'll fly through the sky collecting them for you if you'd like."

Charles threw back his head and roared. How grand it was to see his old friend so happy.

Hearing the music, he muttered, "I suppose I must make my appearance now." He turned and drew Olivia close, kissing both her cheeks. Then he offered his hand to Quenton. But instead of shaking hands, the two men embraced.

"Be happy, my friend. Happy enough for both of us."

"Aye."

They clapped each other on the back, then stepped apart.

"Come, Liat." The king took the boy by the hand. "Let's get you ready for your walk up the aisle."

Olivia watched them go, then turned to Quenton. "I've brought you a bride's gift."

"You've given me quite enough already."

She shook her head. "This is very special to me." She held up the small embroidered coverlet.

"Your shawl?"

"Nay. My mother made this coverlet for my father

when they were wed. It covered them every night of their wedded life.''

"Then I shall cherish it, my love.'' He pressed his lips to the soft fabric, and then to her hands. "And I pray it will bring us as much love as it gave them.''

He set it on the table and turned to regard her. He was standing very still, staring at her with a strange look on his face.

"What is it, my lord? What is wrong?''

"Nothing is wrong, Livvy. Everything is suddenly so right.''

She smiled. "The music has started, Quenton. Bennett and Minerva will be starting up the aisle. We must go.''

"In a moment. Come here.''

She walked to him and slipped her arms around his waist. "Are you having doubts, my lord?''

"Doubts? Oh Livvy.'' He pressed his lips to her hair, breathing in the fragrance of lavender. "I have never been so sure of anything in my life. I just need a moment to hold you.''

They stood, feeling their two hearts beating in perfect rhythm.

"I've been thinking that we might take a little journey. Aboard the *Prodigal*. It would give Bennett and Minerva some time alone here at Blackthorne. Give the servants a rest as well. And it would give us an excuse to avoid the coming winter, and a chance for Liat to see his island once again.''

"Jamaica?'' She drew a little away to look up at him. "You wish to sail to Jamaica?''

"You'd like it there, Livvy. The sun is warm, the air sweet and the people friendly.''

She chuckled against his throat. "You have no need

to persuade me, love. I'll go anywhere you ask, for as long as you ask. Lest you forget, I am a simple country lass who has never been away from England. I am eager for any adventure, as long as it's shared with you."

"Oh, Livvy. How did I live before you?"

"Very badly, as I recall. You were the blackhearted villain of Cornwall. The despair of your housekeeper, the bane of your butler's existence, and..." She caught the gleam in his eye and took hold of his hand. "Come, my rogue pirate. It's time someone tamed you."

As they stepped into the chapel and took their places behind Bennett and Minerva, she felt a sudden, unexpected rush of tears.

Quenton turned to her with a look of love so blinding, she felt her heart nearly explode with feeling. She placed her hand in his and felt the warmth, the strength, the tenderness. She gave a sigh of anticipation as she prepared herself for a life as his wife. This would surely be the greatest adventure of all.

*   *   *   *   *

AWARD-WINNING
AUTHOR
TORI PHILLIPS
INTRODUCES...

An illegitimate noblewoman
and a shy earl to a most delicious
marriage of convenience in

THREE DOG
KNIGHT

Available in October 1998
wherever Harlequin Historicals are sold.

**Harlequin®
Historical**

More Medievals are coming!

A WARRIOR'S PASSION

by Margaret Moore

&

THE SHIELDED HEART

by Sharon Schulze

Available in November 1998
wherever Harlequin Historicals are sold.

Harlequin®
Historical

Harlequin® Historical

From rugged lawmen and
valiant knights to defiant heiresses
and spirited frontierswomen,
Harlequin Historicals will
capture your imagination with
their dramatic scope, passion
and adventure.

Harlequin Historicals…
they're too good to miss!

COMING NEXT MONTH FROM

HARLEQUIN
HISTORICALS

DON'T MISS THESE FOUR GREAT TITLES AVAILABLE NOW!